Surviving the Last Refuge

Book One of The Bowl Series

By R. R. Hutchinson

For Lorna, for always believing in me

Chapter One – Out in the Wilds

'Almost time to call it a day, Nothro,' Julius Dominguez called out loudly without seeing his workmate, then marked a large white X on the bark of the nearest tree before he put the stick of chalk back in the work pouch which hung at his waist. He pulled the collar of his jacket higher about his neck as he finally began to tire of the cold for the day. There was a small settling of snow on top of his dark hair, left somewhat long to keep warm; those snowflakes which landed on his tanned, cheerful face melted after a moment and went unnoticed. He looked around for where Nothro had got to but saw no sign of him. 'Nothro?' Julius called out, realising he received no reply earlier. 'Where are you, you big lummox,' he said to himself. Staring hard, he eventually managed to pick out the brown bulk of his friend slowly inching up a tree a considerable distance away.

*

A branch wobbled high above the large predator as a squirrel-like rodent clambered along in search of food, unaware of what lurked below. It scattered powdery snow gently downwards into Nothro's eyes, which he silently blinked away; further snowflakes clung to the short fur of his face. Just as the creature started to move toward a cluster of leaves at the tip of the branch, Nothro launched himself up the trunk to close the distance, all attempts at stealth now abandoned. He surged upwards and in a crash of foliage was level with his intended prey – which was now painfully aware of Nothro's presence – before he used his strong hind legs to kick laterally off from the tree trunk.

The furry mammal ran toward the end of the branch, fearing for its life and desperate to survive, and leapt for the closest adjoining branch of a neighbouring tree. It had spent too long unaware of being stalked, however, and it was now too late to save itself. Nothro sprang forward, surprisingly streamlined as his bear-like mass sailed through the air, and outstretched a large paw to successfully snatch the unfortunate creature in mid-air.

Clutching his catch in one hand, he used his other, unencumbered claws to dig into the neighbouring tree's trunk to arrest his rapid descent, partially succeeding. He managed to slow himself down and achieved a controlled fall before landing heavily on the frozen ground. The noise made performing this manoeuvre was considerable, but with prey already in hand it was of no concern. He simply put the small body, now limp, atop a pile at the base of a nearby tree where several other similarly sized creatures lay, unmoving.

Nothro straightened up to stretch out his limbs and peered off into the distance for a moment before turning and scooping up his catches into a sack. He then hitched up his load and headed back toward his friend, the raw ingredients for their dinner sorted now. Along with wormroot – a thick, starchy tuber that grew abundantly in the woods, some of which they had already dug up and stored in their hut – they would have a filling and nutritious evening meal.

*

Working outside in all weathers was not a job for everyone, and the outer territory of Thorntuft, which reached right up to the cliff-encircled limits of the Bowl, was anything but a hospitable place. Anyone unprepared was easily disoriented as the landscape turned people around without their knowledge. Julius gazed through the trees at the perpetually snow-covered, undulating rock-strewn slopes topped by thick clusters of fir trees, as a wind stirred and brought the piney woodland scents to his attention anew. The vast stretches of windswept heath between the woods could also be seen covering the rest of the area, with only patches of low bilberry bushes and heather to provide sparse shelter from the elements. Few creatures made this area their home; hardy, thick-furred wild goats surviving on the grasses growing in the thin soil, a few small rodent species hiding amongst roots and tree branches, and grey, orange-spotted lizards which sunbathe on boulders on bright days. The outer cliffs curved around to the west and towered over the edge of the territory, as it did on all sides of the Bowl, forming an impassable border – though one which delineated the relative haven from the frozen wastes. The inner Bowl, many miles away to the east and a much safer, warmer area in which to live, meant that few people settled in Thorntuft. Most who chose to live in the snow did so for the meagre goods which could be gleaned from solid hard work, or else simply to live a quiet, simple – albeit hard – life.

Julius relished being out in the woods, using his youthful energy to work hard and keep himself busy to fill the long days. His employment utilised his mind as well as his skilled hands as he expertly selected trees ripe for felling without depleting any single area. Then came the splitting and seasoning of the logs in preparation of distribution as raw building supplies, or firewood in the case of the poorer cuts. The latter was essential to ensure the survival of those citizens who lived away from the naturally-heated city of Dralcea, located as it was around the caldera with magma roiling at its base, and thus needed additional warmth.

Spending months at a time at work kept Julius away from almost all human contact – an arrangement which suited him perfectly, having never been particularly interested in being around other people. This accounted for part of the reason he chose to work one of the least popular jobs available. His work mate, Nothro Grafanc, also made life easier for Julius – being Ananeptide, he spoke as little as Julius did and they found each other's quiet presence made for easy company. The almost seven-feet-tall, brown-furred creature's superior strength was useful when moving the heavy loads of wood around, and his predatory instincts also usually succeeded in providing them with meat for sustenance.

Despite enjoying his work, Julius always looked forward to the end of the day, when he would head back to their shared cabin and prepare the cooking fire. *You just can't beat warming the ache from your bones by a fire after a hard day at work*, he often thought. In the day he wore a thick jacket trimmed with fur to keep the worst of the cold out, but there was only so much he could do to keep his hands warm. That was the part he relished the most – finally getting to place his hands by the fire and have his fingers gradually become dextrous again was a small but welcome luxury. Julius habitually started the fire and prepared the food, his human hands being much more adept at those tasks than Nothro's much larger, less nimble paw-like hands. They were different in many ways but having worked together for several years, their varied attributes complimented each other and as their familiarity grew it made them an ever more productive team.

Julius was in the minority where they lived – Ananeptide comprised by far the largest portion of the Thorntuft population. Their generally solitary nature meant that the woods far from the urban sprawl was a more natural fit for their kind than the bustle and intolerance of the crowded city of Dralcea, and their thick fur kept the climate from bothering them. Many humans who spotted an Ananeptide and weren't familiar with them saw their long, sharp teeth and claws and instinctively clenched their muscles, their brain recalling primal fears and reacting the only way it knew how. It seemed to most Ananeptide that no matter what they did, humans always mistrusted and treated their kind badly. Occasional outpourings of frustration from the Ananeptide side did nothing to change these attitudes. Nothro walked the line between civil obedience and actively winding up his human contemporaries. Julius was the only human Nothro had ever trusted, and he trusted him with his life.

Nothro trudged slowly but steadily toward where Julius stood by a broad tree, the Ananeptide dragging a large log up the track using a chain tied around a knot in the wood. Having caught Julius's eye, Nothro tossed his head backward, gesturing toward the way he had just come. 'Visitors,' Nothro rumbled, his pointed teeth briefly exposed.

Julius could just make out some movement far down the track, but it was much too distant for him to make out. 'Your eyes are good. Did you call for someone from Dralcea?' Julius asked.

Nothro snorted. 'Not me. Who would I know there?'

'You're mysterious. You could easily have contacts over there in the city,' Julius shrugged.

The pair stood and watched the contingent approach for several moments, eager to pick out more detail. The reason for such a visit was unclear – it was an exceptionally long way to travel for a social visit. Nobody got visitors out in the wilds.

Chapter Two – First Patrol

The recruit adjusted his grip as he tried his best to keep a steady step in line with the others. The rough spear he had been issued with was surprisingly heavy and was causing his arms to ache even as he held it against his shoulder, despite being a young man and by no means unfit. Marching along the worn path was taking a long time too – he had expected to be at the outpost within an hour or so – but he had no real idea of how far outside of the city it was, and had failed to account for the journey through Dralcea itself. As he thought about this gap in his knowledge, he misstepped as the track rose slightly and consequently stumbled forward, trying and failing to cover it up so his new comrades wouldn't notice and give him a harder time than they already had.

'Having trouble, young Gantle? Walking shouldn't be beyond you,' said Gantle's commanding officer, Branch Matthew Arnold.

'No, I'm fine, sir. Just getting used to my boots.'

'You won't be used to such fine garments as those you've been issued with, I suppose. You're lucky to have them. All those unfortunates you left behind when you crawled out of the Warren would probably gouge each other for the chance to keep their toes warm with the storesmaster's finest hide clodhoppers, instead of scraping their claws around in the dirt – isn't that right, recruit?'

'Yes, sir, of course,' Gantle replied through gritted teeth to give the appearance of agreement.

He was sure he was meant to agree with his superior's suppositions, regardless of what he believed, though it burned at his pride to say the words. Prior to signing up to the Dralcea Guard, Paul Gantle had been the proud owner of a pair of rat-skin moccasins his mother had carefully made for him when they had finally caught two of the pests infesting their hovel. The items had made him proud, and on more than one occasion he had been forced to violence in order to safeguard possession of the footwear from jealous neighbours, children and adults alike. The accuracy of Branch Arnold's guess about their coveting of such items made the feeling all the worse to bear.

'That's right. You're in line for the good stuff now if you keep your head up and follow orders. This city is kind to a hardworking guard. Now keep up, you're making the watch look untidy.'

Gantle kept quiet apart from the standard reply of 'sir'. He did not trust himself to make any further reply. Gantle saw their other two companions, both more senior than the young recruit, exchange glances with a grin. He imagined they both knew he was in for a rough time as he learned the trade.

It had been almost a mile since they left behind the outer walls of Dralcea. The dry and dusty track wound through sparse scrub, slowly gaining elevation until the sprawl to their backs seemed to shrink into miniature. Cresting the next ridge, the watchtower that was their destination finally came into view. Gantle tried to ignore how uncomfortable his new uniform, armour and apparently high quality boots were, along with the discomfort of the blisters he could feel forming from the incessant rubbing on his feet.

Gantle fixed his gaze on the middle distance to focus on arriving instead, hoping to distract himself. His rough wool cloak, dyed royal blue, flapped about him as a breeze stirred the previously still air of the chilly early morning, also ruffling his wavy blonde hair as it passed. The air brought with it a vaguely familiar scent, just barely noticeable.

*

As they drew near, Branch Arnold held himself further upright to better display his authority to the trio of guards to be relieved from their watch. Being of a sufficiently senior rank, he possessed a simple iron helmet with a hexagonal crown. He had been carrying it on a belt loop for comfort, but now slipped the dull pewter-coloured helm on to complete his light armour outfit. His face was somewhat lined and his hair greying, having borne the brunt of all the weathers that visited the region as he journeyed to and from outpost towers outside Dralcea's protective walls. Arnold could not see any of the three at the simple doorway at the base of the square, rough-hewn grey stone tower that formed the shelter for those on duty, nor on top where the elevated position provided a better vantage point and beacon to be lit in case of emergency.

Arnold called out to them in his loud, somewhat raspy officer's voice, honed to perfection over the years. 'On your feet, gentlemen! Time to change over. Present yourselves!'

Following a silence that grew more tense with every passing heartbeat, Arnold saw Guard Potas and Guard Hornak catch each other's eyes with a glance. Arnold knew that having joined up and mostly serving together in their two years on the job, the pair would know trouble was ahead for the current watch. They ought to be filing up near the wall or at least shouting back to express the reason why they were not doing.

'Come on, you bastards,' Branch Arnold hissed through clenched teeth, striding further ahead of the group as his frustration rapidly built. The path twisted left around a smooth, mossy boulder and brought him in at a sharper angle to the quietly looming tower. The unfolding view brought forth a dark pool with a long rivulet running down the sloped track toward them, its edges dried to a brown crust. Arnold caught the metallic tang as the breeze picked up, instantly recognising it from brawls and previous engagements when blood had been spilled. Adrenaline flooded his system, quickening his heart rate in preparation for a fight. He readied his spear, levelling the point at waist height, prepared to strike if necessary. Branch Arnold also had a sword hanging at his side but would reserve that for whatever was to come, if necessary. The extra reach of his spear was most useful for now.

'Form diamond on me, lads. Gantle – take rear position,' Arnold said quietly but with an authority that ensured everyone heard. Potas and Hornak instantly split apart from one another, Potas slinking behind and to Arnold's left whilst Hornak mirrored this movement to the right; the formation came together seamlessly as their training showed through. Gantle duly took up his place at the rear, his face flushed with sudden alertness. Together they trod through the spilled blood lying directly in their path and left dark red boot prints in their wake as they pushed forward, the smears marking their passage on the cold, dry path.

Moving as one, they rounded the gap in the low stone wall that separated them from the tower. Gantle struggled to keep pace with his more experienced comrades; Arnold heard him treading heavily in his haste to keep the formation tight.

The first member of the previous watch came into Arnold's view and it became clear that he was the source of the stained ground. The man lay face down on the dusty ground, one arm outstretched toward the tower as if trying to pull himself to it. His other arm lay at his side, torn and bloody, whilst his legs lay at odd angles behind him like the broken wings of an insect. The most unsettling part of the image was the large, ragged hole in the man's lower back, and Arnold had to tear his eyes away as they moved past the dead man. The group pushed forward and quickly discovered another deceased guard slumped against the outer wall of the tower, broken spear shaft still clutched in one rigid hand. His head was a misshapen mass, the features unrecognisable, giving the appearance of having been crushed somehow. Arnold spared a quick glance backward to check on his men, and noted Gantle looking queasy and Hornak, the man closest to the second body as they came close to it, clenching his teeth together in a tense grimace. Arnold had witnessed some grisly sights after years of patrolling the Warren, but this was particularly disturbing.

Ignoring the body, Branch Arnold held his left arm out as they neared the open doorway to the tower. His eyes were trained on the entrance, constantly scanning for any movement that would betray the presence of an interloper.

'Hornak, Gantle – stay out here,' Arnold hissed. 'Potas, stick close to me. Whatever you do, *do not* get jumpy and stick me.'

He paused to check on his men. Potas only just managed to nod his understanding. Paul Gantle hardly moved but seemed focussed enough to do his job. Hornak continued to bare his teeth and said nothing, but he swung round toward the body and stiffly kept watch of the approach to the tower, his back to the stone structure. Gantle followed Hornak's lead, visibly sweating, and he noticeably struggled to keep his gaze off the two bodies lying deathly still.

Arnold led the way into the dark interior of the guard tower with Potas warily following behind. The pair trod slowly and purposefully as they allowed their eyes to adjust to the gloom inside. Despite starting to pick out lighter greys within the darkness that smothered the room, Arnold could see no sign of the third guard who should be present. 'Guard, show yourself,' he called out. He started toward the simple stone steps on the left that would lead up to the tower's flat top when his boot struck something heavy which shifted slightly. His attention snapped down to see what he had kicked.

'*Hold*,' Arnold whispered. As he used the butt of his spear to prod at the object, willing his vision to adapt further and update his situational awareness, it yielded fractionally. *Was that some sort of string at one end*? With a creeping wave of realisation, he recognised it was a boot on the end of a detached leg he had just shifted across the floor. His vision finally fully resolved, and he saw the remnants of the third guard in the middle of the room, limbs severed and spread in a radius around the torso.

Branch Arnold let out a long, stuttered breath. He turned to Potas, who had also belatedly taken in the grisly scene, and despite the dark interior had turned noticeably pale. 'Check the roof, Potas – carefully,' Arnold commanded, nodding toward the steps. Potas duly obliged and shakily ascended the stairs without uttering more than the obligatory 'sir' in response. Arnold stepped over the leg and crouched down next to the largest remaining part of the body, his spear grounded to steady himself as he looked it over. A protrusion from the upper chest caught his eye, and reaching out to it, he found it stuck fast. It was not a weapon Arnold recognised.

Studying the object more closely, it was a glassy-looking shard that protruded roughly seven inches from the dead man's torso. The dimpled surface was very slightly curved and a dappled azure colour; it was utterly unlike anything Arnold had ever seen. Small beads of moisture clung to its surface. He gave the item another heave to attempt to free it from between the man's ribs, but to no avail. He gazed at it a few moments more, tilting his head to either side slowly as if to better understand what he was seeing. It did not help. 'What is this?' he muttered to himself. Arnold then reached into the breast pocket of the deceased guard, pulled out a small hexagonal token and placed it into a pouch attached to his belt.

Potas came back down the stone steps, taking each one carefully and steadily, as if still partially dazed. When he reached the bottom, he turned to look at Arnold, awaiting his orders. 'The roof is clear, sir. No sign of anyone having been up there.'

'Well then,' Arnold said, standing up in one quick motion. He strode over to the door leading outside, gesturing for Potas to follow, and emerged into the bright light outside, eyes narrowing against the sun. Potas shuffled out behind him. Arnold went back to the other bodies and similarly took stamped tokens from them. The three lower-ranking guards kept silent and still, but all looked expectantly at Arnold.

'I have their enlistment tokens, get them buried a little way off the track and scrub the tower as best you can,' he addressed them curtly, looking each guard solemnly in the eyes in turn; each returned a look of bewilderment. 'Replacements will be sent from the Promontory to relieve you in due course. Stay alert today, lads,' Arnold said, turning and striking out for the road back to town and leaving his men to their task and the unexplained terror attached.

Chapter Three – The Crimson Duck

'Ah! Best stuff around, this.' The big sergeant wiped his mouth with the back of one hand whilst slamming his carved stone mug down on the wooden table with a loud rap. His helmet sat in its usual place on the thick table beside his mug.

The tavern was far from full, but enough people were sitting around the variously sized tables and barrels stood on end to keep the atmosphere warm and a friendly murmuring filling the place. As always, Janos was the loudest. Other regular customers of The Crimson Duck had long since learned to ignore him, and more than a few of them had found out the hard way not to intervene in his drinking or boisterous behaviour. He had even come to blows with a few of his fellow guards – those who had experienced this generally found another establishment to drink in thereafter or else kept quiet indeed when sharing the room with him in future. Few came off unharmed in a fair fight with the experienced guard; at 6'4" and built like an ox, Janos was a natural brawler. The routes he walked whilst on duty were always less troublesome afterwards.

The familiar clatter of stone on wood brought the establishment's young barmaid, Ryx Haþingvoð, over to where Janos sat.

'Another, big man?' Ryx asked.

'Always. It's a thirsty job,' Janos replied.

Ryx grinned at him. 'Coming up,' she said, and swiped his special mug in one easy movement. The other customers were all served with cylindrical wooden mugs – these however had proved too flimsy for Janos's big hands and tendency to slam his vessel down once it had been emptied. Rather than fobbing off their best customer with a ban for wrecking their property, and thus depriving themselves of his considerable custom, the Haþingvoðs who owned the pub had decided to adapt and had made him his own mug, one suitable for his considerable strength.

Janos watched as Ryx moved back to the bar, eagerly anticipating his next drink. Ryx tied her braids of red hair behind her head so that they would stay out of her face as she fetched his drink. Her blonde-haired mother, a strong woman in her mid-forties with an abundance of nurturing instincts named Skula, was already behind the bar breaking the seal on a fresh barrel set down by the wall. She smiled as Ryx joined her. Through an arched doorway into the back room, Janos could also see his friend Fyrir, husband to Skula and father of Ryx, busily chopping snippets of meat and vegetables to make the inn's infamous pies. Fyrir stood side-on and his stout frame, short blonde hair and full but well-trimmed sandy-coloured beard were visible as he hummed tunelessly. Janos smiled to himself, amused at seeing Fyrir relaxed and acting as though unobserved, absorbed as he was in his usual task of baking the inn's pies.

Janos's sturdy stone mug was filled with a strong-smelling liquid from the newly opened cask. An oily film sat on the surface until disturbed by Ryx with the intruding decades-old ladle. Her youth growing up in and later working in the inn had meant she was hardened to the powerful fumes that emanated from the drinks purchased by their clientele.

As Janos waited for his next drink to arrive – one of many to come – the pub's adopted mutt, a tamed mlem-mlem and their unofficial mascot named Piecrust, wandered around the tables, tail lazily swishing from side to side. Piecrust had simply wandered in one day, taken a liking to an offered crust leftover from one of Fyrir's pies, evidently decided that this was a good place and had never left again. Everybody who visited The Crimson Duck enjoyed the friendly presence and Janos now absentmindedly patted the furry back that passed by as Piecrust completed a slow circuit of the pub.

Ryx whisked the mug back to Janos, who gratefully took it from her with a big smile for his favourite server.

'What's this galumph called?' Janos asked.

'New one in – Wakelin's Wonder Water. It seems to be going down all right, we're onto the second barrel already. Are your bosses keeping you busy?' Ryx inquired.

'Yep,' Janos said, taking a big gulp of his galumph before continuing, 'there have been a few attacks recently. We need a presence out on the streets, so we're doing extra rounds to discourage whoever is behind them.'

'Well, nobody has rolled out of here in any fit state to go causing mischief! You know that's not our style,' she said with a grin.

Janos was frowning as he turned to face her fully. 'A bit worse than that, love. Nasty stuff happening, a few grisly ones. Probably just one nutter though. We'll get him.'

'Oh,' Ryx said, straightening up and crossing her arms. 'Do I need to start keeping the bat from under the bar close to hand?'

'Having seen you throw more than your share of drunks and perverts out on their arse,' Janos said, '…I doubt you have much to worry about.'

This drew another big grin from Ryx. 'Thought so.'

'Doesn't mean you can go pushing it though, Ryx. I don't want to see you lurking down any dark alleys,' Janos said, slightly slurring his words as the potent liquid started to take effect. 'I won't always be around to watch over you.' Knowing the family as well as he did, Janos felt an almost fatherly duty to help protect the young woman, capable of defending herself though she was.

Ryx walked past Janos and bumped his shoulder with hers playfully; she barely succeeded in moving him much at all. He idly watched as Ryx strolled off to attend to the other customers in the inn and gently cajole those who had yet to drink themselves into a benign stupor to partake of some more. Ryx simply received sluggish smiles from the first few who were clearly quite merry, until she stopped in front of one startlingly sober young man. He appeared to be staring at the barrel top that served as a table he was sitting at.

Janos saw Ryx gently slide her hand onto the top of the barrel in front of the young man until catching his attention. He slowly turned his head to look up at her with a blank expression. An awkward moment passed and still he kept staring, eyes somewhat unfocused, even after she smiled at him. Ryx looked a little uneasy to Janos, something he had rarely seen.

'Everything ok here? Want a drink?' she asked him.

The young man continued to stare blankly at Ryx for a moment. Working his mouth slightly as if to practice for the words about to be spoken, he quietly broke his silence.

'What have you got?'

'To drink?' Ryx asked. 'You haven't had anything here before?'

'No. First time I've ever been in a place like this.'

'I'm sorry, I thought you must have been in here another time. Lots of new faces coming in these past few days. How about the house galumph? It's popular with the big man over there, your colleague. You are in the Dralcea Guard, aren't you?' Ryx asked. Janos turned to watch the conversation as he overhead the mention of his profession and noticed the man had mostly covered his uniform with a dark cloak draped around his shoulders.

The young man nodded. 'I only just joined recently...was told this was where we go after a hard shift.'

'The best place you'll find, lad!' Janos chimed in at last, loud and cheerful. 'Have one of these,' he said, holding up and wiggling his mug so the contents sloshed over the sides and dribbled over his fingers. 'On me. What's your name?'

'Recruit Paul Gantle,' the young man replied. 'You're Sergeant Boltfoot, right?'

Janos raised a thick eyebrow. 'The very same. Have we been through this before? Because if so, perhaps you owe me one instead.' Janos's mood was on the verge of souring, as it was prone to doing on occasion with little warning.

'No, the other guards, they pointed you out a couple of times. Not that you needed pointing out, you're...' Gantle trailed off.

Janos had bristled, his shoulders bunching up without him even realising. 'I'm *what*?'

Gantle was silent for a moment before he replied, sounding nervous. 'Noticeable.'

Janos's posture softened. 'Hmph. Can't really disagree with that.' Janos took a big swig from his mug and with the mug was in front of his face, allowed Gantle a moment to recover his composure. The sergeant put his mug down and noticed Gantle glancing at his hammer with a look of horror. It leant by its handle against Janos's table, the weighty head resting on the floor, and was far from being standard issue equipment. 'Don't mind Hilde,' Janos said. 'She's not on duty.'

Janos was well aware that Hilde inspired terror into the hearts of those facing her in anger. The long wooden handle, inscribed near the tip with the carpenter's business name of Hurst's Hefty Handles, had strips of tarnished metal wound around it and riveted on at intervals to serve as gripping points. The brutal hammer featured an octagonal face six inches in diameter and seven inches deep. On the opposite side of Hilde's shaft sat a counterweight crow's bill, a vicious curved wedge measuring six inches long with two small recesses running from the tip back down its length. The mere sight of Hilde often put potential opponents off any altercation – exactly as Janos liked it to. It never hurt to have such an item to enhance his already fearsome reputation.

Ryx returned with a fresh mug and put it down in front of Gantle with a natural smile. 'Been a rough day has it?'

'You could say that...I didn't expect to start the day stepping over the bodies of my colleagues at an outpost, that's for sure. It's all I can see when I close my eyes.' He visibly winced as he brought his drink up to his face and evidently caught scent of the potent fumes emanating from the vessel.

Ryx looked concerned. 'Oh, that must be a shock to see all that blood if you're not used to it.'

Gantle looked at her directly. 'I've seen blood plenty. Stabbings, mob justice, the stuff that happens in the Warren...but not this. This was different. It was brutal.' He looked distantly at his mug. 'Inhuman.'

Janos took a special interest at that. 'What do you mean, lad? Wasn't it just an attack on the outpost from some exiles? It does happen now and again, given that we're charged with defending the last refuge in the world and all. Losses do happen, and sometimes must, since there's nowhere else to fall back to if there is a large attack.'

'No...it wasn't exiles. There were no stab wounds, axe blows or anything like that. It looked as if...something wild had got in there unexpectedly, something big and vicious.'

Janos took a swig. 'Those lot out there, they're savage bastards. They'll do anything to amuse themselves or put one over us Dralceans. I once saw...' he glanced at Ryx, wondering if he should relay details of the grim scene he had witnessed. A group of exiles had found their way through the outer walls one night when the gate guards on duty were lax to the point of negligent. The intruders happened upon a citizen on the street who had imbibed a few too many galumphs. They had surrounded the unfortunate man, taken his eyes with a knife then drawn their weapons and baited the wailing man as he stumbled around. Every time he came close enough to one, they would slash or stab at him, causing him to back away each time in agony as wound by wound he slowly bled to death. Janos had heard the despairing moans and come running with his small squad on their rounds and got stuck into the outlaws before they could flee. The image of the blinded man panting on all fours with his lifeblood spread in a broken spiderweb pattern all around him as yet more dribbled from his uncountable wounds came to his mind, unbidden. He decided to leave that particular memory inside his own head. '...the point is that they're as cruel and bitter as they come.'

'It wasn't them, I'm sure – they weren't killed in any way a person could do it. And there was something in there that didn't make sense. One inside the tower had something stuck in him, not a weapon...I don't know what it was though. Looked like a bit of an animal.'

'What do you mean?' asked Ryx, who hovered by the pair. 'A claw or something?'

'It looked like a bit of a shell. Glassy, and blue, similar to the crayfish you can buy at the market.'

'Pfft! You think a vicious bit of food killed our colleagues? Watch out for the pies in here then, they'll tear your tongue out!' Janos laughed at his own joke. Galumph dribbled into his greying, crescent-shaped beard that stretched from ear to ear, omitting his upper lip. He wiped it away with the back of one huge hand.

'Be nice, big man. And watch what you say about our pies too, Dad will have you out on your ear if he hears that,' Ryx said, tapping him on the shoulder. Janos knew this was not at all true, as he was a great deal larger and stronger than Fyrir, but the authority of inn stewardship had to be maintained. Janos respected Ryx's father out of a friendship built over many years and would do as he said regardless of any differences, the same being true for Skula and Ryx too.

Gantle looked frustrated with Janos dismissing what he was trying to convey, yet wary of openly challenging him. 'Look,

I'm not saying it *was* a crayfish. But *something* was there. I had to bury him. This...thing, it was wedged in his chest and wouldn't come out. I saw it up close, and the wound it left. I don't know what it was, but it wasn't something some escaped criminal would be toting, or even a weapon from what I could tell. I've seen the knives and broken tools thugs carry – this wasn't one. No handle or anything, and it was sort of broken off.' His eyes looked hollow, but his voice carried a conviction that showed he had already reasoned it out. His tone was starting to convince Janos, though what he would say next made him reconsider. Gantle continued. 'Could it...could it have been a frostmite?'

Janos could scarcely believe what he had heard and spluttered with laughter at the mention of such an idea, spraying his mouthful of galumph in an arc in front of him. 'You think it was the things your mum told you about to keep you safely indoors at night, the creatures that have taken over the frozen world beyond our borders now coming to claim this final haven of ours? How old are you, lad? Give over.' Ryx nudged him disapprovingly.

'All right.' Janos softened his stance. 'Calm down, have some of your drink. Sometimes these things happen in our line of work. You have to take it on the chin and carry on.'

Gantle followed Janos's advice and took a swig from his mug. He gagged as the flavours and pungent smells of the galumph filled his mouth and nose, threatening to overwhelm him. He forced a mouthful down and coughed afterwards.

'Definitely the first time you've had it,' Janos grinned. 'If nothing else, it can help you forget. And warm you for the walk home. And let you take a few more punches in a fight.' He picked up his own mug and, holding it high, studied it as if for the first time. 'It's really quite marvellous when you think about it,' he said in wonder at his revelation.

'That's definitely the galumph talking. I believe you've had enough,' commented Ryx.

Gantle had been quiet but suddenly swept up his mug and downed the contents in one long, gulping effort before placing it down and gasping for breath. Ryx looked at Gantle with raised eyebrows, then took his mug. 'I don't think you'll be wanting another, either.'

Janos felt compelled to finish his own drink and did so quickly without any coughing or spluttering. 'All right, lad. That stuff will kick in soon and you'll either be happy as a snorthog in muck or spoiling for a fight. Let's go before we find out which one it is, eh? Leave this lass with all the other drunkards to look after.' He stood up, patted Gantle on the back a little less gently than he intended and then motioned to the door.

'Take care out there. It'll get easier,' Ryx said to Gantle, who returned an appreciative smile as he got to his feet unsteadily. Janos fumbled in his pocket and produced an assortment of coins totalling a few somoni and handed them to Ryx. He then plonked his helmet back on and strapped Hilde to his back before setting off toward the door. The other customers adjacent to the big man's path, fellow guards and citizens alike, habitually shrank away to preserve the peace. Gantle followed behind obediently. Leaving the warm glow of the inn behind, they started out on the dark road, each heading their own way home.

*

Slumped in the shadows under the small window at the front of the inn, the young boy went almost unnoticed by the two men leaving to go their own ways. The stained rags he wore were a familiar sight to both and they paid him no heed; just one of the countless street urchins living in the Warren. Gantle had hardly been different as a child, nor Janos so dissimilar.

Keeping his head down, the child waited until the two had disappeared in their separate directions before he unsteadily got to his feet. He had sensed an intense foreboding aura surround the two men that passed him by and immediately recognised the significance. It was much too strong to be ignored.

He headed toward the nearest rough stairs leading upwards, jinking to his right along the way to kick a stray clod of earth with his bare feet and sent it spinning off down a nearby set of descending stairs. The boy scampered up the stairs and away into the night, heading east toward the city walls of Dralcea.

Chapter Four – New Creations

Candles lined the alcove above Alfred Omphalos's head as he worked, bathing him in a wavering golden glow as the flames sputtered at the impurities in the wax. The air in his workshop was thick with the accumulated smoke of candles left burning for long hours mingled with fumes escaping from chemical mixtures kept in stoppered jars on his many shelves and from frequent spillages. He was well used to the warm fug surrounding him and paid it no heed, always too fixed on the task at hand. His latest work in progress was proving difficult to complete but showed much promise. The incessant pestering of the project's commissioner did little to help matters, always interrupting when he was busy and stealing away his time which was better spent on working through the issues he faced.

One of those challenges kept him occupied as it had for the previous few days. He held a wooden apparatus with a recess to which he attached a small copper vessel, shaped like an acorn. Omphalos carefully tipped a stream of fine black grains into the vessel, gave it a jiggle to ensure it held its contents sufficiently and then reached for his nearest lit candle. To this he offered a long wood shaving until it crackled with its own flame. Omphalos proffered the lit end to the vessel, and, before he could retract his hand, the powder ignited in a flash. The small explosion and resulting shards of copper receptacle narrowly missed Omphalos's face as they flew past, some of which broke jars lining his walls or lodged in the rafters. He raised his eyebrows at the result. 'That bloody chemical supplier,' he raged. 'This stuff will never catch on.' He put the wooden frame aside and looked at a particularly large splinter stuck in the wall which had destroyed one of his largest jars of stored preservative oil. What remained of the glass jar's base could not hold all the contents and oil steadily glugged out onto the lower shelves and the floor. Omphalos sighed.

He turned back to the tweaks he was working on, but as he did so, an urgent *rap-rap-rap* at the door disturbed his work. 'Probably that same bloke again,' he muttered with annoyance. 'What is the rush all about? Just let me get on with it and get it right.'

Alfred Omphalos was used to taking his time with his inventions, and generally the process he went through was a long one. An idea would gradually evolve as he tinkered with it through the long nights where he took no heed of the time, too involved in the cascade of ideas that crashed through his mind. He liked it that way. Sometimes it would take days to complete a creation, but on other occasions it would be months on end of struggles and mental dead ends, a maze of half-formed thoughts that took a lot of exploring just to decide what would realistically work. The difference was that usually he would create something and then try to sell it; this time, he had the pressure of a demanding customer before it was even finished. With a frustrated sigh he got up from his stool and ambled over to the battered old wooden door. The ancient hinges squeaked a protest as he inched the door open to peer out at the visitor.

'Yes?' Omphalos could see who it was but refused to make it easy for the bothersome man.

Branch Godfrey Vilipas pushed his way inside, past Omphalos without a word. Omphalos was well used to Vilipas being in a rush from his previous dealings with the man. He looked like bureaucracy personified.

'You know why I'm here, Mr Omphalos. Don't play silly buggers with me.'

Omphalos pointedly slammed the door shut with a speed that belied the difficulty he seemingly had opening it. The loud noise made Vilipas jump and look around sharply.

'I don't know what you mean,' Omphalos replied, who struggled to keep the grin off his face at having nettled the man so easily. He scratched habitually at the dark, empty left eye socket he had left uncovered. Omphalos noticed that Vilipas had seen this and suddenly looked uneasy – he always appeared uncomfortable when he looked Omphalos full in the face and consequently only did so rarely.

'Of course you do, but enough bickering. We need to equip our guards with Ejectors as soon as possible – time is of the essence. I need to know when you'll have the prototype working and are ready to start full production. Well?'

'When will it be ready? When it's all finished and fully tested, which isn't yet. You must understand, if you insist on having such a *complex* project completed, you will encounter many more difficulties to overcome than with a simple one. These things take time, and it all needs testing more thoroughly the more complicated it is, and so it takes more time...when you keep telling me that it must be completed yesterday, you are just asking for the impossible and invite more problems to arise if I start rushing. You must realise that.' The inventor noted Vilipas's expression change to one of exasperation at the vague response he had fed to the branch. 'You're getting it in the neck from your superiors, I would wager. They must not understand the process either.'

'They are naturally keen to see something come of this investment. So, how long? Can you show me what you have ready? These are overdue, Omphalos. We need to see results.' Vilipas's voice began to change from authoritative to whiny.

Omphalos gave a derisory snort. 'Overdue? I never agreed to any date, sir. You really don't understand the intricacies involved, the tension required for the flaps adjoining the chamber alone is—'

Vilipas slammed his hand down on the nearest desk, sending several tools into the air before they clattered back down again. The man looked to be a little panicked to Omphalos, which presumably fuelled his actions as his frustration noticeably started to boil over. '*Look*. I need a solid answer here. The situation out on the streets isn't getting any better, nor will it any time soon. You must have made progress since I was last here!'

'What situation on the streets? And you only came here two days ago,' Omphalos pointed out in his calmest voice.

'So, you must have made two days' worth of progress!' Vilipas shouted in anger.

'It's not as simple as that, as I've said before. I've made *some* progress, of course, but that doesn't mean it's almost ready to go. You also cannot expect a continuous, consistent amount of progress for each day that elapses, that isn't the way it works with something as unknown as this. This is something I have never attempted before, and nobody else has either, so why do you think it will be easy?' Alfred Omphalos enjoyed making talking to him difficult for people he didn't like – the conversation was akin to trying to wring galumph out of a drunkard's shoes; possible in the end, but bloody hard and you were going to suffer for it before it was over.

Godfrey Vilipas rubbed his temples tersely. 'We don't think it's easy,' he conceded. 'But it *must* progress, and that's where we are having the problem. We came to the best for a reason,' he added, his flattery to try to grease the wheels painfully obvious to Omphalos. 'We *must* have one to work with as soon as possible, to see how useful they can be. Please, *please* have one ready for us by the end of the week. Can we agree on that?'

Omphalos could see the man was gambling and trying to tie him to a date that was simply unfeasible. *He really must be in trouble to be acting this way,* he thought. 'I can't agree to something that I can't foresee. I am getting there, but the progress is hard to measure and there are problems yet to be conquered. I won't put my name to an inferior product. I will have it ready when it all comes together. On the positive side, the trigger mechanism is coming along well!'

Branch Vilipas straightened and drew himself up to his full height with chin aloft. 'The end of the week, and I'll be back. Make sure there is something solid for me.' He turned on his heel and Omphalos watched with amusement as he struggled to let himself out, unfamiliar with the technique required to free the door from the slightly twisted doorframe that caused it to bind.

Omphalos stared at the door Vilipas had let himself out of with an impassive expression. 'Massive prick,' he grumbled.

Chapter Five – The Bakery

Harold Jenker had already been downstairs in the shop for a couple of hours. He had padded down the earthen stairs from his bedroom above whilst the sky was still black and studded with twinkling stars. His daily routine demanded that he rise early to rouse the fire that kept the great stone oven hot and ready to use for the long day ahead.

He yawned and began rolling and shaping more dough into small spheres and ellipses, ready to add them to the oven once the first batch was completed. The motions came naturally, reflexively, and his eyes were glazed and barely focused on the task at hand. The sun had started its slow rise from the grey murk on the horizon and began to send rays creeping down the length of the street, illuminating it gradually with a golden hue. Jenker rarely had much time to look out at the sight, but he was grateful for its presence all the same. 'Hello, sun,' he mumbled to himself. 'Good to see you. I can't imagine what it must be like down in the Warren where you barely reach.' Living in the gloom appealed to him even less than waking up without the sun.

After an hour or so the first of his regular customers came in and handed Jenker a battered somoni coin, took a canoe-shaped bread roll and left without a word. Jenker sighed. 'Another day like the last then. A conversation with an actual person to make the day less dreary would be good,' he said to himself. This was not the life he had imagined having. Sometimes he wondered if this was what his father had intended; if he would have been happy to see what his life amounted to.

Mentally pushing the introspection aside to carry on baking, he went over to the oven to replace the baked rolls with the next batch. Numbness set in as routine took over and muscle memory played its valuable role. The opening of the oven door flooded the bakery with the wonderful smell of freshly baked bread, something Jenker had long since become accustomed to.

Two guards entered noisily, their boots scraping on the big stone slab in the doorway. Jenker turned to see – he was not inundated with the custom of guards. The pair looked young and wore ill-fitting uniforms; he assumed they were newly recruited. They looked unsure of themselves, even a little jittery as they held their spears. Jenker tried to put them at ease and hopefully make a sale by giving them a warm smile.

'What can I get for you two fine gents?'

'We're not here for anything to eat. Official business. Are you Harold Jenker?' the more forward of the two asked.

'I am indeed,' Jenker replied warily at the use of his full name. 'What can I do for you?'

'We are here to invite you to the Promontory for a ceremony. The Ambassadors have decreed that you are to be afforded a great honour!' The guard spoke the last few words with forced enthusiasm. It seemed obvious that he had been given those exact words and made to memorise them. Jenker was taken aback to say the least.

'Is that right? That doesn't sound right. I'm just a baker, I don't deserve any recognition...I'm not even that good at it.'

'It is correct, no mistake. You are to be awarded the Heart of Dralcea in light of your service to our great civilisation...' – *more scripted hogwash*, thought Jenker – '...and you will experience the unending gratitude you are due at the ceremony to take place tomorrow morning. The exact location to report to is on this sheet, Mr Jenker, so please make yourself ready for the event and arrive in plenty of time.' The second guard, ever so slightly older looking, remained silent but kept a supportive and friendly expression on his face as he placed the invitation on Jenker's countertop.

'But...what have I done? I don't understand,' Jenker said, ruffling his short, brown hair and rubbing the side of his pale face; he didn't get many chances to stray outside. 'Who decided this?' he asked, suddenly suspicious. 'The Ambassadors, you said?'

'Yes,' the previously silent guard piped up, forcing a smile through impatience. 'You wouldn't want to risk offending those in government that recognised you now, would you?'

'But I can't go, I have the shop to run. There's no-one else to take over for me.'

'Don't worry about that, your pay will be covered. Everything will be taken care of – now, please, remember to dress in your best clothes and check the location carefully,' the more talkative of the two said as he asserted his authority.

Jenker was confused; had they been sent to wind him up? Were they really guards? He had initially thought their uniforms looked odd. His mind raced. A scam, a rival out to distract him whilst they burned down the premises that were his livelihood, perhaps? He noticed that they carried spears, despite being on messenger duty. That changed matters somewhat; he could hardly turn the offer down. Perhaps if he could run upstairs, he could clamber out of the window...and go where? Even if he were able to manage that and elude the guards, he lived here, above the shop. There was nowhere for him to go to.

'Mr Jenker,' the older guard prompted. They did not look as if they wanted to be kept waiting much longer, Harold thought. Presumably they wanted a positive response to confirm his attendance so they could consider their task completed.

Jenker exhaled. He had no choice but to go along. *It could be interesting*, he told himself. Perhaps they would feed him some of the good stuff he knew they had first dibs on in the Promontory. At least it would be different from his usual day of sleepwalking through rolling, putting the dough in the oven, removing the finished article and repeating. That was some comfort.

'Ok, it would be nice to be appreciated for once I suppose. I'll be there,' Jenker said as much to himself as his guests as he continued about his tasks which required attention and careful timing.

The guards visibly relaxed as Jenker gave his assent and he saw them share a pleased look. He continued with his work and tried to establish in his mind just what could have led to this award, the Heart of Dralcea. *Never heard of it before*, he mused. Jenker was vaguely aware of the guards curtly thanking him as they left to continue their day delivering these invites, a relatively safe assignment compared to patrolling the streets around the Warren, he was sure. The baker racked his brain further but, coming up with nothing convincing, contented himself with the thought that the following day would be a welcome break to his usual routine. He was thankful for that.

Chapter Six – The Capital

'Do you think they'll catch up with us?' Julius Dominguez asked as they left their busy surroundings for a quieter area.

Nothro Grafanc snorted. 'Not if they have any sense.'

Both had taken exception to being herded around Dralcea by their escorting guards, and it particularly rankled with Nothro since it seemed that they were not trusted. They were there to be awarded the Heart of Dralcea the following day, so they were informed, and had been brought from Thorntuft especially. When Nothro eventually noticed an opportunity whilst walking through one of the narrower side streets of Dralcea, purportedly on the way to their provided lodgings, he dropped back a little from the trio of guards. He held a hand in front of Julius to slow his progress too, letting the guards unknowingly drift slightly ahead. Seizing his chance, Nothro utilised his enormous strength to flip a tall-sided cart over onto its longer axis, forming a barrier between the two parties and separating them rather effectively. Nothro made no mistake in making a hasty exit back the way they had come with Julius scrabbling close behind.

'Well even so, we should probably find somewhere a little less public to be. Who knows when they might turn up again? They must know this place far better than we ever will,' Julius supposed.

'Probably.'

'Why were they being so clingy with us anyway? They seem a little overzealous for glorified watchmen. I'm sure we don't need babysitting.'

Nothro snorted again, a deep gruff sound with a growling undertone that would unnerve humans unfamiliar with his species. 'Probably bored. Doubt they have much to do.' He looked at the shabby streets surrounding them. 'I bet we were the most interesting job going.'

'Could be. They'll be in for one hell of an arse roasting, though, after we gave them the slip. Should have stuck to a boring everyday rota, patrolling or such,' Julius said with a big grin spreading over his face. He stretched his arms up and behind his head, bringing his hands together as he did so. 'Poor bastards,' he said with little sympathy.

Julius saw in Nothro's expression that he spared them no compassion either. Julius looked curiously at one of the stalls they approached, packed with unfamiliar items on display; some sort of glazed pottery in bizarre shapes that looked to be of no practical use. It was one of many stalls he had seen displaying wares completely alien to him. Ever the pragmatist, he was not interested in anything he could not eat, shelter under or defend himself with. Living their lives out in the remote wilds of Thorntuft led them to value the things that truly made life tolerable. A little hot food, a dry place to rest your head. Those held value.

Nothro waded his way through the market crowd and sped up, seemingly following his nose. Julius tried his best to keep up but was caught in the backwash of people from his friend's passage. Julius knew that Ananeptide were much less common in the capital than in Thorntuft and were generally afforded more space by their human compatriots than was strictly necessary. Taking a sharp left turn around a stall, Julius would have lost him from sight amongst the crowd of traders and customers if not for Nothro's large stature; he stood out in all crowds bar those of his own kind, so Julius easily spotted his friend's head bobbing along.

Julius caught up to Nothro as he had halted at a stand dominated by a large cauldron of aromatic, bubbling stew of indeterminate content. Since living out in the province meant less choice in what to eat, Nothro would eat anything even vaguely digestible which came within range of his pointed teeth and strong jaws. The Ananeptide ordered two large bowls and dropped the required value of somoni coins into the wary human vendor's hand as payment. Julius was still weighing up the food on offer as he was less easily sold on the unknown mixture.

'Perhaps I could go first in future? These bastards make getting anywhere like wading through a river of your crap after you've gorged yourself all night,' Julius spat. He watched Nothro demolish his stew, noisily slurping at it with great gusto.

Julius sighed. 'One for me too, mate,' he said, handing over a three-somoni coin. He took his bowl and saw the lumpy contents swimming in a film of grease. He poked at one of the floating chunks which bobbed under the oily surface before it stubbornly resumed floating. It was a hot meal at least, and he started to consume it as Nothro finished the last of his own.

The satiated Ananeptide returned his emptied bowls to the vendor's stall and wiped at the greasy streaks either side of his mouth with one huge, furry hand. The fur around his mouth remained ruffled and glistened slightly. 'Not bad,' Nothro growled. 'I almost tasted some meat in there.'

Julius was used to such talk from his friend. Whilst Nothro rarely spoke, when he did it was usually cynical. Eventually Julius finished and returned his bowl, whilst Nothro surveyed the crowds around them impassively.

Julius grinned as they left the market, intent on enjoying his newfound freedom of the city before the sun rose on the following day with all that would entail. He would find them both somewhere to stay himself. In the meantime they would enjoy the warmer climate of Dralcea, making the most of being positioned around the roiling magma of the caldera and thinking how much better it was than Thorntuft's expanse of snow and frozen earth.

He was enjoying not having to wear a thick fur coat as he usually would at home; it was tied to his back in a bundle, and he wore a simple shirt and his usual trousers. Despite his thick fur Nothro showed no outward signs of any discomfort, or much else for that matter. Julius sometimes thought that he would not show that anything was amiss if he had been grievously wounded, he would just carry on as usual and keep his thoughts to himself, barely saying a word. At this moment in time he was gazing about, silently taking in the sights on offer.

'It's so loud here compared to the woods, everybody seems to be constantly trying to out-shout somebody else. I wonder how long it takes to get used to being deafened.' Nothro did not respond, not unusually for him.

Julius kept his head on a swivel to seek out any places where they might purchase a room for the night. He would not be particularly choosy – after all, he lived in a cabin with only the essentials out in the frozen woods, where comfort came second to keeping warm and safe by whatever means. Provided wherever they found had a door they could shut securely, a soft place to lie down would be a real luxury for him.

'Over here,' Julius called to Nothro. Julius had spotted a lodging house in a side street once they had roamed away from the main streets, simply painted white with a red door which looked ideal. He had dismissed other, more expensive-looking options closer to the centre of Dralcea – neither was keen to part with a large chunk of their earnings. 'This place looks reasonable.'

Nothro looked over the building Julius was now inclining his head toward. 'Says you.'

'Gods, what do you want? A mossy nest all ready and waiting for you like your mother used to prepare? You take what you can get in this place, especially when you don't want to pay through the nose for it. It's a safe place behind a door, hopefully, which is all we need – even if you have to sleep on the floor as you so often do anyway.'

'We'll see.'

'Misery.' Julius gave a series of firm raps on the well-painted door with his knuckles. It was kept in good condition, unlike some they had seen which bore merely a few splinters of their original paint and looked sporadically covered in creeping insects. This one was cared for.

After a few moments, the door opened fractionally to allow an aging gentleman to peer cautiously through the gap at Julius. Apparently satisfied it was not a bandit knocking on his door in preparation to rob him, he opened the door slightly more before he noticed the bulk of Nothro looming behind Julius and opened the door no further. 'Yes, what is it?'

'We're looking for a room for the night.' The man's suspicious tone had made Julius doubt himself, even though he had seen the sign outside. 'You do offer that, don't you?'

'Yes, we do offer rooms. Well, for people we do anyway. We don't have the...facilities for your associate there I'm afraid.'

'Facilities?' Julius asked. 'What do you mean?'

'I don't demand much,' Nothro added. Julius knew from experience that Nothro did not appreciating being discussed without being addressed directly.

'Our rooms are human-sized, that's the problem. We're not equipped for someone of his size to stay. I'm sorry,' the proprietor said in a manner suggesting finality.

'If I fit through the door, that's enough. I don't need galloping room,' Nothro said, frustration starting to show in his voice.

'Come on now, he's not that big. Look,' Julius said whilst he grabbed a handful of Nothro's dense fur on his stomach and jiggling it slightly to help illustrate his point. 'He's all fluff, and soft as snow in temperament too. Would I do this otherwise?'

The man appeared slightly more at ease after seeing this, although he still looked doubtful. Julius knew the direction of the man's thinking now and pursued it further. 'He won't be any trouble. Believe me, I've known him for years and I get into more trouble than he does.' Aware that he might have said something that would harm his cause, Julius relented. 'Which of course is still very little trouble indeed. We're just after a room for one night is all.'

'Just one night?' the man said. He seemed to be calculating how much destruction could be wrought over the course of a single night and weighing that against his potential monetary gain.

'That's right. We're here for an award to be presented tomorrow and then we will be back on the road home. All we want is a safe place for the night and thought that your establishment would fit the bill.'

'An award? What is that for?' The proprietor sounded intrigued, even bordering on impressed. Julius imagined that if they were presented as customers of renown then the owner could use that to his advantage in the future. In Dralcea, nothing compared to being able to brag about famous clientele to drum up business and raise your rates.

Julius sought to press the advantage; he dreamed of not just being allowed to rest for the night but being bestowed with the best room on offer. 'Yes, a high honour indeed. We are each being awarded the Heart of Dralcea for...' Julius realised he wasn't really sure what they were being given it for and blustered as best he could, '...recognition of our efforts to help the community, and society in general. The presentation is being held at the Promontory,' he added, hoping the name would add a little lustre to his appeal. Nothro kept quiet and instead of contributing, the Ananeptide folded his arms across his chest and did what seemed to be his best impression of a respectable member of society.

'The Promontory you say...well, I can hardly turn away anyone who is being recognised for an award, can I?' His tone was still somewhat begrudging, despite having relented.

The owner opened the door fully, revealing his appearance. He was dressed in clothes so thin and casual-looking that the patrons assumed that it was his nightwear despite the early hour, and his feet were bare, exposing unkempt toenails to their unwilling eyes. Julius had not expected this after the disapproval they had just encountered. 'If you will follow me, I'll show you to your room. Or would you prefer to have separate places to stay?'

Julius assumed this was going to lead to further charges, and so replied quickly, 'We'll share.'

The man shrugged. 'As you wish, if you think you will have enough space.' He beckoned them inside and shut and chained the door behind them once they were safely inside. 'Can't be too careful after recent events,' he muttered by way of explanation.

The owner led the way and they traversed a dreary corridor sporting several badly rendered paintings of the outer Bowl on the walls, along with a mirror that looked to have been neglected since the day it was hung. The grime coating the surface made it nearly impossible to see your reflection, and Julius noted that as they passed by, he and Nothro simply appeared as undefined smears. A vaguely fungal smell pervaded the hall.

They passed by a simple staircase, and upon reaching the end of the corridor, found themselves outside a plain wooden door. Their host withdrew a set of keys from his pocket and carefully selected the correct one, eventually unlocking the door and pushing it open. Julius shot Nothro a look.

'Here you are,' the man gestured into the small room. 'It might be a little cosy, but the beds are top quality. Please help yourselves to the water over there on the table and do let us know if you require feeding. We offer a very reasonable rate for dinner here, too – my wife cooks a fantastic snorthog chop, our specialty. Make yourselves at home, gentlemen. If you need anything, give the bell in the hall a ring and we will see what we can do.' With that, he left them to settle in.

Julius entered the room and sat down heavily on one of the pair of beds. They were little more than a basic wooden frame with straw sacking and a thin blanket laid on top to enhance the appearance. Neither were too bothered about the state of the beds – Nothro would sleep almost anywhere he could curl himself up – but Julius noticed a few stains on the walls that had not been cleaned. The small, barred window set high up in the wall facing him admitted a paltry amount of light, thanks to its cloudy nature and the closeness of the neighbouring building.

Nothro squeezed through the small doorway and surveyed the room his friend was already making himself at home in. He sniffed the water jug from a distance to check its freshness – his Ananeptide nose was adept at tracking, and so a jug across the room was little challenge – and gently sat on the remaining unclaimed bed which bowed significantly under his weight.

'Not the worst bed I've ever sat on, but pretty far from the best too. I take it you saw him unlocking the door – what do you think of that? Reckon we might be labelled as a threat and locked in?' Julius asked.

'Possibly.' Nothro gestured at the door with his large head. 'I doubt it would stand up to a kicking though.'

Julius laughed at that. 'True enough,' he said. 'Always nice to have personal security on hand.' He folded his arms behind him, supporting his head. 'Do you want to take him up on the cooked dinner offer? It might be your best chance of getting some real meat. I'm not entirely sure what it was that we ate earlier – was it even from an animal?'

'Wouldn't put money on it,' Nothro commented. 'I could go for some snorthog. It's been ages.'

'Same. Seems as if we've just been eating goat and squirrel for as long as I can remember.'

'Don't moan, or you can catch your own dinner in future.'

'You know I appreciate your hunting efforts. Whilst here in the big city though, I'm going to make the most of it and try something a little more –' he paused to think of the word '– refined. I might even go so far as to sample one of those flammula the Crinochin seem so keen on. Or maybe an egg – you know they are laid already hard-boiled? No need to cook! If I can get any Crinochin to part with one, that is.'

Nothro huffed. 'You think there's much on those little birds? You'll be disappointed.'

'Compared to a fantastically meaty squirrel?' Julius laughed.

'Good red meat on those,' Nothro said defensively.

'Yes, yes. We'll get you some red meat for your dinner. We need to keep your strength up for the big day tomorrow, after all. Come on. Let's see what the city has to offer two hungry travellers.'

Chapter Seven – Reassurances

Branch Godfrey Vilipas was pleased with the turnout of civilians for the reassuring speech he was about to deliver. He stood at the head of a carefully picked selection of his sergeants who would best represent the Dralcea Guard and impress those assembled for the recruitment drive which was to follow. His men were dressed in their best uniforms, buttons and medals polished to a high shine, whilst he wore his best robes and stood atop a small set of wooden steps to increase his stature and oratorial range. Whilst he would not admit as such, he got a thrill from being able to emphasise his importance by standing above the men he commanded and the ordinary people gathered there.

Thinking there was no better time to start now that a sizable crowd was present, Vilipas drew a large breath before addressing those before him. 'Good citizens of Dralcea! Thank you for joining us here today for this important announcement.' He took a moment to smile at his audience in the hope of appearing sincere to win over the notoriously fickle residents, and took note that it was mostly comprised of humans, with a dozen Ananeptide sprinkled throughout and a small number of Crinochin meandering through the others restlessly, trying for as good a viewpoint as their small stature would allow.

'As you may be aware, there have been one or two incidents occurring within the city walls recently. You should be reassured that these are nothing to be worried about, but all the same we would advise you to take care when out in the city at night. We recommend returning to your homes before nightfall in order to be completely safe – danger is always best avoided when you have the choice, after all.' He paused momentarily to see what effect his words were having.

Perfectly timed, a voice in the crowd piped up. 'Aren't you the ones meant to be keeping us safe? We shouldn't have to be hiding away!' This drew a few angry murmurs of agreement from those waiting around.

'Of course, your security is our top priority. It is our very reason to be,' Vilipas said soothingly, hands spread wide. He was trying to lay it on just thick enough to ignite the passion of the people, knowing that playing on their emotions was his best tool in achieving his aim. 'This is simply advice that will help you keep yourselves safe. Small actions that are easy to follow and benefit everyone.' Knowing that the way he was talking would lead to one of a handful of inevitable responses, he waited for the next predictable step to be taken so that he could lead on to his next topic.

'How come you've let those folk get hurt so far then?' an angry woman shouted at Vilipas, waving one fleshy arm as she did so to emphasise her point. 'We've heard about those things attacking people – you can't keep it secret from us, we've seen the evidence. Your lot should have been there to stop it happening! I don't want to be the next one to end up in pieces spread across the cobbles!' She paused to take a deep breath before continuing her tirade. 'You get paid to keep us safe, but you aren't doing it!' Her face was red now, anger building rapidly.

'My good lady, I understand your fears but there are no vicious creatures roaming around our streets. Somebody has been misinformed or else has a fanciful imagination.' Vilipas had heard the rumour that had quickly done the predictable rounds and reached many ears willing to listen and, for the most part, believe. 'You do lead me perfectly on to my next point to raise with you all though. Yes, we patrol the streets and watch where we can, but our scope only goes so far. We cannot be everywhere at once. However, we have recognised that because of this we cannot fulfil our duty as we should at this time, and so we are expanding the ranks.'

Vilipas gazed around at those in front of him to assess the quality of the crowd. There were a good number of the youths who usually haunted the busy streets of Dralcea or else lurked in alleys, along with those older folk who would otherwise be out shopping in the markets or running errands and had stopped to see what the occasion was for such a gathering. His target was the former, but in reality he was happy to appeal to all – the reactions of the older people would easily fuel the actions of the young. 'As such, applications to join the Dralcea Guard are now open and we encourage anyone who feels the urge to serve their city to come forward and enlist. We will need you.'

'Not good enough to keep control as it is, eh?' one older man near the front sneered. He clearly thought he was being hilarious and turned to see the reaction of those around him, only to be disappointed when nobody thought it was funny.

'We always do what is necessary to ensure that we can do our jobs effectively,' Vilipas replied with authority. 'We see where change is needed, and we take action.'

These words brought a mixed reaction but Vilipas could tell that he had elicited some excitement from elements of the crowd. The Dralcea Guard was generally respected in the city and in some quarters feared – both of these views were voiced in the crowd now, along with those who disapproved and believed that the current numbers ought to be enough to keep order. The humans in the crowd who needed work or wanted a taste of authority were the ones most interested. The Crinochin contingent appeared unmoved, simply curious in their own inimitable way, whilst the ever hard-to-read Ananeptide just appeared to be listening without reacting. His humble approach appeared to be working on the humans at least.

'Who will be the first to sign up? This is a worthy calling with plenty of work to be done for good pay. A smart uniform to be proud of, too. Come and talk to us about what we do and about the many other benefits of our organisation.' He hoped that dangling that vague carrot would let their imagination fill in the blanks to a larger degree than was true. It could only help.

The angry voices in the crowd died away as they were unable to think of a suitable argument against this. It was hard to decry their intent to do better by taking more guards on. Vilipas let a small smile escape from his serious façade as he indulged himself with the knowledge that he had calmed the dissenters. He would let them amble over to his men now and get them to sign their futures into the hands of the Dralcea Guard. He was confident that many would do so.

Vilipas made an elaborate welcoming gesture in the direction of the table they had set up which was now covered in official documents ready to be signed. A couple of human teenagers stepped forward, assured in their snap decision-making in the way that only the young can be. Vilipas stepped down from his perch and snapped his fingers for one of the more servile guards present to take the steps away. He moved to the rear of their stall to watch more people come forward to sign themselves into the service of the Dralcea Guard.

It was also a good opportunity for him to observe his sergeants and how they would fare interacting with members of the public in a more casual setting than usual. It could provide him with valuable insight, he thought. Their behaviour was certainly of interest to Vilipas, considering what he knew of the storm brewing on the horizon.

Chapter Eight – New Faces

'Come on you two, at least attempt to look as if this is a job worth having. Sluss, I fear you'll headbutt anyone who dares approach and Souo...well, the less said about the expression you're wearing, the better. It'd put a goat off its mating ritual,' Janos commented. The attending sergeants manned their stall in the parade ground at the fore of the Promontory, left to their own devices after Branch Vilipas departed. Sergeant Egil Sluss was all business and stood for no levity whatsoever – he was serious to the core and always operated with complete formality. Sergeant Younes Souo was simply an old hand at the job, not adept at playing the friendly recruiter that his superiors had intended. His attempt at a welcoming smile came across as an off-putting leer as the heavy jowls of his face contorted and his white handlebar moustache puffed out obscenely. Janos wanted to avoid a dressing down just because his colleagues were useless at recruitment; he at least would do his best to ensure that something positive came out of the day.

'You there, lad! Ever wanted to be the pride of your neighbourhood? Our medium-sized uniform would fit you perfectly. Come and try it on,' Janos called enticingly.

The rather lean-looking youth who sauntered by at a short distance, on his way to who knows what appointment at this time of the day, looked over at their recruiting stand with a look of surprise on his face. 'Me?' he asked.

'Yes lad, come and have a nosey,' Janos replied in his best matey voice, as if they had already been introduced and gotten along famously. 'It costs nothing to have a look!'

The young man approached hesitantly, unwilling to get too drawn into a conversation with members of the infamous Dralcea Guard and his wariness was plain to see. The sight of the towering Janos, the intimidating visage of Sluss and the sheer mass of Souo were enough to make anyone think twice about approaching.

Souo interjected. 'Do you not get fed at home, lad? We would make sure you put a bit more meat on your bones here,' he said, obviously doing his utmost to sound appealing but not realising how ludicrous it sounded. This drew a hiss from Janos in reply.

'Shut up, you'll scare him away! Don't be negative about them or they'll tell you to piss off!' Janos whispered angrily to the much heavier, older man.

'If he does that, I'll shackle the bugger and drag him back to the holding cells,' Souo grumbled.

'Great, just the incentive we need,' Janos said quietly to himself. The young man looked at the neatly folded uniform placed on the desk in front of him.

'Looks good, doesn't it? Just think how smart you would look in that. Have you ever considered a life in the Dralcea Guard, young man? You look as if you were born to do the job.' He was laying it on thick now, but it did not seem to be scaring the lad off. It might even work with a little luck. 'What's your name?'

'Can't say I've ever thought about it,' the youth said. 'My name is Helfred Onnson.'

'Well, Helfred, let me tell you, joining the Guard is the best thing you could ever do. You gain a trade, a good honest wage is yours, and you make a difference. You want to make a difference, right?'

'A difference to what, exactly? Most of the guards I see are just strolling around the streets, not really doing anything.'

Janos was slightly taken aback by this statement but did not allow it to show. '*Patrolling,* my boy, keeping the streets safe. You know there have been those incidents lately? We keep it all in check and keep people safe. That's the real value of our work. Security.'

'But wouldn't I be the first one in the way of these attacks if I joined up? I don't want to be the one getting ripped apart by whichever god's evil creation is out there doing these things. Who would?'

'We're the last defence of civilisation against those barbarous exiles and whatever else lurks outside the city walls. It's noble work, and we work together as a team, lad. You always have your mates by your side, and what could be better than that? You get to know each other, rely on each other, and together you're unstoppable,' Janos said as he gestured to his fellow guards. 'Right, sergeants?' Sluss nodded in reply whilst Souo just grunted. *Thanks for the support, lads,* Janos thought.

'My mates are all dickheads. I wouldn't rely on them to piss on me if I were on fire.' Helfred turned to make his leave.

'Don't you want to attract the girls, Helfred?' Janos quickly asked in an amazed voice.

This made Helfred turn back sharply, one eyebrow raised. 'What do you mean by that?'

'I mean,' Janos said in a confidential manner, 'that signing up makes you a certified hero. You're keeping people safe – it's an honourable, selfless profession, lad. Not everybody can do it, they don't all have the balls. But I bet you could. And you know what? The girls love to see a strong, brave man in uniform. They go mad for it.' Janos could tell that with those last few words he was starting to get Helfred's attention.

'Really?' Helfred looked thoughtful. He ran his fingers over the folded uniform, stroking the material as if sizing up how attractive it would appear if he were wearing it himself. Glancing over at the rotund Souo standing off to one side with his uniform straining to contain his size probably gave him more to consider.

'I can *personally* vouch for that,' Janos said with a sly grin. He knew he was getting somewhere after the failures they had previously overseen. 'What do you say, Helfred – or *Recruit*

Onnson? How does that title sound?' Janos knew that using his name in such a way would surely tempt the man.

Helfred was clearly considering it but still looked slightly hesitant to commit himself so quickly.

'What else have you got to do today, eh? Are you on your way to your job?'

'No, I...I don't have a job. Not right now,' Helfred said with dismay in his voice.

'Well, the pay isn't bad either. Fancy joining up with us and having a good job where you make a difference?'

Helfred looked at Janos with a smile beginning to form on his face. 'You know what? Yes, I will. I need something and maybe this is it. What is your name, sir?'

Janos smiled in return. 'Sergeant Boltfoot, son. Glad to have you on board. You've made a good decision today.' He reached out his massive right hand to shake Helfred's. 'Just sign on this document here and we'll do the rest.'

As Janos ran Helfred through the formalities, Sluss and Souo watched from close by. Once the newly enlisted Recruit Onnson went on his way with instructions to report to the Promontory barracks the following day, the two sergeants engaged Janos in conversation.

'What was that all about back there?' Sluss growled.

'What do you mean? Talking to somebody interested? It's the way to get things done, Sluss,' Janos responded.

'It's not how we usually do it. It's misleading.'

'You can't go being *nice* to them,' Souo spluttered.

Janos laughed. 'Misleading? Hardly. Sometimes you just have to tell them what they want to hear. You know, play on what they think is an aspect of the job anyway, emphasise it a bit.' Janos looked at his fellow sergeants a little more searchingly. 'It seems to work, anyway. It certainly works better than the *traditional* way where we stand there looking authoritative, hoping that civilians will overcome their fear of us looking scary and come over to say hello.'

'It's not right. You'll get them expecting us to be their mates, and that ain't happening,' Sluss said with feeling. 'You'll get done by Vilipas doing stuff like that.'

'What, actually signing up some new recruits? That's the whole idea! He's desperate for us to get the numbers up, at least I'm trying to do that. You really think he won't be more pissed off if we don't get any new names? We've got to try.'

'Well, what's in it for us?' Souo huffed. 'We're not getting any sort of bonus for signing more up.'

Janos gave his colleague a pitying look. 'Think about it. Once there are more folk in the lower ranks, your position becomes more important, right? And, if there are more enrolled, you might even get to spend less time out on patrols. They'll need organising and directing. This is a good step for us sergeants.'

Souo looked pleased with this answer. Janos had no doubt his fellow sergeant had been hoping for more coins in his pay packet, but this must be attractive too – the potential for a promotion and reduced time on his sore feet. Who would be first in line for such a move upwards too, but the most senior sergeant in the Dralcea Guard? 'Well, that wouldn't be so bad,' Souo conceded to Janos. 'Perhaps we should play our part.'

Sluss gave them a look that could break glass. 'I don't know about any of that, but we have our instructions. We had better follow them,' he said, voice full of disdain. Sluss turned to face forward with his best imitation of an approachable face. Other onlookers began to arrive, having seen Helfred come and go with a satisfied expression that salved their fears of approaching.

The sergeants were kept busy for the next few hours with applicants and interested parties out to learn more about the peacekeeping force of their city. The guards did their best to stay civil and perform their unfamiliar role.

*

Grand Branch Drachvas Rizon stood with his hands held tightly behind him as he faced out of the tall, narrow window at the city spreading below. His chamber, a hundred feet up in the pointed front of the Promontory, overlooked both the upper level of the city and the caldera alike as it loomed over them. His mind's eye overlaid scenes onto the streets as he gazed down at them far below; blue-cloaked guards at every junction, standing sentry with spears leaning on shoulders whilst others slowly stalked the roads, both a calming presence and walking deterrent. All the citizens would be together, working alongside one another, strong in doing so. The thought relaxed him to the extent that he became lost in the fantasy for a few moments.

A cough destined to catch his attention snapped Rizon back to the present, and he realised he had been daydreaming a little too long. He banished those thoughts of order then straightened his face as he turned away from the window. The source of the noise seemed to be his Crinochin assistant, Sergeant Gengran Dalbahan, who had allowed Branch Vilipas to enter the room whilst Rizon was in his reverie. Dalbahan made eye contact with Rizon and gestured at Vilipas as if to apologetically announce the branch's arrival. 'Thank you, sergeant,' Rizon said.

Rizon simply stared at the new arrival without uttering a word. Sergeant Dalbahan resumed buzzing about busily in his office, his miniature blue tunic fluttering slightly as he moved from task to task with his wide Crinochin hands. He was better off busy, as his necessity could be questioned otherwise. If he was forced to return to his previous life it would be difficult for him to integrate with his family again after such elevated service in the Dralcea Guard; he had come a very long way from the streets in which he had grown up. Dalbahan had valuable qualities, which although not utilised continuously, Rizon was determined to retain. He would do whatever Rizon needed without question.

Vilipas looked uncomfortable and was clearly waiting for an instruction to start talking. After a few awkward moments, he hesitantly broke the silence. 'Grand Branch...you called for me?'

Rizon continued his impassive stare. *Always good to intimidate the underlings*, he thought.

'Yes,' he eventually said with an annoyed edge to his voice. 'How is the intake going – are we moving forward? How many were enrolled today?'

'Yes, Grand Branch, we have the men out busy with signing up those interested—'

'How many?' Rizon interrupted.

'Well, we haven't managed to add—'

'You realise we need to bolster our ranks immediately? We face unprecedented threats to our very lives, here in the very last vestige of humanity! Our bastion of civilisation itself is at risk. Don't forget that outside our city walls is nought but barren ground, earth as hard as rock, stretching out toward the outer rim itself beyond which lies nothing but a frozen death. We must protect the caldera around which Dralcea is built since it provides us all with the life-giving warmth which lets us survive – humans, Crinochin and Ananeptide alike.'

'What of Olrof and Thorntuft, sir, and the other minor settlements? They survive without our input,' Vilipas said.

Rizon frowned severely at his subordinate. 'Although Olrof and Thorntuft are our allies, I wouldn't describe life there as really *living*. They're brutish and unrefined, unlike Dralcea. If push comes to shove and they are attacked, without the walls or resources that we have, they will quickly fall. This city is the place which must endure – there is nowhere else to go from here. We are walled in around the last refuge in our otherwise frozen world, after all. Would you see this oasis of life in the icy wastes be corrupted and overthrown because of your lax efforts, for want of doing all in our power to change for the better? We are but a speck of light in the vast darkness. Gonnar Muldullah and his fellow Originators fought through unbelievable hardships to ensure that all of us, their descendants and the last people alive in this world, had the chance to live on. You know that their long journey traversing the cave systems leading through the edge of the Bowl were hellish, and they would not have wanted it to be in vain. Would you be the one responsible for dousing our spark?' Rizon kept his voice calm as though talking to a child throughout his tirade until the end when his voice rose to an incredulous tone.

Vilipas stammered back a reply. 'I – I understand the need sir, and we're doing all we can to make everyone safer. We are being aggressive in our recruitment.'

'As aggressive as those exiles that lurk out in the wastes, scratching a living by whatever base means they can? Those who would come and sack the city simply to take pleasure in the cruelty they would inflict? They covet our way of life and would do anything to see it in their hands, debased or wiped away forever. Always remember that. And that's before we even consider the disturbing reports of creatures encroaching on our lands from the frozen world encircling us, and doing unspeakable things to those they find. Gods know there are enough species already crammed into our lands, and the peace between species and different human groups fragile enough, without whatever abominations can survive out on the ice adding themselves to the mix.'

'You're referring to those gruesome losses we suffered recently, sir?' Vilipas asked. 'They did sound nasty.'

'That's putting it mildly, branch. I don't think many people would choose their last conscious moments to be ones where they're being pulled apart by something with more legs and claws than sense.'

'They've been spotted then, sir? We know something about the creatures behind the attacks?'

Rizon stared at him hard. *I didn't think he'd be coming up with the smart questions so quickly*, he mused. *That's not like Vilipas at all.* 'One or two vague reports from witnesses, so we have some idea. The important thing is that they're not good news and we must be ready to stop them.'

'I see, sir. Hence the need for more recruits to be enlisted.'

'Exactly. There could also be any number of other beasts out there in the far reaches of the Bowl, the places untouched by our explorers. Humans and Ananeptide flocked here, so perhaps other species sought shelter here too. Remember, we must have all new recruits trained as well – this does not happen instantly. Time is something we are short of, if you will please remember that. Failure to accomplish this task would weigh heavily on a man of your position,' he said pointedly.

Vilipas paled at the comment. 'Yes, of course Grand Branch,' he opted for, giving the safest answer possible.

'We must also consider internal threats to the city – the last thing we need at this time is interference. It's vital that those we identified are nullified; those citizens capable of intervening, the ones who we know have already gone against the grain, been bold and acted on their own when they should have left the policing to us. We can't have them deciding to speak up and getting in our way. So, how are the preparations going for the Heart of Dralcea award ceremony?'

'It is coming together, sir. Those invited have either been notified or escorted to the city to ensure their presence. There is still the matter of—'

'Just get it done.' Rizon wandered over to his desk near the main window illuminating the room. With his back to Vilipas, who he assumed would now leave, Rizon picked up a long object lying on his desk. It was the first fully working Ejector, finally mastered by their commissioned inventor, Alfred Omphalos. Rizon knew that Dalbahan wished for one himself, if only it were of a size and shape that would enable him to use it with his short arms and oversized hands.

Rizon looked around to be sure that Branch Vilipas had exited the room before speaking. 'Dalbahan – I need an audience with Gate Guard Roque. I have another task for him to help convince the public of our necessity,' he said. 'He has been extremely effective at performing them so far. The mess he made of our unfortunate associates manning the south-western outpost was really quite spectacular. He has talent.'

'Yes, grand branch,' Sergeant Dalbahan croaked in reply. 'I understand it made an impression and the rumour is now doing the rounds. I'll call Roque in to see you.'

'Thank you, sergeant. This campaign is going well. The more scared the population are, the more new guards we can hire.'

'Your plan is coming together, sir,' Dalbahan rasped in his guttural, strained voice that grated on many but did not affect Rizon.

'We will have sufficient numbers,' Drachvas Rizon said to himself more than Dalbahan. His mind's eye active again, Rizon envisaged row after row of uniformed guards marching down the streets, all holding Ejectors of their own – a force embodying strength, and order. More importantly, a force acting on his orders. 'And we will have the means.'

Chapter Nine – Journeyman

'Just how does this city work? Each layer is dug down into the earth surrounding this chasm?' Molefi Cronto mumbled to himself. 'The books don't do Dralcea justice. It's far more confusing than they said.'

He tried to understand how the network of streets worked as he wandered around the Warren; Cronto was a learned man employed as a judge in Olrof, but found that navigating Dralcea was a difficult business despite his reading. He had followed a set of descending steps leading down to the second layer to further investigate the city and satisfy his curiosity. He cut a striking figure in the Warren; those surroundings rarely saw anyone from the north-eastern territory of Olrof. He wore the traditional clothing of his people – a loose fitting ochre-coloured smock bearing a zig-zagging red line around the chest at breast height, somewhat tighter fitting beige leggings with additional strips of a darker brown material wound around the outside and wide sandals on his feet. Sitting on top of his head was his hat, a terracotta-coloured, rounded dish shape three inches high with an intricate dyed pattern of right angles and chevrons around the entire circumference. Olrof received a significant amount more sunlight than the other areas of the Bowl – such hats were necessary to minimise exposure to it.

'At least it's warmer here than back at home,' he continued to himself. Cronto's home region was no warmer than anywhere else outside of Dralcea; it was a mostly featureless, flat and dry area with shifting sands and near-constant winds blowing. Olrof was not considered a comfortable place to inhabit by those who did not live there, though its people had mastered the difficult terrain and accepted its traits for what they were.

The travelling bag across his back was also noticeable. The long, tubular canvas bag had a rope running through it in a loop which he wore over one shoulder, across his chest and under the other arm. It contained his essential washing supplies, currency, changes of clothes and the slightly less usual travelling item – his broad-handled axe named Bulwark, the end of the stave protruding from the top of the bag. He had traversed the dangerous roads leading from Olrof to the capital for many miles and protection was necessary. Carrying a weapon openly on the streets of the capital as an ordinary citizen was not a good idea, however.

Cronto strode along happily whilst peering in at various dwellings and dark, dusty shops of various kinds. He received a few stares of his own in turn – Cronto however took this in good humour and whenever he noticed anyone looking at him, he just flashed a smile right back from his dark-skinned face.

One enterprising shop owner loitered near the front of his shop in which he sold various pieces of worn and battered furniture and cheap ornaments. He sidled out at the sight of Cronto approaching and opened his arms up wide in an exaggerated gesture of welcome.

'My dear distinguished sir! You look to be a man of fine taste. Please come in to peruse what I have to offer!' He swept one arm behind Cronto to usher him inside, hovering his hand over his bag.

'You're right on one count,' Cronto replied calmly. 'Just what do you have to offer? I can't see your wares.' The shop windows admitted little of the already limited light creeping down to the second level of the Warren due to being thickly encrusted with dust and grime.

'The best housewares sir, the best! All kinds of furniture, everything you could need for your home! Or for more decorative purposes, we have...well, all sorts! Jars, clocks, forks, doorstops, nutcrackers, candleholders, tongs, and a particularly fine mirror which I think would suit you perfectly! Do come in and see…'

Cronto held up an appeasing hand. 'Thank you, but I live far from here. Furnishings are of no use to me, as I have much more time on the road ahead of me. I am however sure the mirror you have for sale is magnificent indeed!'

'You will surely be enchanted if you gaze upon it, the opportunity to see such an item should not be missed…,' the merchant said as he tried again to guide Molefi inside his shop. Cronto simply continued to walk on and gave the man a gracious smile as he did so. 'Prosperous times to come,' Cronto said graciously as he walked on.

I have all I could need right now on my back, Cronto thought. He saw another shopkeeper emerge from the dingy door to his own shop and anticipated a similar sales pitch, so Cronto steered himself into the middle of the road and looked thoughtfully at some withered produce for sale on the opposite side. He was thankful that the owner of this shop was less intent on making a sale and allowed him to simply pass by without a haranguing.

He reflected on why he had been summoned to this place which he had seldom cause to journey to before. As a judge in Olrof, most of his professional time was spent settling disputes and sentencing those who did wrong, so travelling was not much of an option; he was always needed at his place of work. Having been made to leave on this occasion, he had left his young deputy in charge for the minor judgements to be made, a responsibility that would add to his experience. More serious cases involving major crimes would have to wait until his return.

Cronto had been surprised when a local boy, around ten years old, turned up at his door and banged on it with his fist until opened. The lad bore a slate with hastily scrawled instructions upon it to make his way to Dralcea. He had been dubious until Cronto eventually wheedled out of the child that he had been paid handsomely to come and find him. He gathered that a pair of Dralcea Guards had been making their way to Olrof to escort him to Dralcea before becoming tired – and presumably scared – of continuing their journey, being so far outside Dralcea's protective walls. They had entered one of the small settlements on the outer edges of Olrof and found the boy, looking in need of money. They had sent him ahead and waited for the child and their charge to return, intending to then resume the journey back, each a coin lighter but with their feet less sore and their throats uncut. Cronto however judged the men's actions – this was the basis of his career, after all – and ensured the boy returned safely to his village before carefully avoiding the guards and making his own way to the capital. Cronto gave the young man instructions to notify the guards that he would be travelling ahead alone, once he had made a sufficient head start, of course.

Cronto did not relish the thought of being frogmarched to the Promontory by guards, no matter what the reason. He was also suspicious of the explanation – he was to be awarded an honour, but why? He did his job as necessary and left it at that, so long as he was content that he had made the right call. As a humble man, he did not believe he deserved any recognition. The message he received was clearly a much-shortened version as it contained no specific details. He felt obliged to make the journey since ignoring such summons was unlikely to be a sensible course of action. In any case, it was a reason to get away for a while and enjoy some solitude. He could do with a change.

Whilst still walking, he passed a pair of guards walking together slowly and having a private conversation in hushed tones. Thinking it best to minimise contact with any guards given his recent shirking of their colleagues, he saw another stone staircase leading up to the surface level approaching to his right and aimed himself at it. He slowly took the first couple of steps, then dawdled until the pair were safely past him before hopping back down and continuing his way. They did not appear to have noticed him, being too involved in their conversation. Cronto paused at a convenient alcove a little way along the tunnel-like street and swung his bag around so it came to rest on his chest. From the bag he drew a small slate with a few scrawled lines on it.

M. Fala

159 Unity Tube

2nd stratum

N.W.D.

Dralcea

He frowned at the address held before him. The system used to denote where people lived in Dralcea was far from simple, mirroring the complex structure of the capital city itself. The name was self-explanatory, and the street name and number were the same as the established system in Olrof. The strata system also made sense when first entering the city, as it was obvious when you could descend through them when starting from the top, the first stratum – albeit utilising the ramshackle sets of steps at seemingly random intervals. An aid was being able to judge which step you were at by the steadily diminishing amount of light outside the further you descended, though with the added complication of radial distance away from the central chasm around which the city was built. The following part of the address was more of a puzzle with its abbreviated form; *N.W.D.* Cronto had eventually realised that this referred to the specific section radiating out from the chasm as if seen from above, like a wedge-shaped slice of a pie, and disregarding the specific stratum – *North-Western District.* He could descend directly down through any number of the strata, stairs allowing, and remain in the North-Western District but could move laterally down a side street and find himself in a different district altogether.

Cronto sighed as he looked up again at the street he found himself in as he continued walking. 'Am I close to this street, Unity Tube?,' he asked himself. He couldn't be completely sure; the structure of the city was too complex to be rendered in map form. He saw a smartly dressed trader at a stall just ahead, the man sporting a neatly trimmed beard and with dark hair oiled and carefully shaped to sit atop his head in a neat pattern. His shirt quality seemed to belie the modest stall he tended.

'Excuse me – do you happen to know where this place is? Would you be so kind as to send me in the right direction?' Cronto asked, showing the man the slate bearing the address.

'Of course.' The trader smiled pleasantly. 'Not from around here, are you? You're almost there. Just up there on the left, where that street leads down the side of that big woodturning workshop,' he pointed, 'it will take you right there.'

'Thank you, good sir,' Cronto said with a smile. As he approached the junction, he glanced back to see the trader looking sidelong at him from a distance but trying to hide it. Cronto stopped short of taking the indicated turn and peered into the gloom of the small road facing him. He could just make out a handful of shadowy figures, some leaning against the walls of the buildings and others sitting on discarded crates.

'No,' Cronto muttered to himself. 'I am not from around here.' He turned back to look at the trader, ensuring he caught his attention and looking him straight in the eyes, then shook his head. *This place,* he thought to himself. *They would slit your throat and leave you face down in the street just to empty your pockets. Looks like they might even do it to TAKE your pockets.*

Cronto sighed and continued along the main street he had been following, ignoring the side street and the thugs lurking down there. 'I'll take the long way round to find this address, thank you.'

*

Cronto double-checked the scrawl on his slate. This appeared to be the correct place, from what little he could tell of the door to the small dwelling; it appeared humble yet respectable, though not marked with a name or number very obviously. It was tucked away in a quiet courtyard off from a minor street and had taken some intuitive navigation on Cronto's part to find in the first place. He stepped up to the doorstep and rapped on the thin wooden door.

'Yes? What do you want?' a thin, reedy voice called from inside.

'Hello, I'm looking for Ma Fala. Could you tell me if she is here?'

'Fala? Ah, yes, the Olrofi. Who are you?'

'May I come in? My name is Molefi Cronto, I am an acquaintance of Ma Fala. I would very much like to speak with her, if she is at home.' He gently pushed on the door but found it resisted the pressure he put on it. A moment later it crept back a fraction and an eye enclosed by ancient, lined skin appeared in the gap, darting around as it studied him.

'She's not here,' the old woman said, pushing the door closed again.

Feeling his efforts being on the verge of going completely to waste, Cronto persisted and called through the door again. 'Could you tell me when she is likely to be back? I would be endlessly grateful.'

'Not here,' the voice repeated through the closed door. 'She hasn't been for months. Moved out, said the rent was too much for her.' The old woman snorted. 'Can you believe that? One of the most reasonable rates for a place of such fine standing. And I never have rats, ever! She won't have got better for her money, I'll tell you that for nothing.' She paused. 'Do you need a room?'

'No, madam, thank you – I have accommodation. Could you perhaps furnish me with her new address?'

'She didn't tell me – was off in a hurry. Things must not have worked out how she wanted them to. Shame. She always paid on time, too. I don't know where she ended up.'

'I thank you for your time, madam. Good day.' The old lodging house owner could be heard to mutter something incomprehensible as she shuffled deeper into the small building's interior.

Cronto's heart sank. Another citizen of Olrof, drawn in by the pull of Dralcea and swallowed by its uncaring vastness. He had wanted to check in on the young woman he had known in their homeland, to show a familiar face and ensure she was on the right path. Ma Fala had grown up a few houses down from Cronto's own house and he was good friends with her parents. There was now no way for him to find her; where to start in such a huge, confusing city? It was hopeless.

He turned away and wandered despondently up the nearest steps leading upwards into the brighter light above. Cronto resolved to see more of what the city had to offer in the surface-level market, rumoured to contain the pick of the produce from the encircling provinces, before the light failed. He hoped the rest of his trip was going to be a happier affair to have made the journey worthwhile.

Chapter Ten – Treats and Intrigue

Molefi Cronto continued to wander the market streets, not particularly looking for anything. A gloom still clung to him at his failure to locate his compatriot and he felt strangely responsible despite having no control over the situation. It was a sobering thought that a place such as this could lure people in with promises of high living and then have them become anonymous, or worse, disappear altogether. He shuddered at the realisation that he could not know which one was true in this instance. Being used to delving through facts to make proper judgements, this frustrated Cronto in the extreme.

Whilst normally vigilant and watchful, Cronto realised that in his reverie he had been staring at the roughly cobbled street rather than looking where he was going and had wandered down an unfamiliar street. The shadows were beginning to lengthen and stretch down the length of the street, further increasing the dinginess of his surroundings. He realised it was approaching the hour his landlady had mentioned as being the cut-off for returning to his lodgings without being charged extra. 'I have to think of myself as well you know,' she had said to him, 'I can't stay up all night waiting for you to come back whenever you feel like it.' That sentiment was fair and Cronto agreed with the principle, but the time she had set was six o'clock. *She most certainly is thinking of herself*, he thought at the time, *she must make a fortune from people like me staying and being rinsed for every somoni coin they're carrying.*

'I wonder what food this city has to offer, I could really use something to eat,' Cronto commented to the street in general. No food was available at his accommodation; he had asked his host about this and she had glared at him and mumbled something about not being a cook of repute in an offended tone. He had not pressed the matter after the strange response he had received. Looking around, he spotted a brown, crescent-shaped sign with its two points directed upwards and short chains leading off them to the supporting bar to allow it to swing gently in the breeze. 'A bakery! Perfect. They must have something hot on offer. It might cost a small fortune but I should really sample Dralcean cuisine, and perhaps a galumph to wash it down.' He assumed the tradition of backyard galumph brewing which used any available scrap of fermentable food was also practiced in Dralcea as it was back in Olrof. Cronto had heard the rumours about the frivolous living in the capital and how all but the best parts of food were discarded, though he doubted it was true. With the wide range of classes of society in this city, surely every morsel of food must be used in some way, be it as the building blocks of stews sold on vendor stalls around the city or in people's homes, filling the bellies of ordinary families. Reaching the shop front, he entered its doorway under the creaking chains of the suspended sign.

The pleasant aromas of baking caressed his nose as soon as Cronto stepped inside, only intensifying his hunger. The smells brought back a rush of memories of his mother baking at home when he was young.

'Hello there! What can I get for you?'

Cronto smiled warmly at the proprietor, thankful for the pleasant greeting despite the late hour. He looked at the racks of pastries displayed for customer perusal. 'I can't see what I would really enjoy...do you have any beasts' horns? Cone-shaped things with a red berry filling. They were my favourite as a child.' They were intended to mimic a bloody horn cropped from a goat or similar animal and were what Cronto had always craved growing up. He felt a giddy rush of childish delight at the thought of having one again after so long. Adulthood usually seemed to deny him the opportunities to enjoy himself.

'Erm...not ready yet, sorry. If you can wait, I have some almost ready to come out of the oven?'

'That would be fantastic! Thank you very much. It has been many years since I've had one.'

'My pleasure! So, are you new to town? You haven't visited us before. By us, I mean the bakery, of course. Jenker and Son, Bakery. That's our name,' he finished lamely.

Cronto was unfazed, being used to talking to people of all different origins, walks of life and levels of sociability. He smiled back politely. 'I'm just visiting for a night or two from Olrof. I have an appointment to keep tomorrow. Does your son work here too? I like to see a family coming together to run a business.'

'Oh, no, I'm the son...my father established the bakery. He's...er...he's not around anymore...' Jenker trailed off.

'I'm sorry to hear that,' Cronto said sincerely. 'While I wait, would you mind me asking a little about Dralcea? I read about it and know the chasm above the caldera marks the centre of the city, but I'm finding it difficult to understand the rest of the structure now I'm here.'

'It often does confuse visitors! Well, you probably also know that everything is built radiating out from the caldera, with its bubbling magma far below where anybody lives. The Crinochin were here long before any humans or Ananeptide fled here from the big freeze, and they dug the tunnels down into the rock and soil, like a huge ant nest. It's a habitable honeycomb.'

'Crinochin dug all this out? That I was unaware of.'

'The original tunnels to shelter themselves, at least,' Jenker replied. 'We humans widened and expanded a lot of them to accommodate us since it provides so much warmth and shelter, and so we now have the six different levels, including this one on the surface. I'm glad of being up here in the light, even if it isn't as warm as further down, though I've heard it's almost unbearable to live in the lowest levels due to the heat and near-darkness. The space up here allows buildings to be taller too, of course. No doubt you'll have come across the stairways that lead between levels, and perhaps seen the cramped streets of the Warren.'

'I've used a few stairways in my exploring, yes. Navigation is certainly difficult, though – not only knowing which level you're on, but which direction you're heading, and in which district. I don't know how you do it.'

'It's easy for me, I don't go anywhere beyond buying baking supplies and my own food,' Jenker shrugged. 'Be careful if you go wandering. It's dangerous out there, especially further down through the tiers.'

'Thank you, I'll be careful – I'm due at the Promontory so won't have much more chance to explore. I read that it's built on the most solid bedrock on the north-east side of the caldera's edge and has no streets underneath it, since as the seat of government it has to be strong and secure. It certainly looks impressive from afar, leaning forward and looming above the caldera like that,' Cronto said.

'The parade ground to its front is even better, projecting out over the chasm and supported by those two gigantic struts. They're anchored at points around the pit's edge – a real feat of engineering, that.'

'Something to look out for. It sounds impressive.'

'Certainly is. I just need to see how the pastries are getting on,' Jenker said. He turned to face the oven set into an alcove behind the counter and gazed through the sepia-tinted tempered glass. 'Damn thing,' he muttered. 'Sorry about this. They aren't baking through as they should – sometimes the oven goes out and this happens. The fuel isn't smouldering enough to properly provide heat. If you'll give me a moment.'

'Of course. I'm sure they will be worth the wait,' Cronto replied pleasantly.

Jenker turned to the left side of the oven and crouched down by the alcove's edge. A small white nub protruded from the wall, a jagged hole visible at the tip and two much smaller openings, parallel to each other, above the larger one. It gleamed with an ivory shine, polished smooth from constantly being touched to use it. Jenker tentatively reached out to the projection, putting his hand around it and then quickly retracting it as a gout of flame shot from the holes and into the grate at the side of the oven's bottom. Jenker groaned as he got up from his squat, meeting Cronto's intense gaze, his eyes wide and ablaze with thought.

'If you don't mind me asking, how does that work? Is that a normal way to light ovens here in Dralcea?' Cronto asked.

'I assume so, it's all we have ever had here. It just stops sometimes – well, quite often, actually. It needs tweaking all the time,' Jenker explained awkwardly.

Cronto looked thoughtful. 'It has been set up in this manner for a long time? Interesting. And you say your father established this place? There wasn't a bakery here before that?'

'No, we lived here before the shop opened but this was just a plain front room, nothing special.' Jenker looked back into the oven to check progress and stared at the contents for several long moments. He looked back over his shoulder to Cronto. 'They should be just about done now.'

'Thank you. How much does it cost?'

'Two somoni, please,' Jenker said.

'Here you go,' Cronto said, handing over a pair of one-somoni coins retrieved from his pocket. Jenker extracted the tray of pastries and put one on a scrap of cloth to cool briefly before Cronto picked it up. The customer glanced outside at the lengthening shadows in the street. 'I had better go, or I will be locked out. I gather it's not a good idea to spend the night on the streets in this fine city of yours.'

Jenker coughed nervously. 'Erm, no, it's not really recommended,' he said. 'Take care out there, sir. Oh, and enjoy that too.'

'I most certainly will,' Cronto said as he lifted his steaming snack upwards slightly in a sort of salute and smiled before making his way back out into the rapidly darkening street, striding purposefully toward his guesthouse. He tore into his treat as he walked the cool street, relishing every hot mouthful. Cronto found the tanginess of the tart red berries was the perfect contrast to the rich, buttery pastry enveloping them.

Chapter Eleven – Gamechanger

On the side of the dusty arena closest to Dralcea's centre, the blue-cloaked figure of Branch Godfrey Vilipas was just visible as he stomped toward the waiting sergeants. Late the previous night Janos had been disturbed by a runner sent from the Promontory and had been ordered to report to this place in the morning. His head was still foggy from the previous night's galumph, having already imbibed it in quantity by the time he received the message. Evidently the runner had been told to try him at his favourite watering hole, The Crimson Duck, and had been successful in locating his recipient on the first attempt, having not bothered trying to reach him at his lodgings. They clearly knew his habits well. Janos tried to peer more closely at the figure across the stony ground from him.

'Just why the hell have they got us out here in the arse-end of nowhere on a morning like this?' Janos said, turning to his fellow sergeant next to him, a stocky figure with wide shoulders and a slightly square head by the name of Zygfryd Tanbry. The weather was actually quite mild, and with the sun still low in the sky it sent rays angling toward their faces at unavoidable angles, making them both squint. Pleasant and putrid scents alike wafted across to them as they waited. 'And who's that approaching? Looks like that gutworm, Vilipas. I've seen his face far too much recently, strutting around giving orders as if he's actually earned his position.'

Tanbry flicked his eyes to regard Janos but didn't bother to turn his head. 'Gods know,' he said in his deep voice with an air that suggested he did not care for the reasons, but just resented being present at all. 'I just got told last night, same as you.'

Janos stood to Tanbry's left, and Sergeant Sluss stood silently to Tanbry's other side, his stony gaze casting across the open ground. Sluss was taller than Tanbry but not as tall as

Janos, sporting a gaunt face that appeared to have too little skin stretched over his head – which was bald save for a tuft of light brown hair in the centre above his forehead. Some of the braver men under his command called him Death Baby, his appearance reminiscent of a portmanteau of a skull and infantile features. This was of course spoken of purely behind his back; nobody in their right mind would be so openly disrespectful to their commander. The punishments meted out by Sluss for such infringements, or any other infraction, were without exception unerringly harsh and inventive. His fellow sergeants kept their opinions of him to themselves, but all knew him for his lack of humour and few words; in fact, many of them secretly envied him for the unflinchingly stern persona he projected and consequent respect he commanded.

Egil Sluss continued silently surveying the area as if nothing perturbed him, as Tanbry and Janos stood and waited impatiently. Janos eventually saw Vilipas gesture off to his left and a group of four men in plain shirts dragged two heavily loaded carts, two pulling on each, into view. 'What have they got in those carts? Looks like jumbled piles of wood,' Janos commented to Tanbry.

Branch Vilipas arrived, carts in tow, and drew himself up to his full height. Hands clasped behind his back, he looked the three sergeants in the eye one by one.

'Good morning, sergeants. I trust you are all in a receptive mood to take on today's training. You should feel honoured to be here today, getting to grips with our latest equipment that will revolutionise the Dralcea Guard – and getting to give them their first use too, ahead of your colleagues.'

'I might if it wasn't so bloody early,' Janos muttered under his breath. His head throbbed from his overindulgence in galumph the previous night, but he noticed Tanbry try to suppress a grin, whilst Sluss simply maintained his silence and impassive gaze. Sluss was never one to go along with any humour to endear himself to his colleagues. That was of no interest to him – he did not care what others thought of him, just that the job got done, and done properly.

'We've requisitioned the finest quality hardwood for the crafters to make these,' Vilipas continued, oblivious to Janos's mutterings. He patted one of the long wooden handles protruding from the pile, which made several others stacked on top of it wobble and threaten to tumble off. Vilipas started and withdrew his hand. 'Yes, the very newest kit. Gone are the days of the spear ruling the land. Anyone can wield a spear, as some guards down in the Warren have found out to their peril recently. These, my good men, are Ejectors.'

Sluss spoke abruptly in his gruff, no-nonsense voice. 'What are they exactly?'

'*Ejectors*,' Vilipas said, sounding irritated at not being given the chance to elaborate before being interrupted. 'A distance weapon. We need no longer be limited by the reach of an arm, or the length of a weapon shaft – or be stuck training with a bow for years to become even halfway good at making arrows end up where we want them to. These will let us take internal and external security by the scruff of the neck – firm control of the streets and protected borders, gentlemen. You are to familiarise yourselves with them and will then be instructing the other ranks on their use in turn. I suggest you make good use of this morning. The first set of enlisted men will be here at midday to learn their use.'

Janos looked at Vilipas incredulously. 'We've got a few hours to master some daft new weapon we've never even heard of before? Excellent idea, sir.'

'If you don't think you're up to the task, sergeant, then perhaps one of your men would be a better fit for your position.'

'How about you show us, sir? You are evidently much more familiar with them,' Janos said with a grin, knowing he had trapped Vilipas.

'*I'll* have a go, sir,' Tanbry cut in calmly.

Vilipas glared furiously at Janos at having his authority undermined so easily. 'Leadership is about setting an example,' he said acidly to both Tanbry and Janos. He grabbed one of the wooden shafts protruding from the cart nearest to him and with some difficulty extricated it from the pile. 'So, it's a three-foot long weapon, has a small rectangular box at this end, and this cable which runs from the back of the box along the shaft to the far end. There it joins this wooden peg with a deep groove in the butt of the handle.' He held the object unsteadily whilst describing it, as if at any moment it might bite him.

'This chamber at the front,' Vilipas said slowly, as if working it out for himself as he said it, 'is where the real power of the weapon lies.' He let go of the Ejector with his left hand and tried to take up the full weight of it with his right. The Ejector pivoted crazily as he struggled to control it, the load clearly exceeding what he had accounted for. The three assembled sergeants did their best not to flinch as the tip swept across the front of each, only their eyes narrowing betraying any sense of nervousness. Vilipas eventually got it under control and set it down handle-first on the ground, the firing end pointing straight up. 'On this end,' Vilipas tapped the forward end of the chamber, 'goes a thin square of tanned animal hide. The iron loop clamps it on securely. Think of it as one weapon, which is full of a mass of other weapons.'

'How does that work? Like a deadly cabinet filled with knives or something?' Janos asked sarcastically.

'Do you enjoy being a sergeant, Janos? If so, I suggest you shut your mouth right now unless you want breaking back to the ranks. I'm sure some of the men would have a few things to say to you about that,' Vilipas retorted. Janos looked sternly back at his superior with barely disguised contempt but refused to be drawn into saying anything further that he would regret. Vilipas gave him a smug smile before continuing.

'These are what make this a formidable tool.' Vilipas dug around in a pouch suspended from his belt and withdrew a handful of small objects, opening his palm to let the others see the contents. 'Sweat of Hephaestus. The power of an ancient god – power imbued into our hands. These,' he continued, removing the loop and then the hide cover of the chamber and pouring the small pieces of iron inside with a light clinking sound, 'will fly out in a swarm faster than your eye can blink, and wreak havoc on the poor unfortunate you've pointed your Ejector at.' He then carefully pushed the skin and loop back in place until it fit snugly, having contained the Sweat of Hephaestus in the chamber. He paced past the three men and stopped ten metres from a wooden post sporting a shirt stuffed with dried grasses.

'What the hell is this all about?' Tanbry grumbled quietly. 'This is stupid. The bloke's waving a big stick around as if it makes him invincible. Bollocks, the lot of it. I had deadlier-looking training weapons before I could tie my shoes.' Janos grunted his agreement.

Vilipas raised the Ejector, left hand supporting the shaft three-quarters of the way to the front and the other held the thicker handle at the rear. He lowered his head and squinted so that his view was down the length of the weapon before he stood completely still. 'Hold it this way and put the chamber in front of your target as you aim at them, like so.'

He moved two fingers of his right hand to find the rear-mounted lever just ahead of the handle and firmly pressed down on it. At once a loud clack could be heard as the lever dipped down and released the cable which, suddenly relieved of its immense tension, raced forward and set in motion another reaction in the chamber at the front. The cable, having rapidly slackened, let the rear flaps of the chamber, which had hitherto been pulled back, pivot forward and forcefully eject the small projectiles through the thin membrane to the front. The Sweat of Hephaestus exploded from the chamber, reaching the target within a few fractions of a second. The effect of the shot was devastating. Vilipas turned to the sergeants, smiling. 'Convinced yet, men? Rather effective, I would say.'

Janos was shocked but noted Sluss remained impassive, whilst Tanbry's mouth sagged open a little in astonishment. Janos was the first to speak. 'Hell's teeth.' He exhaled loudly. 'It certainly made a mess of that fence post.' He led the way over to inspect the damage, his colleagues following behind.

'So those Sweat of Hephaestus ripped right through the shirt,' Tanbry said, poking at one particularly large hole. 'Shredded the thing.'

'More than that,' Sluss said scornfully. 'They've gone right through the stuffing and then some. Look, the shirt is rent to pieces. Not bad going.'

Janos moved the remaining scraps of cloth and grass clinging to the post to one side. 'They're embedded in the wood, too! There is some force behind that thing.'

'Yes, precisely. Think about what it'll do to a pissed off Warren mongrel charging at you with his dagger flashing, eager for it to meet your neck.' Vilipas patted the Ejector cradled in his hands. 'It'll do more than just stop him. Or any other thing that might want to harm you, come to that,' he said. He walked over and pressed the Ejector into Sluss's hands. 'Have a go, sergeant. Get familiar with it, learn its quirks and intricacies. The same goes for you two. I need you all to be experts in their use, today. As I said, the men will start arriving and they must be up to speed as soon as possible...which of course means that you must be even better so you can teach them. There are sacks of gravel in the carts to be used for practising. Aim for the targets already set up and nothing else.'

'Gravel? What about those metal bits, sir?' Tanbry enquired.

'The weaponsmiths are working on making as many Sweat of Hephaestus as possible, but it's slow work. We can't use all the ones we already have in practising; it would slow down production even more. So – we use the fine gravel for now. That's one of the strengths of the Ejectors. If you run out of your official missiles, you can use other, similar materials instead. So long as they are a similar size and weight, they should work in the same way.'

Sluss nodded his head. 'I approve. It's flexible.'

Janos eyed Vilipas with wonder. 'In a pinch, use a pinch of whatever's available.'

'Correct. One more thing,' Vilipas said. 'For the love of the gods, don't point them at each other, even in jest. See to it, sergeants.' He turned on his heel and strode off, evidently needed elsewhere on important business – or so Janos assumed.

Once out of earshot, Janos retorted, 'Thanks for that wonderful piece of advice, sir.' He and Tanbry went over to the closest cart and picked up Ejectors for themselves. 'Let's get on then, lads, before the rank and file arrive.'

Chapter Twelve – Practice

After many hours spent by the sergeants at the practice space, the sun began to set, slowly dipping down below the rim of the Bowl far away on the horizon. Those last golden rays sent long shadows emanating from the clothed posts along the open ground. Many of the enlisted men there drooped visibly under the weight of the Ejectors they held; the long hours of practice had drained most of them physically and mentally, learning the complicated new way to use the Ejectors and focusing on trying to aim effectively.

'Remember, men – make sure you aim properly before you fire. Otherwise, your shot is as good as useless, and you might just hit someone else. I'd rather that wasn't me out in the field.' They had made good progress despite some of the things he had bawled at them. 'Algunas! Stand up straight, or so help me I will kick your arse every time you slouch!' A healthy dose of fear and berating was useful to push them along – after all, they would not be using these weapons under calm conditions in the course of their duty and they had to gain experience using them under pressure. Janos did not know why they needed such firepower, nor why they needed to be trained on their use so quickly. He assumed he would be informed eventually.

Janos saw the signs of fatigue in his section of men and decided to leave the training there. 'All right, lads. You've made the smallest possible amount of progress, but that's not bad considering it's you lot and all. Get home now, or whatever hole your fancy it is to crawl into at night. Fulfil your normal rounds tomorrow, and we'll have you back here the day after that to continue training. Maybe one of you will hit the damn target then. I won't be putting any of my hard-earned somoni on it, though.'

His men began to file wearily away and placed their Ejectors back into the carts in untidy heaps. Janos strode over to where Sluss was standing stiffly, hands folded behind his back. He appeared to be trying to wither his section of men into breaking down and stopping without being ordered to through the sheer repetition and being subjected to his icy glare. Janos stood aside Sluss silently, taking his lead from his fellow sergeant, and took note of how those recruits were getting on. He noticed one or two cast occasional glances in their direction, trying not to be noticed doing so. They were clearly exhausted and once they saw Janos's section trooping off, they looked even more dispirited. Janos knew what awaited them if they were to give Egil Sluss any excuse to mete out his own sadistic brand of punishment, which was motivation enough for them to continue.

'Making even less progress than my lot, eh?' Janos commented.

'Not likely,' Sluss snorted. 'Nothing wrong with working them hard. Make them earn their money; now that would be a first.'

'Well, your call. They won't be much use if they drop face-first into the gravel though,' Janos said, clapping Sluss on the shoulder with one of his gigantic hands as he made to walk off toward Tanbry.

Tanbry had just dismissed his own section when Janos arrived at his side. One particularly bulky recruit appeared to have managed the heavy work better than most and swung his Ejector by one hand as he left his post. Janos overhead a snippet of another of Tanbry's charges remark to the bigger man as they walked away.

'Wish I had your energy, Oso,' the smaller man said. 'It'd be useful on days like this.'

'Family trait, that is – don't show any weakness, just keep going. It's all in the name. Oso means "brave" in the old language from way back.'

'Does it?' his companion replied.

Janos turned back to Tanbry as the pair conversing moved almost out of earshot. 'That lad of yours there is almost as big as me,' he commented.

'Nearly. He talks as much rubbish as you do, too.' Tanbry turned away from Janos for a moment. 'Remember to put those Ejectors back in the carts – carefully!' he yelled after the departing men.

One man, however, remained standing in his designated position whilst all the others trudged away, grateful to be let go. Janos watched him carefully add a fresh handful of gravel to the front chamber, place a new skin over the end and secure it with the metal loop. Tanbry seemed impressed with the extra effort being shown. 'This has certainly been a different morning,' he said.

'You've got that right,' Janos said. He followed his colleague's gaze and recognised the young man who continued to practise. The man raised his weapon, aimed at the tattered post some distance away, then released the tension on the cord with a loud *thwack*. A fresh assortment of splinters flew outwards from the target as his shot found its mark. 'Not a bad effort. Any others of yours learning anything?'

'Mostly just how to complain as if their lives depend on it. They just want to give disapproving looks, strut around with a spear resting on their shoulder and occasionally prod folk with it when they want them to move on. Can't say I blame them in all honesty, that's how this job has worked for hundreds of years after all. What is this all about anyway?'

'Beats me. That dick Vilipas keeps mentioning the need for us to be better armed, as if there's something happening that changes our situation. Thing is, we're the ones out wearing our boots down on the streets every day, and it's not as if they're crawling with muggers or outlaws – well, no more than usual. What's he alluding to – have you come across anything?'

'Not a sausage, just the usual stuff, you know. This all seems excessive to me, spears still do the job after all. Or, that bloody great hammer you insist on carrying around with you. That's as much of a deterrent as most knife-wielding idiots need, if your reputation is to be believed.'

'That's half of the fun of it,' Janos replied, stretching his massive arms behind his head. 'Let them hear the whispers and worry about Hilde and me, then I don't have to do half as much as I ought to.' He grinned at his companion. 'Works a treat!'

'Yes, well, we don't all have a back the size of a wagon to carry huge hammers around on,' Tanbry grumbled. 'Some of us have to make do with what we're issued.'

'Come on, you miserable sod. There's nowt you can do about how tall or otherwise your parents are. Fancy one or two down at The Crimson Duck? I've worked up a real thirst doing all this instructing.'

'Not if it's me buying them. You drink enough to fill the caldera over the course of a night.'

'Of course you're buying them! I might wear big trousers, but I don't have deep pockets. Come on, before they sell all the good stuff. You might need to tell your man to give it a rest though. He's certainly keen.'

'We'll be lucky to find any good stuff, the dives you drag us to…' Tanbry grumbled as they turned to make the walk back to the city proper. 'Gantle! That's enough, good work there. Get yourself a rest. We're off.'

*

‘I’ll be amazed if any of those Ejectors become used regularly. We’re better off with our spears. There’s nothing a good pointy spearhead can’t fix, right?’ Janos asked.

‘Mmm,’ Tanbry agreed. ‘Too much f-faffing for my liking,’ he struggled to say through the alcohol.

‘Exactly, Zygfryd. Your lad Gantle seemed to like his though. I never thought I’d see the day a guard needed telling twice to knock off for the day.’

‘He’s eager to learn, that one. Noth-nothing wrong with that. Some of the others could take a leaf out of ’is book, some of ’em would rather sc-scratch their arse all day than learn anything. I even caught him giving pointers to a few of the other lads around him who weren’t doing so well.’

‘Maybe he’s trying to get ready for the day the frostmites come for him, so he can put up a decent fight.’

‘What are you on about? He’s a bit old for those s-stories.’

‘Tell him that. He reckons there’s one wandering around out there, says it tore up some lads on sentry duty at an outpost.’ Janos sighed. ‘These new lads do believe some bollocks.’

‘Well, to each their own ‘n’ all that. I’m more co-concerned about the buggers out there looking to do in a poor innocent sergeant so they can sell his boots,’ Tanbry replied.

Janos took another big gulp of his drink then wiped his mouth with the back of his hand, clearing the frothy residue away before rubbing his hand on his thigh – the area already somewhat soiled from previous wipes. He blinked slowly, his eyelids impeded by the effects of the galumph he had been imbibing since he and Tanbry settled into their seats many hours previously. ‘I think I’m about ready for another,’ said Janos, who had been going at it heavily with barely a break to empty his bladder, true to reputation. His companion had been more reluctant to take on so much intoxicant. It was true that Janos required a copious amount to become drunk, owing to his massive size, and Tanbry's much smaller, squat frame could only absorb so much. Consequently, despite taking on much less galumph, Tanbry was far from sober himself. As he reached for his own tankard, he merrily misjudged it and pushed the vessel away with his outstretched fingers. He giggled as some of the malodourous liquid sloshed out and down the sides, pooling on the table.

'I think that might be a s-sign to have galumph enough. I mean, that I've had enough,' Tanbry said. His head rolled a little as he spoke, Janos noticed.

'But, my friend, the night is young! And, more importantly, there's more galumph left here, yet to be enjoyed.' Janos tilted his unique stone mug from side to side, making a sloshing sound, to show that he had nearly reached the bottom of it again. 'It'd be a shame to disappoint it, and let it go undrunk.'

'Well, do what you like. You're big enough to make your own mind up.' Tanbry looked at Janos. 'More than big enough. But I've had my fill...and then a bit more.' Tanbry hiccupped suddenly and looked a little sickly afterwards.

'Pfft. Suit yourself. It won't be much different company if you go in any case.'

'Ah, shut up. Here comes that bar maid you hand far too much of your money over to, anyway. She can keep you company if I'm so bad.' Tanbry looked up and affected a gentler demeanour for her. 'Ryx! You can tell when a big lump like this has had enough, right? Tell him. He listens to a pretty face.'

Ryx was smiling as she approached from behind Janos. 'You know I'm the best judge of his sobriety, comes from years of practice. This place doesn't seem the same without him taking up a big chunk of the space, he's here that much.' Janos smiled stupidly at the comment, looking proud.

Tanbry continued, 'He's talking a right load of—' he checked himself just in time to avoid swearing in front of her. '—rubbish. Monster stories.'

She moved round to Tanbry's side of the table and bent her legs so she came level with Janos's face to study it. Her eyes darted back and forth as she examined him. 'Yep...look at that. You can see it all in his eyes. Very telling, are the eyes. He's had enough, as my empty barrels attest to. Time to go...unless of course you want to drink yourself into even more of a stupor and fill my pockets up even more. Just so long as you don't start making a mess or causing trouble, that is.'

'A fine offer!' Janos roared cheerily. 'One I think I might just take you up on,' he said, pushing his mug toward Ryx.

'Don't encourage him,' Tanbry said with a sigh. 'I'm making this call for you. Come on,' he said firmly, putting his hand under Janos's arm and exerting pressure. Although this did fail to move him – few people could affect him in such a way – Janos did not resist, and stood with the prompt.

'Fine, you boring bastard. My coins will weigh down my pockets for another day.'

'Probably just as well, it's just me tonight and you'd keep me twice as busy fetching drinks when I'm already rushed off my feet,' Ryx said.

'The parents bunking off?' Janos asked.

'Gone to some circus show in the arena on the outskirts, they do all sorts of tricks and performances apparently. They've been after a night off for months...but the demand for refreshments is usually quite high,' she said with her eyebrows raised. 'I can handle this place alone for a night once in a while though.'

'No doubt you can – just don't work yourself too hard, lass. I'll need more of these fine drinks again tomorrow.'

'Of course you will. Goodnight, gentlemen!' she said as they passed her, already turning to deal with her other thirsty customers vying for her attention. The two walked unsteadily to the door; Tanbry led the way with his best attempt at sober authority but did little better than his companion. Another pair of men in Dralcea Guard garb also made their way out in the wake of their colleagues leaving.

*

Ryx left the inn by the side door now that she had finally moved on the final customers who had dragged their feet well after closing time. She hauled the newly emptied and particularly sharp-smelling barrel into the alley to scrape out the remaining scum. It was hardly the most rewarding part of the job, but it was easier to do now than leave it to dry on and become even more stubborn. Ryx crouched down to steady herself as she began working at the clinging substance using the same trusty ladle used inside to serve up the intoxicant liquid. Consequently, she was engrossed in the task and did not notice the two figures approaching from further up the dark side street.

'You're very friendly with those sergeants,' one of the two men said in her direction.

She looked up with a start, having not even heard them approach, but now saw the pair had stopped a few feet away from her. She noticed they wore the guard uniform she was so familiar with and realised they had been inside the inn before leaving some time earlier. 'We're shut now. We open the same time tomorrow – come back then.' She had no desire to be drawn into another long-winded conversation with the inebriated, so she looked back to her barrel and continued scraping, wanting to get the arduous task completed as quickly as possible.

'Very friendly, inside,' the second man agreed. 'Especially to a man in uniform. How friendly are you out here to us fine working men?' He advanced and as Ryx stood up, he grabbed her left wrist. 'Let's find out,' the man said, his voice dropping an octave.

‘Don’t do anything you’ll regret, boys,’ Ryx said in a warning tone, having stiffened at the unwanted contact. The guard went to grab her neck with his other hand. His companion had drawn a knife and moved closer.

Adrenaline flooded Ryx’s system and her free right hand clasped the ladle tighter. In one rapid movement, she lifted her arm up and swung the implement in a vicious arc that connected heavily with her attacker’s left temple with a dull *thump*. The guard staggered back a step sharply from the blow, then stood bolt upright as his eyes lost focus and his pupils dilated. Without warning, his legs collapsed from under him and he fell in an untidy heap, completely unable to stop himself as he lost consciousness.

The second man’s jaw fell slackly open in shock. Ryx, her senses heightened and body primed for action, took the opportunity afforded her and leapt forward, barrelling into the other man. He was knocked back against the wall, causing him to drop his knife before he stepped forward and squared back up to her. She lurched forward, bringing her forehead down and savagely headbutting him in the bridge of his nose with a wet crunching sound. Blood gushed from the wrecked nose and he gasped in pain and surprise. Ryx followed this up with a swift kick between his legs, causing him to gasp again with a sharp intake of breath and quickly shield his groin with both hands as he slumped to the ground. Blood leaked out over his lips and chin and he moaned softly between snorts through his bloody nose as he lay on the cold ground in misery. She made to kick him again in his prone state, but just managed to break through her crimson veil of rage and stopped short. Instead, she scuffed a little dirt into his face to demonstrate how utterly bested he had been. Turning around, she glanced at the first man, still lying in a pile of his own limbs, out cold. She stepped over him and back to her ladle and barrel, resuming the job.

'You don't grow up in an inn without learning a few things, boys.' The one conscious would-be attacker simply whimpered on the floor. She ignored them both until she completed her undertaking, then went back inside without a backward glance.

Chapter Thirteen – Rewards

Julius and Nothro stood in line, waiting behind two other people ahead of them with a patience borne of bemusement. 'I still don't really know what we have done to deserve being here for this ceremony – not that I'm complaining about the change of pace. It's nice not to have frozen fingers for once,' Julius said.

Their surroundings were quite unlike anything they were used to. The two contrasting figures stood on a cloister running along the western edge of the Promontory, the area itself raised fifteen feet above the ground. Windows shaped with ornate stone swirls admitted dappled sunlight to dance across the people waiting there and gently warm them. The view through these apertures afforded a sight of the luxurious gardens below, the intention being to relax and impress visitors with the opulence of their surroundings. Julius moved to the side so that he leaned with his back resting on one of the windows, inhaling scents of jasmine and honeysuckle climbing up towards them as bees and insects droned about their green paradise. He glanced at the double set of doors ahead of them, then back to his friend.

'This lot here in the capital really love to put a lot of effort into dazzling the commoners like us, eh? This one walkway is fancier than anything in the whole of Thorntuft. I could get used to being treated like this.'

'I prefer the forests,' Nothro replied with disdain in his coarse voice.

'You would. That's where your species generally live, after all.' Julius looked up and around himself, taking especial interest in the vaulted ceiling above their heads. 'Nice to see they spend our hard-earned taxes on such useful social investments,' he said. 'What's the best we can hope for out of this then, matey?'

'I'd take an extra month's pay, or a few weeks off for the hunt.'

'Ever the optimist! I think the reward might be a little less grand than that, given the number of others also due something,' he said, gesturing at the large group of people waiting in line. For the most part they talked excitedly amongst themselves, relishing the thought of what was to come. 'I wonder what they're being rewarded for? Presumably they took all their weapons off them on the way in too, if they had any. They don't all look like woodcutters to me.'

Nothro tilted his head down toward his friend whilst remaining silent, in a manner that Julius was used to interpreting as condescension. 'I don't think this is just to celebrate us who work in the woods.' The large creature looked down the line. 'Look at them. They look like they do all sorts. There, that little one. He looks as if he clears other people's plates for them.'

Julius looked up at Nothro, searching his furred face for any evidence that he had meant that as a rare joke, a difference from his usual sombre mood; however, he remained as inscrutable as ever. He gave up and instead turned to look back down the line himself and noted the wide variety of people present.

Julius saw the young man Nothro had singled out; he was short in stature with immaculately cleaned and smoothed brown tunic and trousers covering a slightly chubby frame. The man appeared to be jabbering nervously to the person closest to him. Scanning along, certain people caught Julius's eye: a red-headed woman stood alongside an older woman with blonde hair; a man dressed in clothes of a type he had never seen before, including a round, flat hat; and a tall, thin man in an unusually elaborate black jacket covered in reflective squares and featuring many sets of lapels and a large collar that stuck straight up and rose to a crescendo at the nape of his neck, was standing silently and perfectly still.

'You're right, Nothro, there is a mix of people. Mostly ordinary but there are some interesting-looking characters who stand out, too,' Julius said. 'Definitely not all woodcutters. A good showing of guards too, all lined up here with their unusual helmets on.'

The guards present stood at regular intervals up to the steps descending the far end, each with their backs to the wall of the Promontory so that they faced the people waiting there. Every guard wore extra ceremonial trim to give themselves a more elaborate look for this special duty. Their hexagonal helmets bore metal trim shaped like tree branches clipped to either side above the ears, and a royal blue sash stretching between the two pauldrons protecting their shoulders. Each guard stood upright, gaze fixed straight ahead and held a long-handled spear grounded and tip pointing upwards.

Julius looked forward again to the double doorway and the pair of guards standing either side of it. The one to the left of the door looked nervous; he shiftily glanced at those waiting in line before he snapped his attention back to a point in the middle distance, focused on nobody in particular. Julius sighed and resigned himself to waiting a little longer.

*

Wilfred Wolfscope struggled to contain his excitement. *I can barely believe I'm being recognised for my work so early into my career*, he thought. The young man was also extremely nervous and was babbling to any of those around him willing to listen as he tried to ease his tension.

'The powers that be must have seen the new system for tracking tax payments that I implemented,' he said quickly to a woman standing behind him. She smiled at him politely but did not reply.

'I was working on it for ages too, so that could be it. Spent lots of hours on it, I did. Makes it easier to look up who's paid what.' He ran his hands down the front of his shirt to clear it of some imaginary dust, an obsessive habit of his. 'So, I suppose I've made things easier for a lot of people, and presumably that's why I'm here today...' he trailed off as he fidgeted with the hem of his shirt. 'It's not quite what my father wanted me to do of course, he wanted me to follow him into his line of work, but I wasn't quite suited to that you see.' Wilfred's neighbour in the line did not seem to have heard and was looking intently out of one of the intricate patterns that gave view to the gardens below.

Well, this conversation is hopelessly one-sided, Wilfred thought, and decided to abandon it. Instead, he reached into his shirt where a small wooden box hung from a pewter chain around his neck, and held the box in the palm of his hand. The dark wooden box's lid was hinged and had a clear window set into a brass surround in the lid's centre. Through the window the contents were visible. Wilfred's beloved black and white striped jumping spider, Zebedee, moved restlessly around inside the box, his legs moving in a staccato, mechanical fashion as he waited to be released to go and hunt his minute prey. The sight of his constant companion cheered and relaxed him. 'I'd love to let you out for a feed in that garden below, but now isn't the time,' Wilfred said. *Not everybody appreciates seeing the smaller creatures of the earth roaming freely and doing what comes naturally to them, baffling as that viewpoint is,* he thought.

Wilfred looked forward again to see if the line was making any progress and saw one of the pair of doors at the far end swing inwards.

*

The sergeant paced the quiet corridor inside the Promontory, a slate in his hand with scrawled names on its surface. He stopped outside the doorway to a particularly finely prepared room into which the invitees were escorted singly or in pairs. Two rows of three guards stood either side of a shiny, blue-tiled aisle in the otherwise grey floor. Beyond them a wooden pedestal bore two small statuette-style awards, props hastily made to appear prestigious. These were intended to fool their guests into appearing genuine and legitimising the sham ceremony they attended.

All was calm as the guards facing each other cleaned their swords, in sharp contrast to the carnage they had just been party to. The sergeant glanced through the doorway and saw the guard who had previously been standing behind the pedestal now dragging a body toward a doorway at the rear of the room, a waxed sheet underneath preventing a trail of blood. The hired cleaning team were busy finishing up the scrubbing and drying of the tiled floor.

'Ready for the next ones, men?' the sergeant called into the room.

'Just let him put that one out the back and we will be,' the guard closest to him said, flicking his head toward the rear door.

'Another one out of the way and no longer a threat to us. Well done, all.'

'You should try doing work this hard sometime,' the guard grumbled.

'Perks of being a sergeant, lad,' he said with a grin as he strolled back toward the doors of the outside cloister, where the next in line waited. He composed himself, regaining his habitually stern visage.

'We'll soon be rid of all these fine, upstanding citizens,' he said quietly to himself. 'Then nobody will dare stand up to us.'

*

Julius's attention was drawn as he heard the nearby door open with a squeak of hinges. Another guard cradling a slate in the crook of his arm came through and stood to attention. A slight movement of air from inside the building followed the guard before the door swung shut again. Julius sensed rather than saw Nothro bristle at his side.

'Next!' the guard with the slate yelled.

'All right mate, we can hear you,' Julius responded. The two people ahead of him, a man and a woman of a similar age to himself stepped forward eagerly, as the newly arrived guard glared at Julius, clearly not appreciating the comment.

'What are your names?' the administrative guard demanded of the couple. Julius's thoughts were interrupted by a low, rumbling growl that made the hairs stand up on the base of his neck. He turned to Nothro, evidently the source of the sound, and saw his pupils were wide and his powerful shoulder muscles bunched – subtle signs that only a human much familiarised with Ananeptide would recognise – and suddenly Julius was on edge himself.

'This isn't right,' Nothro said to Julius. 'Something bad has been going on here...we are being deceived.'

'What? What do you mean?' Julius hissed insistently.

'Blood has been spilled...this is a trap...'

Nothro Grafanc's deep Ananeptide voice meant it was hard to keep anything he said particularly quiet. The guard had stopped talking, instead staring at Nothro's broad face with a look of shock at the ruse being exposed. This alarm had spread quickly and the twitchy guard by the door stepped forward, as his partner simultaneously put his free hand out to steady him. It was, however, too late.

To Julius's eye, the nervous guard looked to be overcome with panic and he then acted without being ordered to. He lowered his spear, stepped forward to the left of the newly arrived guard and thrust it at the person in line closest to him, the man at the head of the queue. The long blade caught the man in the left side of his belly, causing a spurt of blood and the unfortunate man to fold over the weapon in agony with a shocked howl. The other guard joined, supporting his colleague before the queueing people could gather their wits, and plunged his spear forward powerfully. It bit into the stricken man's partner, driving between her ribs and into her heart before he quickly pulled it free and let her slump to the ground, eyes roving wildly and gasping desperately as she rapidly lost blood from her ruined organ.

Whilst these attacks took place, the guard bearing the slate dropped his list and quickly drew the short sword on his hip, a weapon showing his superior rank. He was clearly well practised and it came free in one smooth motion. He stepped over the dying woman to advance upon the next nearest targets, Julius and Nothro.

'ADVANCE!' the commander yelled in a hoarse rasp to the guards in his charge as he strode forward. Julius saw the incident-sparking guard struggling to retrieve his spear from the punctured man in which it was lodged; he pulled and twisted in his desperate attempts, jerking the man this way and that in agony whilst the victim's bloodied hands gripped the spear shaft in a vain attempt to stay the shooting pain.

Nothro was breathing heavily now beside Julius. With eyes wide, Nothro lurched forward at this new threat to protect himself through action.

The ranking guard made an incoherent battle cry at the top of his lungs. He swung his sword forward in a vicious arc and it looked destined to bury itself into Nothro's shoulder; the large Ananeptide, however, was packed with more muscle under his coarse fur than the guard knew, and his appearance belied his lithe movements. Nothro thrust his arm forward with the speed borne of his unremitting work, and getting within the swing of the sword, shoved heavily at the guard's armoured shoulder with much of his body weight, spinning the man slightly on his planted foot and halting his progress. The sword's trajectory was redirected with this movement, and the edge flashed across Nothro's front instead, scoring a weak cut across his hairy forearm on the opposite side. The wound was relatively shallow and insignificant, with only a modicum of blood lost.

Adrenaline pumped into Julius's bloodstream and made him feel invincible, so he chose that moment to charge forward, join his friend and influence the scuffle, despite being unarmed. He turned himself into a fleshy battering ram, which was the best he could manage in the situation and screamed incoherently. His wild shoulder charge met the breastplate of the guard at an oblique angle and sent him tripping backward as Julius followed, falling with the guard with completely uncontrolled momentum. The combined force of the impact, Julius's weight and the man's heavy armour meant he could not correct his tumble and he crashed into his comrade behind him – the collision forced the other man's spear to point downwards and away from the guests as they collapsed in a heap. Nothro leaned forward and roughly grabbed Julius by the shoulder, wrenching him up and away from the pile of attackers until he was standing back on his feet by Nothro's side.

'Thanks,' Julius said to Nothro breathily, unable to say much thanks to the adrenaline. He glanced around whilst the two guards in front of him were incapacitated, and noted the third guard still struggled to retrieve his spear, and mentally wrote him off as no immediate threat. Whilst assessing, he felt a pressure in his hand. He looked down to see Nothro pushing his wide-bladed utility knife into his hand. Julius looked up at his companion with a huge grin and saw Nothro's other hand reach into the patch of denser fur around his navel and extract the steel gauntlets Nothro always wore whilst at work. Comprised of overlapping steel plates that clinked gently as they moved against each other, when worn the gauntlets protected Nothro's large hands and enabled him to wield a punch akin to a hit from a sledgehammer. Julius could not keep the grin off his face as he commented, 'Sneaky bugger.'

Nothro looked back to their erstwhile hosts. He leapt forward swiftly and landed a hammer-like blow to the side of the sword-wielding guard's head, causing his helmet to buckle inwards slightly onto the man's temple and knocking him unconscious. He remained atop his subordinate, preventing him from getting up. The trapped guard squirmed under the combined weight of his own and his superior's armoured bodies as he struggled to breathe.

Nothro exhaled a victorious grunt and turned to face the rest of the queue that had been waiting behind him. The guards further down the line had quickly cottoned on to the changing situation and had also lashed out, felling many invitees. He and Julius beheld the slaughter that had already been wrought upon the unarmed people and felt sickened. Many bodies were strewn about the elaborate walkway with blood pooled around them. Those people who had survived so far lay gasping pitifully from mortal wounds whilst others knelt, desperately trying to put pressure on their own or their companion's injuries to stem bleeding. The pair also saw that a small number of people were vainly trying to fight back as they had themselves.

Julius and Nothro caught sight of the stubby young man they had previously picked out for mockery, who was backing away from a guard advancing upon him with spear levelled and a savage sneer on his face. They could hear as he jabbered something incoherent – presumably some appeal to prove his innocence – and waved his hands out in front of him to try to ward off attack, as he rapidly backed up toward the stone edging of the cloister. Both knew that the innocent-looking man wouldn't stand a chance once he bumped into that barrier. They set out at a run, long years of working side by side attuning their instincts to reach the same conclusion, hoping to intervene and save him. Julius felt helpless as they closed the distance and saw the guard make feinting stabs toward the helpless man, delighting in his savagery, toying with his prey. Julius's rage built at this sight and he tried even harder to reach the pair. They were, however, too late.

Chapter Fourteen – Recollections and Rescues

Rundup Ovygdalha stood conspicuously alone, those around him in the queue all with someone they appeared to know or simply opted to talk to and naturally formed pairs. The tall, thin man attributed this to his manner of dress. It was far from any usual attire anywhere in the Bowl – in fact, it was unique, as it had been designed with sheer performance in mind and to make him as distinctive as possible. His large, rounded collar rose to a high point at the nape of his neck from his many faceted, bright jacket which contrasted with his dark skin tone. The unusual clothing had clearly been noticed by those around him and had caused them to give him a wide berth.

Fine by me, he mused at the time. As a performer, he usually dealt with people mobbing him and giving him unrelenting attention. Quite the opposite situation came as a huge relief to him, and he intended to enjoy it. How long that would last, being there to be honoured as he was, Rundup did not know. He was to be awarded the *Heart of Dralcea*, whatever that was. It was completely alien to him, although he was not one for keeping up with those sorts of matters that happened in the city.

With nobody to converse with, Rundup thought about why he was there. He assumed that the award was being given to him thanks to his actions in repelling a band of outlaws that had breached the city walls and were intent on murder and mayhem; his fellow performers had certainly made a big deal about his actions. More specifically, the interlopers had found his troupe's camp and begun to cut their way into some tents or set others alight in the dead of night. He was hardly just going to let them have their violent way with the camp's sleeping and surprised inhabitants, was he? Rundup let his mind drift back to the events of that night.

*

The first exile to have slashed his way into Rundup's tent and stepped through the ragged gash in the canvas was greeted with a thrown mug to the face. Having already been awoken by their less than subtle mutterings outside, he became instantly alert when it became evident those weren't his colleagues joking around outside. They entered his private quarters and Rundup caught a waft of a rancid stench from them – the product of stale sweat, spilled food and the fumes from consuming rough alcoholic drinks. He knew that whilst some of his fellow performers could sometimes indulge in galumph pretty heavily after a performance – and occasionally before one – none of them ever ended up smelling *that* foul. Hearing their muttered and slurred violent intentions confirmed it, and he felt a deep rage grip him at the thought of these villains invading his inner sanctum, their coarseness a stark contrast to the fine furnishings collected over the years.

He had jumped out of bed and hurled the vessel he kept for his night-time drink of water at the nearest man. Having caught his attacker square in the face with the projectile and knocking him unconscious, his companions had followed in behind him in single file in a short procession, and Rundup used his precision skills to keep on targeting them with other personal objects aimed at their heads. With three exiles consequently rendered unconscious on his floor thanks to his water mug, three-legged stool and candlestick – the candle having flown off and extinguished itself somewhere in flight, rolling up to one of the tent sides – he stripped one of them of his woodcutting axe and another of his ten-inch-long dagger to properly arm himself against any other intruders. He made for a chest pushed under his desk which was covered with a check-patterned cloth. Rundup pulled back the cover, undid the catches keeping it closed and looked inside before he paused, gazing at the dustpeppers resting inside. *No use now,* he chided himself as he consciously patted his legs, *nowhere to put them*.

Rundup stepped through the ripped canvas into the cool night air wearing just his long johns and prepared himself to take on any further invaders. He was determined not to be caught unawares by them sneaking about; he was *not* keen to be gutted in his nightwear. Rundup's efforts were aided by a bright moon, only slightly obscured by a thin scattering of clouds, as shafts of silver light picked out the edges of the other tents and buildings. Occasionally he was gifted patches of brighter, argent illumination to see by. Rundup moved inwards toward the busier cluster of living-tents – his being out toward the edge, always isolating himself for a quieter life – and stayed close to the canvas sides as he moved along, seeing no further signs of violation. However, he soon ran into another cluster of outlaws.

These four intruders, having not seen the axe that Rundup held behind his back, must have assumed that they had encountered an easy victim for their night of carnage with Rundup being in his undergarments. They advanced upon him with a swagger borne of confidence. He could imagine their thought process being something along the lines of, *Here's another sap whose luck has run out on this cold night, now we'll have some fun*.

Emboldened by his earlier triumph over their ill-prepared partners, Rundup allowed the leading two to get up close to him with knives drawn before shifting his grip on the axe handle to just below the head. He swung it round in two quick, vicious sweeps that caught one then the other exile around their temples with the handle before either could react and saw them crumple to the ground. Their friends, either enraged at this reversal of fortunes or through concern for their downed comrades, howled and charged the remaining distance to their intended prey. Rundup took a second to line up his aim before throwing the axe at the lead exile, the weapon turning end over end as it flew in a straight line through the air. The axe head buried itself in the man's breastbone with a wet cracking sound as it tore through layers of linen before ruining the flesh beneath. The man tilted backward at the waist under the impact, his momentum carrying his forward a couple of paces before hitting the ground on his back and remaining there, inert. The other man, a skinny wretch with a greasy mop of straw-coloured hair and pockmarked cheeks, met arguably a worse end.

The final raider charged forward with his hunting knife as Rundup drew the dagger from his waistband. Rundup sidestepped the man's wild lunge whilst swiping the newly-acquired dagger hard just above hip height. The blade, well sharpened on both edges, cut through his side with little resistance, causing a deep gash that immediately bled profusely. The sharpness of the cut meant that the man did not realise the full extent of his wound and he turned, snarling, to round on Rundup with a thrust of his knife aimed at his throat.

Rundup only just reacted in time, but he flashed the dagger up to deflect the knife blade and barely succeeded in pushing it away, albeit making the tip slash open his cheek in the process. The attack deflected and the two up close, Rundup acted the only way he could. With his arms inside the other man's reach, he put his bodyweight into a shove centred on the reeking man's shoulders.

Having been pushed back a step, the man made to step forward to attack again but stopped, noticing the wetness at his side and stopped to quickly examine it. He whimpered at the realisation that his blood was leaving his body rather rapidly. He clamped a hand over the wound, barely stemming the flow, and with a terrified look in his eyes made to settle the scores as his last act with his knife raised in his left hand.

Scared for the first time due to the desperation in the man's face, Rundup panicked and lunged forward, striking whilst he had the chance. He stabbed the dagger at the man's throat, piercing the windpipe and then let go, leaving it stuck in place. Unable to breathe and with blood now leaking from his side and throat, he choked and slumped to the ground, the long blade still lodged awkwardly as he lay on his side, gurgling pitifully.

Rundup immediately felt a horrible guilt at the suffering he had inflicted, but he reminded himself that a far worse fate had probably awaited him should he have fallen victim to the four murderous interlopers. The action done and irreversible, he left the two dying men and their unconscious companions behind and roused other able-bodied performers from their slumber to form a small counter-incursion team to repel the remaining invaders. They successfully saw off the exiles left in the camp, the lucky ones having abandoned their attack and fled. Those knocked out by the performers with their array of hastily snatched up cudgels and tools were restrained, and once given over to the Dralcea Guard were summarily executed in public to the cheers of the ordinary folk of the city.

*

Those actions had caused his summoning to his current location. He was a little flattered by it but did not feel that it was deserved. After all, it had been him or them, as they would have surely cut his throat in his sleep had he not awoken, and who wouldn't have tried to defend themselves and their kin? Rundup found himself touching the scar on his cheek at recalling that night's events. He had eventually had the wound stitched after the event by the troupe's oldest performer and resident mother figure, Lady Folodawa. Despite the neat job she had made of closing it, the cut had been deep enough to leave a pronounced scar running horizontally across his left cheek before a curved flick upwards which ended just above his ear. People seemed to believe the marking on his long, elegant face from the incident made him more of a hero. He disagreed; it had not made the encounter any more dangerous, it was simply a consequence of it, and was insignificant compared to what he had done to those opposing him.

Rundup's reverie abruptly ended, his mind snapping to alertness as soon as the first screams sounded from ahead of him; the solitude irrelevant now as he tensed, his fists clenched and blood pumped hard as he felt violence stir the air. Rundup glanced to where the screams emanated from and caught sight of a scuffle occurring at the head of the queue. Whilst there were no guards in his immediate vicinity, he saw others spaced either side of him at intervals in the queue begin to tense and use their weapons on the people waiting there. The sweeping wave of violence seemed to catch up all in its wake. The guard toward where the incident seemed to start knocked a man down with the butt of his spear as Rundup watched, and the sense of outrage overtook him. *We are their guests here, how dare they*!

The performer dashed forward and grabbed the shaft of the spear before any further damage could be done to the man on the ground. The guard's eyes were wild as he struggled to regain control of his spear, and the look only intensified as he failed to win the battle. Rundup did his best to stop the guard using the point of his spear but feared it would end badly as the seconds ticked by and the man became increasingly angry. Rundup eased away a fraction of the pressure from his grip so that the guard sensed the action and yanked the weapon back to him with renewed vigour; Rundup however knew this would be his reaction and pushed the shaft with all his might just as the guard pulled it, and it snapped upwards right into the guard's face at force. The man's eyes seemed to roll back into his head as he crumpled heavily to the floor, out cold. Glancing backward, Rundup saw the victim clutch his gut where he had been struck, but he got back to his feet unsteadily and looked relatively unhurt. He wheezed a word of thanks to Rundup and tried to straighten up and regain his breath. Rundup reached down, claiming the spear from the fallen guard's flaccid fingers and looked around.

Rundup steeled himself as he stepped over a body sprawled on the floor and saw a short young man a little distance away being forced backward by another guard jabbing at him with his own long spear. The man unsurprisingly looked utterly bewildered by the situation, and Rundup moved to his aid as quickly as he could, spear in hand. Time appeared to be running out for the defenceless man as he walked backward and came up hard against the edging of the stone balcony. As he closed in for the kill, Rundup could see the guard's face twist in a mask of triumph as he closed the distance to his victim and drew back his spear to strike the killing blow.

All Rundup's experience performing his balancing and knife-throwing act came in to play as he readied his own spear. He mentally blotted out the heavy pounding of feet and two looming figures approaching from the head of the queue as he thrust with the weapon, just as the guard moved forward with his intended killing strike. Rundup's aim was impeccable, and his spear point went exactly where he intended it to – scant inches behind the steel head of the guard's spear. It lodged firmly in the wooden shaft and fouled the guard's attempt, forcing it wide of the intended victim and down so the point clanged against the flagstone floor. The guard, who had been so focused on his tormenting he had not noticed Rundup approaching, quickly swivelled his head to face him, stunned at the sudden turn of events. Rundup rapidly made up the last few steps separating them and slammed his foot down on the guard's spear shaft with all the force he could muster from his long leg.

He impacted above where he had skewered the handle and with a satisfying *crack,* shattered and separated it from the steel spearhead. Rundup reacted quickest and swept downwards to retrieve his stolen spear before the man could replace his own weapon.

The guard's face dropped at being suddenly unarmed with a strangely dressed and bizarrely capable guest fighting back against him, and without colleagues close enough to help. He stared at Rundup in horror and didn't notice the thundering steps of the Ananeptide rapidly closing on him from behind; Rundup finally took note of the approaching figure and stepped back toward the young man he had just saved, who was leaning against the balcony and breathing rapidly. The onrushing Ananeptide put his shoulder down as he reached his top speed and, not letting up as he approached, crashed into the unwitting guard full on.

None of those present had ever witnessed such a thing before and were unlikely to forget it in a hurry. Rundup watched as the Ananeptide's massive build-up of momentum hit the armoured man like a bat cleanly striking a ball; the guard positively flew in the opposite direction. His feet left the ground and despite the additional weight of his armour travelled fully fifteen feet before he slammed into the cloister's decorative windows further down, then clanged to the stone floor. The guard lay motionless and blood seeped from many of the openings of his armour to coat much of the metal and pool around him. The winded man, Rundup, the young man just saved, the Ananeptide and his companion all stared at the sight before looking at each other.

'My name is Rundup,' he announced in his unintentionally theatrical voice.

'I'm Harold Jenker,' Harold wheezed, still recovering from his winding.

'Julius, and this is Nothro,' Julius said. 'What's your name, mate?' he asked the man Nothro and Rundup had just saved.

'W-Wilfred Wolfscope,' he stammered, looking frightened out of his wits.

'Nice to meet you all, though I wish it were under better circumstances. I don't feel very welcome here anymore,' Rundup commented drily, shifting his grip on his spear. 'Thanks for the help there,' he said, nodding to Nothro, who now stood slightly apart from the others as he had struggled to stop after shoulder-charging the guard.

'He never did enjoy gatherings,' Julius said with a grin. 'I say we leave before we end up like this lot. Who's coming along?'

'Y-yes! Please, let me come with you!' Wilfred said desperately. 'I don't understand what's happening here...'

'Mind if we join? We managed to evade the attention of the guards, and you seem capable of looking after yourselves,' a tall man with long dark hair dangling down past his shoulders said as he and two other men and a young woman – other surviving guests – ran over and swelled the small gathering's size to nine.

'Of course. It seems we have all been lured into something sinister here,' Rundup said. He reached down to the cold stone floor and picked up the broken-off spearhead, tucking it into his inner jacket pocket. 'Yes, I really don't feel like staying for the festivities,' he said tartly and strode purposefully the way the downed guard had fallen. 'There are others ahead.'

The small group moved forward, and Julius put an arm around the shoulder of Jenker to help him along as he still struggled for breath. Rundup and Nothro jogged forward before they came up to a red-haired woman furiously kicking a downed guard who despite still wearing all his armour, lay curled up in the foetal position. His weapon lay to the side. An older, blonde-haired woman stood by, tugging at her daughter's arm with one hand and holding the other to a wound in her shoulder as she looked around wildly. Rundup saw the blonde woman's eyes widen as he and the huge, shaggy figure of Nothro approached, but visibly relaxed when Nothro slowed and spread his gauntleted hands out high and wide to show he meant no harm.

'Don't worry madam, he means no harm, and neither do I,' Rundup said soothingly in his elegant voice.

'Thank goodness,' the lady said. 'I'm Skula, and this is my daughter, Ryx...'

'...*bastard*! I'll *show* you what happens! You *dare* touch her...' the younger woman screamed, kicking constantly, punctuating certain words with especially hard kicks.

'Are you all right?' rumbled Nothro.

'He got me, but then Ryx flew into a rage as she does, and...' Skula gestured at her daughter still furiously attacking the cowering guard. 'It's not too bad, just a spearpoint stab really, it could have been much worse. What the hell is going on here? We were told to come for an award presentation.'

'We were told the same. We're going, bored of this,' Julius said with forced levity. 'Best come along I'd say, before this bloke gets it any worse.'

'*RYX*! Come along, we must go. Leave him, I'll be ok. Whatever's happening is only going to get worse if we stay here. We need to leave, *now*,' Skula implored. It seemed to snap Ryx out of her fixated attack on the man, and she looked around, face still flushed with anger. Rundup noticed her try to slow her breathing and her pupils visibly dilated as she seemed to calm down slightly.

The expanded group, now numbering eleven, moved off. Rundup picked up the dropped spear and spared the curled-up man a quick assessment as he sobbed lightly from the kicking he had received. Rundup saw him as no further threat and passed him by, then handed the spear to Ryx. 'Take this, my good lady,' he said. *This woman looked savage enough with just her fists, she must be terrifying wielding a weapon,* he thought. *She should be a real asset in escaping from this place.*

'Thanks,' Ryx replied. 'I don't think it'll do as much damage as I would want it to against these thugs, though.'

'Now is not the time for more violence, Ryx. It's not the answer. We've survived so far and should be thankful for that,' Skula said.

'I'm quite keen on being violent after he *stabbed* you, mother,' Ryx said angrily. 'Fair is fair. I'll be thankful if we both get out of here in one piece.'

They carried on down the long passageway before they joined up with another small knot of guests who had avoided – or defused – the attentions of the nearby guards on duty. Rundup saw one man with a dark complexion and stocky build as he wrestled with another guard.

*

Advancing whilst helping Jenker lope along, Julius was impressed with the way the exotically-dressed man ahead of him was dealing with another guard. He had already disarmed the man and held his armoured forearms as they grappled, looking as if he intended to nullify the threat.

'My leg around yours like so,' Julius heard him say, explaining the technique of unarmed combat once it was too late for his opponent to counter it, 'and down you go!'

His movements were smooth and confident, rendering the guard unable to resist and he landed heavily on his back. At once, his seven fellow surviving guests who had gathered around leapt onto the felled guard, wrenched his helmet off and beat him unconscious with their bare fists. 'That should do it,' he remarked. The man noticed Julius, Nothro et al approaching and seemed to realise they had fought back as his own informal group had.

'Nice move there, very effective. I'm Julius, this big lad is Nothro. Were you invited here for a supposed award too?'

'Judge Molefi Cronto, at your service,' he bowed slightly. 'That was the story I was given, although that must have been a ruse. Do you know why they turned on us? All I know is that whatever is happening is a disgrace and will not go unpunished! For now it looks as if getting away from here would be the wisest action, however.'

'Absolutely agreed about leaving,' Skula interjected. 'I've no idea why they attacked us. It was so sudden.'

'Can't say why, but I smelled them spilling blood inside the building once we were near the doors,' Nothro said.

'Is that what got you all het up before? We can discuss it later anyway, I'm sure. Let's get ourselves out of here,' Julius said, and the two groups moved onwards as one, sensing strength and safety in numbers now that nineteen of them had a common cause.

Heading back the way they had all initially entered the corridor, when times had been so much simpler yet occurred mere minutes earlier, they collectively did their best to step around and over the bodies of those who had met the unprovoked rage of the Dralcea Guard and not survived. Julius continued helping Jenker along and watched as Nothro was joined by Cronto heading up the expanded group. The frontrunners found themselves stepping around the body of an Ananeptide, significantly smaller than Nothro was; the fallen appeared to be an adolescent, yet to reach maturity. Julius saw the effect of the sight visually stoking the fires of anger coursing through Nothro, and he mentally vowed to help his friend take revenge for the youngster's needless death.

Julius shouted to Nothro as they pressed on. 'There's at least one more,' Julius noted, gesturing forward. A hundred yards ahead, the corridor arced round to the left and out of sight. Near to this curve, a panicked-looking guard with a bloodied face turned away, then sprinted off as well as his armour would allow and disappeared out of Julius's line of sight.

Just visible through the elaborate stonework filigree enclosing them was a round tower climbing the height of much of the outer building, with similar cut out shapes running up the sides. Julius watched as he ran, seeing flashes of colour and reflective metal as the guard laboured up the spiralling staircase within the tower. Once again, the guard disappeared as he gained elevation. Julius continued and tried his best not to take in too many details of the fallen.

A sudden, ear-splitting pealing sound reverberated down the corridor, making some visibly flinch, and Julius realised the guard had not simply been fleeing but running to sound the alarm and summon his comrades. Evidently the tower he had climbed contained a bell at the top, out of sight.

'Damn,' Julius spat. 'We really need to leave now.'

Nothro gave a low rumble as response. It succinctly conveyed all his opinion of the situation.

Chapter Fifteen – Past the Teeth and Down the Throat

The nineteen survivors pounded along the flagstones and down a flight of stairs, leaving the scene of carnage behind them. What Julius had witnessed would surely haunt his dreams, but he was completely focused on surviving now and fled without remorse. They had originally entered the Promontory through a side street just off the parade ground to the building's front. The small street directed them around the edge of a walled garden, through the gates and along a wall-enclosed corridor which led them to where the chaos had broken loose. As all were aware that the walled corridor led out of the Promontory complex and back to the streets, they headed for it and Julius silently prayed it would lead to their salvation.

As Cronto led the fleeing people round the last corner of the cloister, Julius saw him stop sharply and those following also tried to slow down, many bumping into one another at the sudden change of pace. 'Oh, dear,' Cronto said. 'Those two ranks of armoured guards are not what I wanted to see. Looks as though they are all armed, too.'

Few were covered in the full complement of armour bestowed upon those lucky enough to be on duty in the Promontory, and many simply had a helmet and breastplate on. One guard only had time to don his dark blue cloak and greaves to cover his shins in the rush to assemble at the call of the summoning bell. Those not trying to pull on additional pieces of protection were fumbling with their weapons, trying to ready them for action.

'They're blocking us in. They will stop us getting back to the gate and out into the city...' Cronto said as he looked around desperately. Some of the escaping group watched the guards fearfully, expecting more of the same violence they had already received; there was no reason to believe that they would be treated any better. They were also hemmed in on both sides by the high walls either side of the corridor. 'Our only option is to press on and attempt to force our way through,' he said with surprising calmness. Nothro and Julius respectfully but insistently pushed their way to the front of the group where Cronto stood, closely followed by Rundup Ovygdalha.

'You're right. We have to keep moving, or we're dead,' Julius said, his breath steady but face flushed from the earlier fighting and run that followed. 'More will be coming.'

'We are indeed at a critical juncture. Our actions must be swift and decisive!' Rundup declared.

Rundup turned back to their tormentors and launched into a sprint, heading for the nearest guard. He cleared the distance rapidly by virtue of his long legs and the man visibly panicked. Rundup swung the shaft of his spear menacingly, forcing the guard to topple to the ground in his effort to avoid the blow, and the performer was quickly past him. Nothro gave a short grunt of assent and launched himself forward the same way, issuing his best snarl to aid the terrifying effect of having a huge Ananeptide bearing down on them. Julius was right behind Nothro, yelling for all he was worth and waving his knife. Nothro and Julius each shouldered aside a guard blocking their path and knocked them to the ground, forcing them to drop their weapons.

As the intrepid trio charged onward, Julius heard Cronto begin to rally the rest of the group, and turned back to watch the effect of the man's words. 'Come now, we must not delay!' Cronto swept his arm up and then forward as if to gesture the way and lend their movement more impetus. The mass of bodies rippled on in an unsteady wave, treading the path worn by their vanguard – pushing past those fallen guards in their way without a care, some feeling oddly powerful to be getting by these people relatively easily. Julius noticed with a smile that Ryx could not help but shove a hand in the helmeted face of the nearest guard she passed by, stunned as he fumbled and tried to ready his weapon.

One of the last through was the tall survivor, his long hair swishing as he turned to check who was left to get by; Wilfred Wolfscope also lagged, his fear not completely overcoming his natural sluggishness. He ushered the shorter young man through the broken screen of authority, toward where the others watched from further along, the guards scattered to either side of the passageway, leaderless, as they all appeared to be recruits. The man then turned to follow the others, evidently satisfied that everyone else had gotten safely through.

Unfortunately Julius noticed too late the guard, shoved aside moments before, who had successfully loaded his weapon whilst lying on the dusty flagstones. 'Look out!' was all he could shout. The guard aimed at the closest target to him, a man with long hair turning to run after his group, and pulled the trigger mechanism. This set the levers in motion and forced the Sweat of Hephaestus to burst from the membrane and fly at the man from short range; they impacted across his back, some bursting out of his chest as they passed through his body in a bloody.

Cronto, Rundup and Nothro turned at the strange sound of the firing and joined Julius in seeing their fellow survivor's confused face. He staggered, wild-eyed and bewildered then stopped in his tracks, his shirt shredded and reddening by the second. He seemed to hang there, his only remaining strength engaged to hold him upright. Julius belatedly roared in pain and grabbed at his shoulder as an errant Sweat of Hephaestus caught him, then yelled with rage as he made to fly at the offending guard, only to be caught by the hairy arm of Nothro who scooped him up and turned him around. 'You're not letting your temper kill you today,' Nothro rumbled before pointing after the rest of the group. 'Go.'

Julius took a noticeably deep breath to calm himself, realising that he was powerless to help the man now. He had collapsed onto his hands and knees as blood streamed from the multiple exit wounds covering his upper body. He coughed deeply once, spraying the stones red beneath him, before he lifted his head and rasped one last sentence that only Cronto, Julius and Nothro could hear: 'Get them out.' He then slumped to the floor as his arms gave out from under him, his eyes staring straight ahead with the glassiness of death.

Other guards appeared to be recovering their senses and Julius noted some getting their weapons readied. *This is getting more dangerous again by the second*, he thought. 'Cronto, Rundup! Get far away from them, as fast as possible.'

Julius rejoined the others, shoving Wilfred along after he had stopped to stare at the spectacle against all reason; the young man seemed morbidly fascinated and needed physical intervention to tear his eyes away. 'Get moving,' Julius growled at Wilfred, struggling to keep his voice level through the intense anger coursing through him. A fresh throb of pain in his shoulder did nothing to help the matter. 'That man just gave his life for you. Don't let it have been in vain.'

Tears formed and then overwhelmed Wilfred's eyes as he was pushed roughly in the direction of the others. He seemed as though he might have been rendered insensible if not for those around cajoling him into movement.

'Quickly now. The gates to the street are ahead – we can make it,' Cronto called out confidently. 'We might even be able to get back our possessions if we can access this security booth. It looks quiet there.' Cronto quickly reached the small booth and cautiously snuck inside before he reappeared in its gloomy doorway.

'All clear! And a big chunk of luck, those guards back there must have been those meant to be on duty here. Quickly, grab what is yours if it's essential and let us leave this foul place behind, physically if not mentally,' Cronto said, waving those who approached inside, looking eager to take back what personal protective items they had been stripped of on their way into the governmental complex. Julius noticed Cronto had already grabbed and slipped on his own bag and now stood watchfully as others frantically rummaged inside the hut. Julius was surprised at the efficiency with which everybody collected what was theirs, and in no time at all they were finished, standing ready outside.

'Never before have I seen such wanton violation of the law. Good riddance to this foul place,' Cronto said as he led the way back into the alley that led along the side of the Promontory, toward the parade ground and the chasm below it, none knowing yet what other horrors Dralcea had in store for them.

Chapter Sixteen – No Safety in Numbers

The group's collective footfall clattered down the street as they made no attempt to be quiet in their haste. Their primary concern at this moment was to put as much distance as possible between them and the scene of slaughter they had narrowly escaped.

Julius paced forward to the head of the group where Cronto ran, having been out at the fringes shepherding the others following his earlier charge forward. Some struggled to keep up but were helped along by Julius's encouragement, whilst Rundup also did his best to cajole people into keeping pace. Julius's rigorous outdoor work meant he was in excellent fitness and had no trouble with the speed they attempted to maintain. His increased heart rate gave him a renewed reminder of the wound he had sustained, as it throbbed anew.

They had turned right through the gate; to the left was a dead end as the outer walls of the Promontory's guard barracks cut across the street, preventing any travel in that direction. The survivors moved steadily down the long but narrow street which channelled them toward the grand front face of the Promontory, its ceremonial parade ground and the huge chasm beneath.

Nothro pushed up alongside Julius and Cronto, his large legs powering him along seemingly effortlessly. Julius knew that Nothro could easily run at a faster pace and for a longer time, but here he was restricted by the humans accompanying him and he slowed to accommodate them and stay with the group. If nothing else, Julius could count on Nothro to stick with him. They had worked and lived in close proximity for long enough to be so connected that they instinctively looked out for one another.

The three slowed their pace as they reached the mouth of the street and looked around briefly. To their left a handful of guards were hurrying toward them, drawn to the Promontory by the exhortations of the pealing bell in its tower. The wide colonnaded front of the governmental building was to their right and a work gang were busy repairing the pavement at the far end of the street leading past the Promontory's front. The only feasible option was to follow the steps which led down to the parade ground and public meeting place directly in front of the building they had just escaped, open to the hot air that rose from the churning depths far below. None of the three frontrunners realised that they had been heading toward the largely enclosed space, though they were given little choice in the matter. Nothro and Julius dropped to walking speed alongside Cronto, who looked displeased with this development.

'As places to lay low go, I wouldn't pick this as my first choice,' Cronto said. The rest of the group followed the leading three down the wide steps and onto the polished, sandy-coloured stone slabs. The only other people there were those tending a scattering of small market stalls and those citizens interested in gazing at either the imposing frontage of the Promontory or the smoking depths of magma far below the parade ground. 'Perhaps we were a little too direct in trying to escape from that place. We've come back around to the front of it.'

Julius looked over to Cronto, who appeared to be trying to shoulder the burden of protecting them all by himself. 'So, what now? We aren't from the city. Where should we go?'

'Well, neither am I,' Cronto said. 'It doesn't seem wise to stick around here though, that was hardly the welcome to Dralcea I expected. The most important thing is to avoid any more guards – with that call to arms they will be out looking for us now. I've seen them patrolling the streets ordinarily so it must only be a matter of time until we come across them, looking for us or not. Any suggestions for avoiding them?'

'Tipping carts over in front of them seems to flummox them in our experience,' Julius replied. 'Other than that? Run like hell. But really...keep out of the way, stick to the smaller streets and alleys. Avoidance must be the surest way to survive.'

Nothro suddenly exhaled heavily, making Cronto jump slightly; a breath from his large lungs was a noticeable event. 'Won't be easy with eighteen of us.'

'No, you're absolutely right. We will need to be exceptionally cautious and keep quiet.' A look of deep sorrow crossed Cronto's face and he cast his eyes down. 'What has happened here today? It started off so clear and bright, but now it has been sullied by a downpour.'

Julius sought to divert this sour mood; they had no time to waste reflecting on what they had been through, at least for the moment. 'Cautious or not, some of these lot need a rest. We need to get somewhere out of the way so they can have a breather, or they simply won't be able to keep going. This city is built like a maze, maybe we can lose them? Or at least cause confusion. It could even be fun,' Julius smiled wolfishly.

'I really don't think messing with them is the way, we want to get away from them, not closer. And if they were to catch us? Do you think they would show any mercy after what they did to us all back there, and what we in turn were forced to do? No, not a good plan. But your huge friend there raised a vital point. We cannot stay together – even if those guards being sent out to apprehend us have no idea how any of us look, they could realise who we are by the simple fact of us being a large group. Add to that the fact that several of us have weapons, and we must be quite recognisable,' Cronto said.

Julius saw Nothro looking displeased to have been referred to as 'huge', but then saw the small upturn of his mouth and knew he was flattered that his insight was recognised. A young woman from the following group jogged up and stopped dead in front of Nothro. She did not seem at all intimidated by his size.

'Just where are we being led? We seem to be running away – isn't it about time for you to go on the hunt, rip a few of them apart to teach them a lesson? You have the claws and teeth for it,' Ryx said to Nothro.

'It doesn't bode well for your immediate future when you start tearing people into multiple different parts, funnily enough,' Julius commented from Nothro's far side. 'They had some sort of ranged weapons back there too, I've never seen anything like them. Didn't even look as though you needed a good aim with it. Don't you think he would make quite a sizable target?'

'Ryx, don't go volunteering other...folk to go into battle,' Skula said, looking at Nothro. 'I've met a few Ananeptide in my time running the pub and always found them to behave with the utmost respect and politeness. Perhaps they are more likely to go all or nothing when it comes to drinking galumph, compared to humans at least, but they've never been violent on my watch. I wish the same could be said of my own species. At least when there are Ananeptide in The Crimson Duck, the humans are scared into behaving impeccably. That's an invaluable commodity in our business.'

'Yes, I've never had to chuck an Ananeptide out, luckily for me,' Ryx said with a grin.

It was at that moment that the first armoured figures appeared at the top of the steps they had descended mere moments before.

'Over there, on the parade ground!' the man at the head of the guards yelled, audible to the escapees. 'That must be them! Form up, guards!' he bellowed with his hand raised in the air to focus their attention.

Almost all the escapees turned to look at the guard yelling, as did most of the citizens wandering around the space who had up until that moment ignored them. That suddenly changed and those even remotely near to the disturbance backed away whilst staring in wonder at what they could have done to draw the ire of the Dralcea Guard.

'Oh, damn,' Cronto said. More guards filed into view at the top step leading from the street and fanned out along its length. Most carried the weapons they had seen used to devastating effect only minutes before, but even the remainder held more familiar arms, particularly spears.

Julius and his companions instinctively backed away at the sight. They were being cut off at a rapid pace and the only place they could retreat toward were the barriers encircling the far end of the curved space. Upon reaching that limit, the reality gripped them with icy certainty.

There was no safety to escape to.

Chapter Seventeen – Desperate Measures

Dralcea Guards were thoroughly trained and well-drilled, even if that was not shown to be the case very frequently. On this occasion, however, the situation called for concentration and consequently their discipline returned to the fore. Those armed with Ejectors formed the front rank whilst those behind held their spears either side of their comrades to create a bristling row of sharp points and Ejector chambers that would deter all but the most berserk of attackers.

The gate guard who had shown up and taken charge of those guards he had found mustering in the vicinity of the Promontory quickly dressed the line to ensure none stepped ahead too hastily and broke the formation. He kept his bow in its place on his back and instead had drawn his short sword to use for the upcoming fight and pointed it forward as he gave his instruction.

'Forward, and hold the line!' he shouted at high volume.

The men of the guard paced forward steadily and carefully to negotiate the downward steps onto the flat expanse beyond. They managed to maintain their step despite their eagerness to fight and avenge their fallen comrades. Those with Ejectors had them loaded and ready.

*

Julius, Ryx, Skula and Cronto waved the rest toward the metal railings to distance themselves from the advancing guards as much as possible. Nothro stood in place and faced the guards whilst the others moved behind him, his aim to give some semblance of a defensive front. Julius hoped their actions would buy them some time in which to come up with a plan, though it seemed hopeless.

He cast around desperately. As the more frightened milled around in a tight press by the barriers, he glimpsed something through the railings. A dark causeway of interlocking stones stretched from somewhere underneath the platform they occupied all the way across to an anchoring point further around the curve of the caldera. It was the closest of the two supporting struts that helped hold the parade ground in place over the chasm and looked to be their only slim hope of escape. It was manifestly not meant to be accessible, however, and absolutely not intended to be walked upon.

Julius caught the attention of Cronto as he also looked around to find a solution to their problem. 'There's something we could do, but it's risky...I mean, it's crazy really, but we obviously don't stand a chance against that lot.' He beckoned Nothro over urgently. 'We need you, big man. Can you get some of those railings out over there?'

Nothro shrugged and moved to where Julius indicated, parting the crowd effortlessly. He gripped a section of the railings three quarters of the way down to where it was cemented into the paving slabs and began trying to wrench it out.

'What's your idea? We haven't got long,' Cronto said.

'There is a support that runs from here across to the other side, see? If Nothro can get that railing out, then we could get down to it, then across and away. *Extremely* carefully, of course.'

Cronto glanced at where Julius indicated and exhaled a big breath. 'That sounds like a pretty fast way to end up dead. Have you seen what is down there?'

'I'm all too aware of what's underneath us, and I'd recommend not looking either. Have you seen the array of weapons they've got to hand? I'd say that staying here is the more suicidal option of the two.'

A screeching sound nearby alerted Julius to the success of Nothro's endeavour. The Ananeptide stood with the section of railing, clumps of shattered concrete still clinging to the uprooted ends, and held it in front of him as though it were a shield. He gestured at the formation of guards marching ever closer. 'Time is of the essence,' Nothro rumbled.

'Gods, it's come to this. All right.' Cronto walked over to the newly formed gap which the railings formerly occupied and looked down. 'Who's first?' he said with his best attempt at levity.

'Any volunteers?' Julius asked everybody. He noted the drop to the strut was around five feet but the width of the curved stone support, at three feet wide, was adequate to walk on. Although a terrifying proposition, attempting to traverse this terrifying tightrope appeared to be the more appealing of the two options since he knew full well what those guards had in mind, although not the reason why.

'I'll go first,' Ryx said. 'Mum, follow me. This is our opportunity to escape. We can make it.'

Skula looked at Ryx in horror, then at the mass of guards approaching before she nodded. Julius watched as Skula allowed her daughter to guide her over to the gap and, after a deep breath, Ryx clambered down. She then helped her mother down and began walking carefully along with Skula following closely.

Those remaining saw the idea coming to fruition and quickly caught on, preparing themselves to follow along and escape the guards. Julius, Rundup and Cronto helped organise them into better order to speed the process, whilst Nothro contented himself with hurling the railings in the direction of their antagonists. The action stalled some of them for a moment as an element of fear entered their thoughts.

In good time the majority made it down the short drop and Julius anxiously stood watch as they shuffled their way along, most trying to keep their gaze facing forward on the slowly nearing visage of their destination. A pair of women held hands as they walked to aid their stability. Jenker helped Wilfred along and encouraged the young man to hold onto his belt to overcome the evident fear he had of every movement. The last to drop down were Nothro, then Cronto, and Julius was last, all eighteen trying to cross. Julius felt that as it was his plan he could not ask anyone else to be the last to go, and was thus the most vulnerable to attack from behind. The stench of gases rising from the depths was sulphurous, acrid, choking.

Those final few endured a handful of pot-shots from some of the more impetuous Ejector-wielding guards before they had the chance to jump down from the parade ground's edge, though Julius was particularly thankful that none of the efforts had yet hit their mark. As he slowly advanced, he felt as if his back was ten feet wide and waited for the fatal blow to land. *We must make quite the sight doing this, with not so much as a rope between us and oblivion,* he thought. *I bet nobody other than the occasional drunk has ever attempted this before. I doubt they survived it, either. At least us being sober ought to give us some hope.*

The rattle and clatter of spears and Sweat of Hephaestus striking the stone around them and under their feet only served to unnerve the final few to cross. They did their best to keep their tread steady and avoid rushing; the very last thing they needed was somebody going too quickly and shoving anyone, as the result would almost certainly be them overbalancing and – well, it was best not to think about what would happen after that.

Julius desperately wished to be further along but forced himself to be calm and maintain a safe distance – he would not condemn someone else to a horrific end just because of his own uncontrolled panic. The stiflingly hot fumes rising all around him noticeably dried his skin after mere moments, and he could feel his eyeballs becoming itchy as the fumes robbed them of their moisture. Julius could hear Nothro, a few metres ahead, muttering something incomprehensible to himself and wasn't sure if it was an outpouring of fury, a calming affirmation or some plea to whatever deity Nothro favoured at the moment – although any would have surprised Julius, given that neither of them were overtly spiritual.

Good progress appeared to be being made further up the line and the survivors shuffled along as quickly yet safely as they could. Several obviously did not trust their balance as much as others and resorted to crawling along on their hands and knees. Julius risked a look along the drawn-out procession. Ryx had reached the far end and was clambering up the five-foot height discrepancy between where the strut anchored against the caldera's side and the street's edge as Skula boosted her up, pushing under one of her daughter's legs. Julius himself was pretty much out of range of the attackers' weapons now; the hail of missiles noticeably tailed off as the guards stayed at the parade ground's edge and dared not follow, contenting themselves with hurling insults instead. That was something that Julius could relax about, at least, as much as he could whilst he walked the narrow strip suspended high above a pool of lava.

*

One of the older surviving couples roughly in the middle of the procession were taking slightly longer than the others. The gentleman, dressed in his formal shirt, trousers and waistcoat was trying to keep his step steady but still missed his footing and started to pitch forward. As he fell, he outstretched his arms reflexively to cushion his fall and protect his face, but he also succeeded in accidentally striking the leg of the person ahead of him, a man of average height in his mid-thirties.

This action tripped the younger man and he fell to one knee heavily then tipped sideways before he could stop himself. His momentum carried his upper half out over the precipice and his arms could only grasp at the hot air rising to meet him, his feet also unable to snag onto anything that could arrest his movement. He was powerless as his weight carried him over the point of no return and he pinwheeled down into the chasm, howling in terror as he went.

The older man's wife, following closely behind and wearing her best green dress and sandals, instinctively reached forward and tried to grab at her husband to help him up. She herself then overbalanced as her husband's leg flailed in an effort to get to his feet, and she fell the opposite way to her husband's unfortunate neighbour. He managed to catch her leg as she toppled but most of her weight already projected over the side and he struggled to reverse the action. The man held on tightly as his wife screamed, facing down into the depths far below, and he steadily slid in the same direction himself as he desperately cursed with his rising panic. With both hands clinging to his wife he had no way to halt his movement and every inch that she jutted out further made it harder for him to stop, until a moment later the inevitable happened, gravity took a hold and he too slipped off the side.

Rundup, who followed behind the couple, was unable to intervene in time and could only watch as they plummeted, embracing each other in anticipation of meeting their doom. He moved on numbly after witnessing the sight and tried to dispel the shock that enveloped him.

*

Ryx, from her position at the far end helping people up onto the street, had also seen the three people fall over the course of just a few seconds and was horrified. Her viewpoint from above and looking back at the rest meant that she saw them fall for much longer than any of the others and it was a sequence that would stay seared into her memory. She continued to haul people up to safety and tried to keep her eyes clear as she did so. There would be time to grieve and process what had happened later, but right now everybody else's lives depended on speed and efficiency. Ryx kept that thought in mind to focus herself on the task at hand.

*

As time progressed, all those remaining ahead of Julius successfully made their way to the end of the strut without further drama, barring the occasional hastily corrected wobble. He could see the steadily increasing crowd on the street that was their destination as Ryx, the first to reach it safely, hauled them up one by one as people reached her. Nothro didn't require Ryx's help, being the tallest and able to leap up onto the street, who by any rate was looking tired from having hoisted so many people up the gap already. Julius looked on, mildly annoyed as Nothro insisted on helping Cronto up and then himself, wishing his friend was less of a gentleman. He had been hoping to be assisted by the red-haired young woman who had led the way on their perilous walk. The relief of reaching the far side made up for his disappointment, however, and those remaining fifteen were soon gathered on the street far across the chasm from the Promontory.

Another feeling mixed with the relief that Julius felt, and it tempered the high from successfully reaching safety. It had been his plan that led them out onto the long supporting strut; nobody would ever attempt something so insanely dangerous without some outrageous benefit waiting at the far end. Julius hadn't wanted to cross the improvised bridge any more than any of the others, but if it was a choice between that and facing a large formation of angry and well-armed guards, then he would choose the terrifying test of balance every time. That thought did little to soothe the awful feeling in his gut that it was because of him that those three poor people, victimised just as he had been, had fallen to meet a horrible end. The responsibility lay with him, and its weight was a heavy burden.

'Well done for making it across, everyone, and thank you for the plan, young man,' Rundup said in his cultured voice. 'Your quick thinking, along with your friend's invaluable assistance,' he nodded graciously to Nothro, 'has saved us for sure. We owe you our thanks.'

'Except those who fell,' Julius said sullenly. He didn't want to hear thanks at that moment. It was not appropriate after their number had shrunk so suddenly.

'That wasn't your fault, it was an unfortunate accident. Think of how many of us would have survived if we had faced off with our over-zealous friends back there,' Rundup inclined his head back toward the Promontory and placed a placating hand on Julius's shoulder. 'I daresay none of us.'

'Did anybody know the names of our companions who didn't make it across?' Cronto asked the wider group.

The shaking of heads and muttering told him that none knew their identities. 'We will honour them regardless, along with those lost at the Promontory, when the time is right,' Rundup declared.

'Yes, and there will be a time, but now we must move,' Cronto said.

Julius looked back across the yawning gulf to the parade ground and could no longer spot the Dralcea Guard by the barriers where they had previously stood and launched their missiles. He looked around the curve of the upper level between that point and their own location but could not pinpoint where the guard had got to. 'I can't see them now, but they will surely be in pursuit of us. Remaining exactly where we've been seen to travel to would be madness.'

'True, and where we go is something we need to decide quickly,' Cronto said authoritatively. 'Any thoughts, anyone?'

'Why don't we all go back to the pub, have a drink and consider things?' Skula suggested. 'Ryx's dad will be able to think of something, I'm sure.'

Ryx's eyes widened upon hearing this. 'Mum! We can't just go home and pretend that nothing has happened, it doesn't work like that! *They* are *trying* to *kill* us! We can debate it all we want but it won't change a bloody thing. We've just crossed *that*,' she pointed at the support with energetic emphasis, 'which I can scarcely believe in itself, and you've seen what they're capable of, and...and I can't think of a damn thing we can do to change any of this...,' she trailed off, sounding helpless; a far cry from what Julius and the others had seen of her up until this point. She gave the impression of being a strong woman, sure of herself and who rarely needed assistance from others.

'Look, it isn't too far to our place from here. If nothing else, we have plenty of room to keep everyone under our roof temporarily, just to get refreshed and then come up with a plan. What else can we do?' Skula said, putting her arm around her daughter. 'I don't fancy standing out here where they can spot us, easy as pie. Speaking of pie, we can get fed there too.'

'A kind offer, but I think it would be best to keep moving, my lady – or make only brief stops at most. Our priority must be to keep away from the Dralcea Guard. They are sure to come to our homes to find us – most of us at least, I have the fortune to not live nearby. Though I'm not sure even that will deter them,' Cronto said.

'Could we go to your home, perhaps ride this out there if you live away from this mess?' Skula replied hopefully.

'I'm not sure it would be wise, it is many miles distant and they know where my home is...I believe there is somewhere that does need a visit however,' Cronto said, looking Jenker straight in the eyes.

Chapter Eighteen – Unknown Treasures

The previous mention of pies made a realisation strike Cronto hard whilst he was speaking. He looked over to where Jenker stood amid the crowd, now recovered from his winding and appearing somewhat shocked by the death-defying walk just endured.

'You want me to take you where, my shop? Why on earth do you want to go there, with all this chaos happening around us? It's no sanctuary. I don't even like living there,' Jenker replied to Cronto's strange request.

'It's a feeling I have, a hunch. Something that was niggling at me when I came in the other day. We really must investigate it further – it might just make all the difference to us. I insist. What else would you be doing right now if not going there anyway?'

Jenker's face was a mask of confusion, but he looked resigned to this course of events. Molefi Cronto's position as a judge meant that those principles were at his very core and he held such authority that most people felt powerless to disagree with him. He adjudged Jenker less able than most to resist his suggestions. 'It's hard to argue with that...where better to hide than in your own bed. OK fine, we can go there, although I think you'll be disappointed,' Jenker said.

'We will see,' Cronto said, smiling. 'Thank you, Jenker Junior.'

'Shall we get going?' Jenker asked.

'No time like the present. I'm not from this city though, if you remember – I had trouble enough finding my own lodgings at night. Would you lead the way, please?'

'Oh, yes, of course. This way, then. We'll go down a level to help stay hidden.' Jenker strode off toward the stairs that lay just across from them.

'*Wait!*' Ryx screeched, stopping Jenker in his tracks and forcing him and all the others who had started after him to turn on their heels to see what was happening. 'You're going off to his shop? That sounds a stupid thing to do. We aren't going to do that, are we, Mum?' She turned to Skula, who looked startled, and continued before receiving an answer. 'We're going to get my dad; he will know what to do. He fought with distinction in the Great Border Raid Retaliation.'

'Do you think that's wise? What makes you think you will be any safer at one shop than another? We ought to stick together,' Rundup chipped in, standing at the edge of the group with his spear like a shepherd guarding his flock.

'Shop? Oh, ours is no *shop,* our place is The Crimson Duck – the best inn on the second tier! Definitely better than those in tiers below, and probably better than those on the surface too, since some of them serve water. *Water*! Ha. Anyway, we're not going anywhere without my dad. We're going there to get him.'

'Well, he does need to know what has happened, dear, you're right. I think we had better get back. Let's go,' Skula said.

'Just you two alone? No, that's not right, no. I will accompany you,' Rundup said. Cronto understood the man's feelings; neither had been in the presence of these people long nor even spoken to most of them, but they had been through a traumatic experience that had silently bonded them in a way that none fully understood. Cronto guessed that Rundup also felt a duty to protect them, as he did, and likely couldn't stand the thought of more people being hurt so unjustly.

'What, because we're female? You underestimate us Haþingvoð women!' Ryx retorted.

'No, not at all, my lady. I mean no offence. My concern is simply numerical. There is safety in numbers after all.'

'That is true. What do you say, big man – want to go along too?' Julius asked Nothro. 'Five would be safer than three. And let's be honest, you count for at least double, so it's more like six. I know how you enjoy a pie and perhaps a galumph too. That must sweeten the deal.'

The big, brown Ananeptide did an impression of a human grin. The result was a terrifying curl of his lips, revealing his frankly unsettling dual rows of dagger-like, inch-long canine teeth.

'A simple yes would have sufficed,' Julius commented drily. 'No need to scare the other humans.'

'All right, if you must go, then go – but we should not separate completely. Is there somewhere we could regroup later? The sooner the better, but perhaps under cover of darkness for safety if feasible. Does anybody know of a reasonable place we could easily find without exposing ourselves to the guards who will doubtless be patrolling?' Cronto asked.

'There is a Flowers of the Sun temple in the east, you can see the golden ball on top from miles away – and it is only a handful of streets away from the gatehouse in the eastern wall. The gardens surrounding it are well tended seeing how they love to make things grow; it's full of bushes, vines and trees. Good cover,' a slim man in middle age who had hitherto been quiet declared. 'Sorry I haven't spoken to any of you yet, this has all been such a whirlwind. My name is Zhin Xofia.'

Julius nodded his acknowledgement before replying with his own name and pointing out Nothro and the others. 'Cover definitely sounds good to me, I really don't fancy being caught in the open by those bastards,' Julius agreed. Nothro nodded his assent.

'That sounds a reasonable enough place to head for. Then it's agreed – we meet in the grounds of this temple as the sun sets. Seems oddly appropriate.' Cronto took a deep breath and drew himself up as straight as his relatively stout frame would allow before looking at each of Skula, Ryx, Rundup, Nothro and Julius earnestly in turn. 'The best of luck to you all.'

With that, those five turned and headed off toward The Crimson Duck, Ryx taking the lead as she was wont to do.

'All right, onwards!' Cronto confidently prompted Jenker to lead the remaining group of ten.

The survivors filed down the steps to the first subterranean level and made their way toward Jenker's bakery. 'Keep watch for guards, and be as quiet as you can,' Cronto instructed as they painstakingly edged through the smaller side streets, taking their time to be careful. Twice they were forced to backtrack into the deeper shadows further away from their intended path to avoid guards patrolling their normal routes. Luckily for Cronto and his band of survivors, this familiarity meant they were not being particularly observant as the routine was now a chore to be gotten through as quickly and perfunctorily as possible.

Eventually they reached the street where Jenker and Son, Bakery was situated on the surface level. Once they had all gathered outside, having carefully scoped it out for guards first, Jenker withdrew the well-worn brass key from his pocket, placed it in the lock and persuaded the door to swing open on its well-greased hinges. He ushered everybody inside and out of sight as the pastry-shaped sign swung creakily above them.

'Here we are, make yourselves comfortable everyone,' Jenker said, sounding slightly embarrassed. Most simply opted to stand given the lack of seats, although the two older gentlemen present chose to sit cross-legged on the floor and rest whilst they had chance. Cronto came through the door last and quietly closed it behind him.

'Zhin,' Cronto asked the man who advised their later meeting point, 'will you keep watch from the window?' A particularly muscular man who gave his name as Cedric Guyal naturally gravitated to stand by the now-closed door to stand sentry.

'What now? Should I fire up the oven and feed these people? I can get it going and throw a few bits in...' Jenker rambled.

'No, that's not the priority right now. It is your oven I'm interested in though...in a way. May I take a look?' Cronto said, bowing his head slightly.

'Of course, I don't know why it's of such interest to you though,' Jenker replied, as he shrugged and stepped away from his oven. 'Seems a strange thing to want to do given what we've just been through.'

'Thank you for indulging me,' said Cronto, moving behind the counter toward the oven. He crouched down on the left of the appliance where a hole on the side allowed access to the fuel at the bottom. 'This part is of particular interest to me,' he said to Jenker, pointing at the small white nub opposite the hole, which protruded slightly from the stone wall. Cronto kept his distance but extended his index finger until he was almost touching the top of the protrusion, ninety degrees from the three holes in it which faced the oven. He inhaled sharply and pressed his finger to the polished surface. Three small jets of flame shot from the apertures, converging into one larger stream a few inches from their exit points. Cronto stood back and grinned madly at Jenker. 'How long has this been here?'

'It's...always been like this, ever since my father built the shop and set everything up. I was young then, so the memories are hazy. It's one of the main things I remember as a child, this oven being here, and then eventually I took over,' Jenker said, sounding wistful.

Cronto slipped his bag off from his shoulder and reached into it before hesitating. 'Would you mind if I investigate this more –' he paused as he thought of the correct terminology for what he had in mind, '– thoroughly?'

Jenker looked even more confused than before. He simply nodded in response.

The older man pulled Bulwark, his distinctive axe, from its resting place in his bag. With a practiced eye, Cronto carefully aimed a heavy blow at the mortar just above the white nub, sending several small chunks of the fastening material showering down on the floor with a tinkling sound.

Jenker looked alarmed at this sudden destructive act and stepped forward with his hands up in the air, shouting. 'Stop! What are you doing? I said you could look at it, not destroy the bloody thing! I *need* that!'

Cronto held his hand up toward Jenker in a calming motion. He resumed his work, chipping away at the loosened parts more softly with the top of Bulwark's blade. His steady hand made it look surprisingly dainty, but he quickly made clear progress. Within a couple of minutes, a more complex shape began to emerge; as he worked at removing the mortar, two almond-shaped eyes became visible along a snout with a multitude of tiny, pointed shapes lining the top and bottom of an opening on the shiny white surface. Cronto sat back on his heels as he regarded his work, satisfied. 'Here. It's as I suspected, although there's a little more to uncover yet. Have you seen this much of it before?' he said, tracing the shape of the eyes gently.

'No, never! What is the point of having such an ornate carved tube, only to cover it up? I still don't really see the fascination with it though, it's just a nozzle – and I especially don't understand why you were so keen to come here.' Jenker suddenly pointed at Cronto accusingly. 'You're a conman, aren't you? You've been obsessed with this place ever since you first dropped in to scope it out. And now you're back with your cronies to take what you want, and I'll be unable to stop you...' he trailed off. He looked around at the armed people at close quarters in his shop.

'No, no. You see the shape – what does it remind you of? Also, I'm not trying to relieve you of your possessions, just to put your mind at ease. If you are willing to believe me, that is,' Cronto said.

'Well, it would be more convincing if you weren't wielding an axe at this exact moment in time. But...it does look like some sort of mythical creature—'

'A dragon!' Cronto exclaimed excitedly. 'It's a carving of a dragon, a flying serpent that breathes fire. They used to roam the world back when...when the world was more than just the Bowl we have today. They ruled the skies, raining down their hellacious breath on those who displeased them or impinged on their territories, or so it was claimed. They became a symbol of power – embodying strength, ferocity and remorselessness. All of which makes them perfect for representing what I believe hides in here.'

'Please just tell me what it is you're after. I don't understand what any of this is about,' Jenker replied, sounding exasperated.

'The best way I can tell you is to show you.' Cronto hefted Bulwark again. With some more worrying at the wall, he uncovered more of the carving. A long, smooth body with a pair of wings that stretched outwards, extending from the body, became visible – all in an ivory white with a dull gleam underneath the mortar dust. Cronto gripped the dragon-shaped carving and pulled at it, to no avail. Bracing one leg against the remaining brick, he tried again, heaving at it with all his strength; after a few moments of inertia, Cronto was on the verge of giving up on this approach when a crack filled his ears. In a rush of dust and crumbling masonry, the weapon embedded in the wall came free in his hands, sending Cronto falling backward. Cronto looked up and saw Jenker staring down at him and the imposing cutlass in his hands with an awestruck look on his face.

'What is *that?* That was in my wall?' Jenker exclaimed.

'This, my boy...this is your inheritance.' Cronto got to his feet, holding the cutlass with its ornately carved dragon handle securely, trying to ignore the dust on his face. 'This belonged to your father, of course. During the war against the exiles he was there leading from the front, turning the tide with this fine, fine weapon in hand. I know his record, I had to review it for some research in a case with some similarities and the same...complications. Anyway, I shouldn't be telling you all about your father, you know that, better than anyone.'

'Well, I'm not sure that is strictly true,' Jenker said, smiling sadly. 'My father looked after me well enough in my mother's absence, but he never really knew how to connect with me. He was respectful but distant. I'm not entirely sure what really happened during the conflicts my father was involved in, other than him being a key figure, an impromptu leader. I know he rallied ordinary people who were desperately needed to defend Dralcea and who would otherwise have wavered in the face of the enemy. Father never spoke much about the details of his engagements; I don't think he felt he could open up to me. Whether that was because of himself or me, I couldn't say.'

'Regardless, I think you ought to take this,' Cronto continued, intending to snap Jenker out of his reverie. 'It's rightfully yours after all.'

*

Jenker accepted the cutlass gingerly with his palms up, but did not say a word, instead staring dumbly at it without feeling comfortable enough to grasp it properly. Eventually he looked up at Cronto, eyes wide. 'One moment,' Cronto said, disappearing through the narrow doorway into the back. He brought back a wooden bucket with iron loops binding its staves together and placed it in front of Jenker, managing not to spill the water it contained. 'Try it out. Reverse the handle and aim it at that bucket – it shouldn't catch. Just don't cut yourself with the blade, then focus on what you want to happen.'

Jenker carefully turned the cutlass round so the dragon's mouth on the end of the ivory hilt pointed toward the safety bucket for his oven, the flat of the blade tucked under his arm. The wings sat at the back of his hands now; they would normally form a guard to shield the fingers when using the cutlass in its usual position. Trying his best to focus, he squeezed his eyes into tight slits as he stared at his bucket. As soon as he thought back on the fearsome day's events, a torrent of flame spewed forth in a cone of orange, rippling and spitting with a white-hot core. He missed the bucket at first, blasting the stone floor before he corrected his aim, spiralling it inward to meet his mark. After a couple of seconds, he scared himself into wishing it would stop, and as soon as he did that the flame ceased to spout from the dragon's mouth. The rapid heating and sudden cooling of the flagstones caused one to audibly crack, whilst the bucket was blackened and scorched, the remaining water inside steaming away and dispersing into the air. He stared blankly at what he had just done for a moment before a big grin spread across his face.

'Pleased?' Cronto asked with an amused smile.

'For the first time in my life, I feel as if I have some power to defend myself. Actual, real power, right in my hands. It feels great!'

'Fantastic! Keep hold of it and treat it with respect – and a huge amount of care, of course. I think you're going to need it in the days to come. As will we all, I suspect.'

'Erm, folks? I suggest we all get down,' their man at the window, Zhin, called over to them urgently. 'There are some of those dicks in blue armour heading this way.'

Chapter Nineteen – Search and Destroy

The clatter of boots on the cobbled street growing ever louder as the runner approached his home failed to wake Janos from his slumber, but the insistent banging on the rough timbers of his front door certainly did.

Janos sat upright in his bed. 'What the hell is this about?' he muttered.

He swung his legs over the side whilst the furious knocking continued and frayed his patience beyond saving. 'Shut it, I'm getting up!' he bellowed angrily. At once the din stopped. He pulled on his trousers clumsily as he staggered to the door, not bothering with a shirt just yet. It could wait, seeing as whoever was at his door seemed to be in quite the hurry to speak with him.

Janos pulled the bolt back and yanked the door open as quickly as he could manage on its protesting hinges that he never quite got around to oiling. He liked to open it rapidly to startle the person waiting on the other side, particularly in this case seeing as they had woken him so rudely. It had the intended effect, and the messenger waiting for him gaped at him even as his chest rapidly rose and fell from the obvious exertions of sprinting there. 'Yes? What do you want, waking me at this hour?' Janos snapped, knowing fully well from the young man's clothes that he had been dispatched from the Promontory and would likely be calling on him to perform some duty.

'Forgive me, sir,' he said between rapid breaths. 'Urgent message from the Promontory.'

'Yes, I worked that out. What the bloody hell is this about? It's my day off and I was enjoying it until you showed up.'

'There's trouble, sir. It's bad. Branch Vilipas demands that you gather your men at once and put them to work finding a group who attacked our lads at the Promontory.'

'What? Somebody had the balls to attack us, in our own back yard?'

'It seems so, sir. There are several dead.'

'Bastards! All right, I'm awake now anyway, I'll just have to take a different day off instead. What do we know about these attackers? Are they exiles? How many?'

The runner looked sheepish in the face of the rapid-fire questions asked of him, and his eyes roved around in his head, trying to look everywhere but Janos's eyes. Janos continued his questions. 'Humans? Ananeptide? Did we take many of them down? Where are they now?'

'The thing is, sir, they didn't tell me. As soon as they realised what was happening, they sent me out to get you.' He tried to pull himself a little more upright to seem as if he had some measure of authority despite his lack of knowledge. 'I got here as fast as I could, sir.'

'All right, very helpful,' Janos replied, without much enthusiasm. 'Nothing like going into a fight without a damn clue what is happening.' He turned away to find his socks and boots before he would consider pulling on his armour and uniform. Comprised of multiple pieces along with the padded garments that sat underneath them to prevent contact sores, his armour would take a few minutes to fully assemble and secure onto himself. Being as experienced as he was, it would be done as swiftly as possible. As Janos turned to the side in his search for the next most sensible part to put on – he didn't particularly organise his equipment when he shed it at the end of a day – his peripheral vision noticed that the doorway was still occupied by the figure of the man sent to collect him. 'What are you standing there for still? I know the bloody way to the Promontory! Go and make yourself useful!'

The man jumped a little at being yelled at, before he abruptly turned away and stuttered his apologies as he set off again, no doubt wishing he had had more time to rest before making the return trip.

'Useless, these recruits,' Janos muttered. 'That's what happens when you just start taking anyone that turns up for the open day.' He pulled on his shirt from where he left it hanging over his only other piece of furniture, a sturdy but roughly finished wooden chair. He glanced at his hammer leaning in the corner of the room, the heavy head sitting on the floor. 'You might actually get to be involved in some action today, girl.' He flexed his biceps and rolled his shoulders; they felt stiff, the effect of the years he had seen pass him by. 'Gods know it has been a while.'

He eventually got all but his helmet on and took one long, gulping drink from the water jug he kept by his bed. Then, helmet under arm and affixing Hilde to his back, he hurried off out of the door to fulfil his duty.

*

Janos strode up the last flight of stairs to the assembly room housed within the Promontory where Branch Godfrey Vilipas and several of his fellow officers stood waiting. Sergeants Egil Sluss and Zygfryd Tanbry were among them and had both put on all their decorations from previous honouring ceremonies. Each sported a small collection of brass shapes with ribbons trailing from them; crescent moons, concentric circles, bars with crosses at the ends, squares inset with other metals and glittering diamond shapes. They had evidently had the same thought to wear their best ceremonial finery to show what they had achieved in service in an obvious effort to lead the inevitable response to the attack. Janos inwardly sneered at them, but then became painfully aware that he smelt of galumph from the previous night and had neglected to shave in his haste to arrive. He kept his armour in a decent state of cleanliness and buffed to a respectable shine, but without his own awards pinned to his chest he looked drab in comparison.

The most senior sergeant present was Younes Souo, a rotund man in his fifties with a frizzy white moustache adorning a bloated face turned a disconcerting shade of purple from too many years of alcoholic excess. He always looked comical in his ill-fitting uniform as the buttons strained to contain their contents and he was a source of quiet amusement for most of the younger recruits. His fellow officers gave him the respect his rank deserved, but all knew he walked the slowest beat and these days struggled to effectively train his new charges. It was Janos's opinion that he would not last much longer in the job, either due to ill health or simply an inability to fulfil his duties effectively. Janos drew himself up as tall as he could manage and approached the others in his best parade ground march to compensate for his own dishevelment.

'Glad you finally decided to join us,' Vilipas said acidly to Janos as he joined those waiting.

'I came as soon as I was summoned, sir. I wasn't meant to be on duty today. What exactly is the situation? The messenger only had the faintest idea, sir.'

'Yes, well, we aren't in the habit of dishing out all the information available to every errand boy and recruit who's just signed up. He served his purpose and got you here eventually, at least. As you must now be aware, we had an incident – an attack – on our guards right here in the Promontory, on those performing ceremonial duty no less. This is an outrage that cannot go unpunished. The perpetrators are at large and must be found, quickly and decisively, before this gets out and a panic ensues. Questions?'

'Complete bastards! Lost some of my lads thanks to them!' spluttered Souo in outrage.

'Yes, Souo, we know. We'll find them.'

'And destroy them! I'll bloody gut the bastards! When I get my hands on them—' Souo blustered, before being cut off by a violent hand gesture by Vilipas. The large man simply huffed after that, his extensive chest heaving. Janos and Tanbry shared an amused glance whilst Vilipas's back was turned.

'What is the force, sir? Exiles? They must have been well organised to have bested our lads in a fight,' Janos said, desperate to make up for lost time and prestige compared to his colleagues. He loved nothing better than a hunt and ensuing fight and was determined to be involved in this one – preferably leading the way. He wouldn't have backed Tanbry to be tenacious enough to mercilessly hunt them down, as would be expected of them given the situation, but Sluss could be real competition for him; he would drive his men just as hard as Janos would to achieve their aim, perhaps even harder. Sluss was known to have pushed his men to the brink of what was physically possible before, and on a few scandalously hushed-up occasions, beyond that which could be endured. Souo would be incapable of moving quickly or reacting dynamically to such a situation, and consequently would never be a threat. Their other two colleagues present, Disheart and Pelovir, were much newer to sergeanthood and therefore less likely to be given any command.

'They were a mixed force,' Branch Vilipas said vaguely, waving his hand around in the air as he said it. 'Unpredictable, a dangerous bunch indeed. Our colleagues who fell are testament enough to that. Their exact number is unknown.'

Sergeant Pelovir ventured a question. 'How are we going to identify them in that case, sir?'

'How about you get the big mass of buggers running away with pleased grins on their faces for a start?' Vilipas snapped. 'They are unlikely to be wearing name badges identifying themselves as your target.'

Pelovir nodded sharply, chastened. 'Yes, sir.' He had reddened at the rebuke.

'Do we know why they attacked, sir? Did they take any prisoners?' Janos asked.

'It is unknown currently,' Vilipas replied coldly. 'We don't believe they took anybody with them, although they did also attack many of the people there for the ceremony. Those innocent people must have been in the way.'

'We must go after them with the fullest use of force then, sir. Which complement is to chase them down, and who will lead our lads?' Sluss asked in his usual growling tone.

Vilipas smiled. 'I know that each of you will want to be the one to take charge of this action and play it your own way. However, you will each be leading your section as usual. You will split up, each taking a different area and sweeping around to meet one another, giving them less chance to elude us. Make no mistake, gentlemen. They *will not* elude you. You are each to act as a spear tip, and I want those tips to return reddened with blood. Do I make myself clear?'

Janos knew what was being asked of them – stay out searching until you find and deal with the perpetrators, however long that might take. They each replied with a serious 'yes, sir', but hid their disappointment in being denied the opportunity to earn a great honour in leading a successful pursuit to defend Dralcea. Such a distinction would have added further lustre to the collections of the four older officers, and much enhanced the reputation and prospects of the younger men, Pelovir and Disheart. Janos knew it was fruitless trying to argue with Vilipas, however. Better to accept the senior figure's instructions and get on with them lest his temper turn and cause him to reprimand those quibbling.

'Good. See to it, gentlemen. Muster your sections immediately and get out there – I want to see results quickly, and report back as soon as you have achieved them. This supersedes any other actions you might have been engaged in or any other event that may occur until you are told otherwise by myself. Our last report of them was that the perpetrators were seen heading east away from the chasm. Sluss, take the Promontory area and sweep it quickly for any stragglers, you can decide the rest of the search pattern between yourselves. You're all to be armed with Ejectors too – they should make a difference, provided you have all paid due care to train with them fully. Might as well make use of the advantage they give, so make sure you collect them from the armoury. Show no mercy, sergeants.' He strode off to let them get the job done. Sluss also exited quickly since he had already been given his own instructions.

Once Vilipas was safely out of earshot, the five remaining sergeants relaxed a little and turned to face each other. Janos broke the silence. 'Not quite an overload of direction there, or information either for that matter, although I've come to expect no less from that tit. Anyway, it's up to us proper guards to get this done – and we're 'ere because we're the best, so let's get to it and show that pillock a thing or two about real work.' Janos received grins in response at the casual way he spoke of their superior, particularly from Pelovir and Disheart, the two newest sergeants.

From there they quickly sorted out who would tackle each area in such a way to cover as much ground as possible in a sweep that would leave the least chance of evasion. Souo would take the shortest distance due to his decreased mobility. He did not argue for a more taxing route; this search was going to be a tough task as it was, given the multiple levels of Dralcea.

'Even though this could be a tough one since they could be anywhere by now, there's one thing to bear in mind,' Janos said to his colleagues.

'What's that?' Disheart asked.

'If they *were* exiles, which seems likely to me, then they aren't going to hang around in the city. Fair?'

'I suppose so, but what's the relevance of that?' Souo asked, sounding huffy at the lecture.

'Well then, they must be heading for one of the city gates, since they are the only way in or out of Dralcea. And, given that each gate is at surface level, you would imagine they won't stray far from it on their way. The second tier, perhaps, but that will be about it. It will help narrow down the search,' Janos said.

'That's assuming that they are in fact exiles. If it was a rabble from Dralcea then they could have just melted away, back into the Warren where they came from. In which case – you are dead wrong,' Tanbry said to his friend, one eyebrow raised.

'Wrong?' Janos replied. 'When is that ever the case?'

Tanbry raised both eyebrows in response.

Their decisions made, the officers separated off to gather their men and head out to do their duty. Janos felt his arm be grabbed just as he started to stomp away.

'Before you go, Janos,' Tanbry said quietly. 'What do you make of all this?'

'What do you mean? Some wrong 'uns got into the city and staged an attack – and it's on us as the go-to arse-kickers to sort it out. It's pretty self-explanatory.'

'I don't know, it just doesn't make sense to me...something about the circumstances. A load of people get right into the heart of our city, into the Promontory no less, kill a few guards and citizens and then flee. They didn't take anything or take any prisoners – even ignoring some of ours that they came across. Why?'

Janos pulled a confused face and narrowed his eyes to look at his old friend and colleague Zygfryd Tanbry as if he was an idiot. 'Who the hell knows? Don't worry about the details, we've got a job to do. And...' he grabbed Hilde from its harness on his back, cradling it across his open palms, '...It should be a lot of fun.' The evil grin on Janos's face said more than any words could ever about how in his element he would be. 'Good hunting, my friend.'

'And you, Janos.' They clapped each other on the shoulder briefly, Janos being more heavy-handed than his friend with his over-enthusiastic pat.

Janos watched Tanbry stride off to perform his duty, and wondered about his friend's words. It was odd that whoever these attackers were had reached the inner areas of the Promontory – the most heavily guarded place in their known world – without so much as being noticed before wreaking havoc and then fleeing. Janos remembered various times past when Tanbry had asked too many questions, insistent on knowing the reasoning behind their orders. Not so for himself. He pushed the thought out of his mind – he would do what he was told and enjoy himself doing so.

Janos idly swung Hilde with one hand as he set off to play his own part.

Chapter Twenty – Inheritance

Julius followed as Ryx led their small group with all haste to The Crimson Duck, her spear levelled all the while, and was thankful that they ran into no trouble. Nothro's presence likely played a part in this. After piling through the door, Julius stopped a short distance inside and put his hand on Nothro's arm, letting Skula and Ryx rush to a man behind the bar who looked busy tending to the needs of the few who sought the comforts of the inn early in the day. The blond-haired man looked surprised at this sudden arrival. 'Give them a minute,' Julius said to his friend. Rundup also complied and the trio hung back. Julius noticed the piney scent of wood chippings and a slightly sour undertone lingered in the air, although the mixture was not entirely unpleasant.

The few grimy windows spread among the walls permitted a modicum of light to illuminate the smoky interior, and a few hardy souls sat slumped around benches and tables, fairly spread out to keep their personal space unviolated. Julius spotted a dog with light brown fur under one of the tables near the bar, sound asleep with its head on its paws.

'Oh, Fyrir,' Skula said tearfully.

'Dad!' said Ryx as she hugged the man.

'You're back early!' he exclaimed, smiling warmly. 'Is that your reward?' he asked, nodding at Ryx's spear. He gave Skula a quick kiss. 'And you brought friends back, too...*or customers*?'

'Definitely friends after what we've been through,' Skula said.

'What happened to you? You're hurt, dear.'

'Yes, something terrible has happened,' Skula said. Even from halfway across the room, Julius could hear her voice crack with emotion. 'The ceremony, it wasn't right, the guards there were in their finery but then something happened – they attacked us…'

'What? You must be joking, right? We get plenty of them in here, and certainly some of them are a bit coarse, but they surely wouldn't turn on people there to be honoured. I'm not saying I don't believe you, of course, my dear – how exactly did you get that wound?'

'It was one of the guards, with their spear...but Ryx sorted him out. She was fantastic out there. So too were these fine gentlemen,' she said, turning and gesturing to Rundup, Nothro and Julius. 'They were heroes there today with everything they've done, and no mistake.'

'Very pleased to meet you in that case,' the man said, offering his hand to Julius. 'My name is Fyrir Haþingvoð. Thank you for helping my wife and daughter today with whatever happened.'

'Julius Dominguez. We just did what we had to at the time,' he said, shaking Fyrir's hand.

'Nothro Grafanc,' Nothro said, gently shaking Fyrir's proffered hand.

'I'm Rundup Ovygdalha, nice to meet you. Sorry about the circumstances,' Rundup said as he followed suit in greeting Fyrir.

'Nothro, Rundup, Julius. Thank you,' Fyrir said earnestly.

Julius noticed that the bulk of Nothro passing close by made one of The Crimson Duck's customers look up from staring into his crusted mug of galumph. Seeing the Ananeptide, he raised his mug in salute and his face split into a huge toothless grin that made his whole face crease into a mass of wrinkles. Nothro nodded in return. Julius knew that his friend had encountered enough of the ill will of humans to enjoy the small gestures in good spirit when offered.

'We really didn't do anything,' Julius said after the introductions, feeling embarrassed by the praise. 'Just looking out for each other and then running head for leather.'

'*Hell* for leather,' Nothro corrected.

'Is it? If you say so,' Julius replied. 'Besides, we did what we had to. Anyone would have done the same.'

'That may well be, but the fact is that you did, and we're grateful to you all. Make yourselves comfortable whilst I get this cleaned up,' Skula said to her guests. 'Fyrir, will you help me see to this wound? Then we'll all have a drink before we go,' Skula said, patting her husband's hand which rested on the bar.

Fyrir looked confused. 'Go – what do you mean go? Why would we go anywhere?'

'We can't stay here, Dad. Guards came after us when we left the Promontory, as though we were some common criminals who had just robbed a shop! Please understand. We were lucky to get out of there at all. We even had to clamber across struts out above the chasm to escape.' Ryx took a deep breath before continuing. 'Others weren't so lucky – people *died* there this morning, Dad, and I don't know why any of this happened. *Normal people* died. They're coming for us, and I won't let us end up like them – it was no accident. We must go, others are waiting for us.'

'You climbed over the caldera? Wait, they actually killed people there at the Promontory?' Fyrir looked flabbergasted, but it seemed that what his family had been telling him was finally sinking in. 'How could they...how DARE they!' Fyrir smashed a clenched fist down on his bar and the sharp noise woke the sleeping dog with a bark of surprise, who then stared at the newcomers before stiffly plodding over to greet them.

'Shh, Piecrust, it's all right,' Ryx said soothingly to the creature who wagged in response to her words.

Julius, Rundup and Nothro each gave Piecrust some attention, either with a pat on the head or scratch behind the ear; Julius was amused to see Nothro being particularly gentle and was engrossed by the small, friendly creature. Piecrust looked delighted to receive this attention, regardless of the species providing it.

'How can this have happened?' Fyrir asked rhetorically, shaking with barely controlled rage. 'So many guards come here, The Crimson Duck is virtually an official Dralcea Guard drinking establishment, and we are nothing but fair with them all. For years we've seen their faces every day, letting them take the weight off their feet and relax after a hard day's work keeping the peace – well, supposedly. Some of those regulars we even call friends.' Fyrir looked up sharply. 'You don't think Janos had anything to do with this, do you?'

'Not a chance, love,' Skula replied. 'It's his day off today anyway, remember?'

'Not really,' Fyrir said with a shrug. 'You're better at remembering all the things our customers tell us.'

'He's more than a customer and you know it, Fyrir. Janos might be big and scary-looking, and admittedly sometimes likes a brawl, but he's no murderer,' Skula said.

'Absolutely. I've known Janos my entire life and there's no way he was involved with what happened to us. He just couldn't be,' Ryx said.

'No, you're right. I'm just angry that I wasn't there when my wife and daughter needed me. That powerless feeling is terrible.'

'Don't feel bad about it, dear. You couldn't have known that something like this would happen. It wouldn't have made any difference if you had gone instead of me as you were meant to, they still would have turned on us. It's not even as though you would have been needed to protect Ryx, since she had the beating of the one that jabbed me,' Skula said.

'Even so, stupid me decided that it was more important for me to keep the pub open longer than go and collect this award.

And for what? So a few old hard drinkers would hand over a few grubby somoni coins as payment for their galumph? If that award was even genuine,' Fyrir mused. 'Never did find out what it was for.'

'We were never told the reasoning either. I don't think it was real to begin with,' Julius chipped in. 'We're woodcutters from Thorntuft, and not to sound modest, but we aren't deserving of any recognition.'

'Doubt it was. They were attacking people inside the Promontory before they turned on us waiting outside,' Nothro said. 'I could smell the blood.'

'So it was on purpose?' Ryx asked.

'With the amount of blood I could smell, it must have been,' Nothro rumbled sadly.

Fyrir dipped behind the bar for a moment before reappearing and putting something on the bar's surface; it had a long handle and Fyrir put it down heavily and caused a loud *bang*.

'Ryx – come here,' Fyrir said. 'I know you always wanted to play with this macuahuitl when you were younger, my girl, and of course I couldn't let you. That all changes today. Take it and remember all the frustration you felt at not being able to use it before. Feel the weight, how the grip shifts under your hands, how easily you can swing it back after a stroke. Use all that, get to know it until it is an extension of your own body, and above all defend yourself with it. I have no doubt you will soon master it. If they want to fight dirty and hit hard, then we will just have to fight dirtier and hit harder.'

Julius craned his neck for a better look at what he thought must be a weapon. Ryx was looking down at it with a look of awe on her face.

'Oh my...I was obsessed with this when I was little. It's been so many years since I thought about it though, with adult life getting in the way, I had forgotten about it. It's been under the bar this whole time without me knowing?' she said.

'Certainly has. Just in case things ever *really* got out of hand in here,' Fyrir said with a grin. 'Never needed, until now.'

'Thank goodness,' Skula said.

Fyrir picked up the macuahuitl to show it off. 'Take note, Ryx. The handle is big enough for you to use both hands, and this spherical pommel at the end has a spiral of steel inlaid in it – you can knock someone out with it if necessary.' He mimed jabbing the blunt end forward at head height to make the point.

'This long, paddle-like part is the body, and the most dangerous. A foot and a half in length is more than enough to protect yourself with.' Fyrir carefully tapped the top end of the wooden weapon, which gradually widened from the handle upwards. 'This end can also be used to help people off to sleep none too gently. The real strength of the macuahuitl lies in these trapeziums of volcanic glass that line these two longest edges. They might be chipped and irregular, but all these facets are razor sharp. If you so much as lightly brush them – well, just don't. They'll slice you open and you might not even feel it. Be *extremely* careful with it, Ryx. This is serious business.'

'I understand, Dad,' Ryx said, staring at the deadly object. She handed her spear to Skula and, once her father put the macuahuitl back down on the bar, she took her turn and carefully picked it up.

Julius watched intently, as did his two companions beside him. He noted that the obsidian blades protruding from the sides of the weapon caught what little light was present in the pub, reflecting off their many facets and highlighting their deep emerald green colour.

'It's so light,' Ryx said as she held it up high with apparent ease.

'Don't let its weight fool you. A good swing using the edged sides will have a devastating effect,' Fyrir told her.

'Looking at the blades on that thing, I can believe it,' Julius said.

'Stay back, Piecrust,' Ryx said before she gave her inheritance a test swing and then grinned.

Julius hastily stepped back in surprise, as did Rundup. Nothro appeared unmoved by the close quarters use of such an item. It took a lot to make him flinch.

'Many generations ago, when the world at large was still habitable, that belonged to your grandfather – well, one of our ancestors, so your great-something-grandfather,' Fyrir said. 'On a particularly long voyage, he headed south and west with his crew and made landfall where the climate was unlike anything they had ever seen before. There he met and spoke with the leader of a warband, and finding that they had much in common, they peacefully exchanged ideas and knowledge. When it came to it, the two warriors exchanged weapons as a token of their meeting. Our ancestor gave his prized steel sword, pride of his clan, and in return the chief bestowed upon him this fine piece of art.'

Fyrir gestured to Ryx to hold it up, and its bladed edges glinted as she did so. 'Look at the centre,' he continued, pointing to the intricate carvings in the dark wood. 'This at the top is the sun, as you can probably tell. And this?' He pointed to another depiction, directly below the sun and stretching to fill the remainder of the flat wooden space.

Ryx shrugged. 'I don't know, Dad. Some sort of animal, I think – or *person*,' she said, glancing at the Ananeptide standing nearby. 'It looks like a predator – you can see the claws emphasised on it.'

'Yes,' Fyrir nodded. 'A big, four-legged predator with large teeth and claws that inhabited the forests of their land. They were sleek, black creatures that slunk between the trees, quiet as the moon. The war-chief intimated that this weapon was meant to replicate their ferocity in battle and its blades were akin to that beast's claws. Your ancestor named it Grænn Klær.'

'It certainly looks fearsome, that thing. Please, *please* be careful with it, Ryx. I've no doubt it gives much more than a scratch if you are careless with it,' interjected Skula.

'Obviously I will be careful with it, mother,' Ryx scowled, sounding annoyed.

'That is a fine-looking specimen there, no doubt about it. I've never seen anything like it.' Julius stared in wonder. 'It must be genuine; we don't get nice dark wood like that here now. Would you mind if I—'

'Hands off, stranger. This is a family heirloom, and now, it's mine. I intend to use Grænn Klær on those blue-cloaked bastards,' Ryx said venomously.

'Woah, I meant no offence – I was just admiring it. Rundup, how about you help me clean this up whilst she has a little practice swinging that thing?' Julius said, patting the blood-soaked patch of shirt over his shoulder, courtesy of his Ejector wound. It gave a light squelch as he did so. 'I would ask him, but his huge hairy paws would make it endlessly worse in trying to dig it out, plus he might be tempted to have a nibble.'

'Shut up,' Nothro replied gruffly.

'Yes, let's have that seen to or it will get infected. Might I borrow a sharp knife, my lady?' Rundup asked Skula.

'Of course,' she replied, hurrying off to the kitchen at the rear of the pub. Skula returned with a thin-bladed paring knife that Julius could see was heated white-hot to sterilise it, and she handed it over to Rundup. 'There you are – but be careful, it's hot. I had better get mine sorted too. Help me with this, dear.' Rundup bowed to show his thanks before Skula and Fyrir went off to clean and stitch her own wound.

Nothro led the way to a quiet corner of the pub as Julius and Rundup followed behind and settled at a somewhat clean looking table. Julius got as comfortable as he could before

Rundup pulled back Julius's shirt to reveal the entry wound on his shoulder. He began to probe the area with the knife's tip to find and remove the Sweat of Hephaestus lodged inside whilst Julius did his best not to pull away due to the pain. Julius was used to a rough outdoor lifestyle and was accustomed to such pains when he had incurred many minor injuries previously through his work.

Julius tried to distract himself by watching Ryx put her new acquisition back behind the bar and out of both his sight and that of the understandably fascinated regulars, then brought a mug resembling a tiny wooden barrel over and placed it in front of Julius. He looked at it and raised his eyebrows. 'On the house?'

'This one is – there's no need for this little operation to hurt any more than it has to. Drink it quick, but enjoy it – it's the only one you're getting for free.'

'Well, I'll drink to that. Cheers!'

Rundup paused in his work to allow Julius to lift his mug in salute and then swiftly downed the entire contents. Julius nearly choked and his eyes went wide. 'Bloody hell, that's some potent stuff! What is it called? I feel as if I could breathe fire.'

'Scott's Skull Scorcher. The strongest stuff, not on sale to everyone,' Ryx grinned. 'Just those stupid enough to dare drink it.'

Julius shot her a look, causing Ryx to laugh and waltz off. Rundup resumed his work and before long had hooked the knife's tip behind the little slug of iron then stopped to warn Julius. 'You might want to grit your teeth for this part.'

Julius did as he was told and braced himself. Without delay Rundup dug further behind the foreign object and into his subject's flesh before twisting the bloodied lump outwards, extracting it within a couple of seconds. He deposited it on the tabletop with a clink.

'We're done!' Rundup declared.

'Damn.' Julius breathed out shakily. 'I could do with another one of those drinks.'

'I'm not sure that would be wise. You're probably going to need your wits about you in the very near future and I can smell the fumes from that drink emanating from you already. At least the worst part with that wound is over,' Rundup said.

'Easy for you to say,' Julius replied, feeling down his back with his other arm and finding the broad, sticky trail of blood tracing a path down his shoulder and back.

'It should heal well enough if you let it, and of course keep it clean. That part is vital. I would offer to stitch it, but...' Rundup shrugged and rolled his eyes, indicating the lack of materials in the inn and the likelihood of them being unsanitary should they be found in any eventuality. 'Clean water, preferably freshly boiled, will be your friend in keeping it healthy.'

'Well thanks, but I can't say I remembered to bring my teapot and firewood along with me on this occasion. Just how am I supposed to get hold of boiled water when we're fleeing for our lives? Come to think of it, what do you two think of this plan anyway? Should we just leave the city? We seem to be completely in the dark about what is happening, and just running. It doesn't feel right to me. We ought to be fighting back.'

'Against a horde of highly disciplined, well-armoured and fully armed lawkeepers of unknown number? Sounds like that extra-strength galumph speaking. We might as well just bash our own brains in right here and now in this charming establishment, using their very own benches and stools. Half of our number are old, or too frightened to be of much use. It was something of a miracle that we escaped from the Promontory at all.' Rundup made it clear what he thought of Julius's proposition.

'So you want to run away from it all?' Julius asked.

'Well, with respect,' Rundup said, 'running has enabled us to survive so far. Don't forget that they not only attacked us under false pretences but then chased us down too. They must know the city inside out. What's to say they will give up now?'

'I wouldn't like to say. They have shown themselves to be quite persistent so far,' Julius admitted. 'Even so, they shouldn't be allowed to just get away with what they've done.'

'He prefers to pick fight over flight. As a human living almost exclusively among Ananeptide, he thinks he has something to prove,' Nothro interjected.

'Wrong,' Julius retorted with a sneer, although actually he was annoyed with how succinctly his large friend had summed up his subconscious feelings, which he barely recognised himself. Nothro had clearly observed his behaviour shrewdly and analysed it, whilst giving nothing away. Julius realised that there must be a lot more going on in that furry head than just deciding what unfortunate animal he was going to hunt next for their dinner, and he had underestimated Nothro's analytical capabilities. 'Those guards have done such wrong to so many people today, we can't just forget that. Good people were killed for no reason whatsoever. I won't ignore that or pretend it didn't happen. I can't.'

'You would throw your life away in some vain attempt to atone for their deaths? All that will bring is more sorrow to those around you. Whilst some of them may be able to take it,' Rundup said, patting Nothro's hairy forearm, 'is it right to inflict it upon them?'

'What is your point?' Julius retorted.

'My point is, unless you want to accomplish their task for them and wind up dead more quickly, there is only one choice in reality; we keep moving, and perhaps we can start again elsewhere. There are pockets of life away from Dralcea, as you well know, so we should put this putrid city behind us and see what is out there. Obviously, you won't want to be returning to

Thorntuft, they'll be sure to go there to seek you out – just as I won't be able to simply go back to my troupe, much as I might wish to. I could however do with dropping by there to retrieve something that could help us. But my point is, go back to our normal lives and they will quickly discover us and no doubt bring plenty of those weapons to aim at us. It's inevitable. So, we rejoin the others and make for the city gate in the east – the closest one to us. They're not fond of leaving their zone of influence, so if we can leave Dralcea undetected, there is a chance they'll just leave us to fend for ourselves wherever we end up.'

'I'll believe that when I see it,' Julius said, starting to slur his words slightly.

'They won't send many after us if we leave – they have to remain here to keep order and keeping trouble outside of the walls makes their job easier. So, we put the city walls between us and them.' Nothro Grafanc always had a way of cutting right to the important parts of any discussion. His efficiency with words often stunned Julius.

'Precisely, thank you,' Rundup replied. 'Somebody sees sense at least. When this family are ready, we should be on our way. If you would be so good as to join me, I'll retrieve some belongings of mine on the way.'

Chapter Twenty-one – Routine, Ruined

The day had so far panned out routinely for Roger Skerrick. The sun still shone weakly overhead and poked through gaps in the grimy clouds, just as it had earlier when he left his ramshackle lodgings and headed out onto the streets of Dralcea as he always did. He was dressed in his usual simple clothing. The beige hessian trousers held at waist height with a length of tied rope, plain straw sandals and loose off-white shirt were purely functional – the only part of his usual ensemble that wasn't necessitated by social niceties was his waistcoat with its long, pointed tails, somewhat battered by daily use. These held an extra use that was not obvious to the casual passer-by.

Skerrick had already spent a couple of hours walking the upper level streets of Dralcea, taking his time as he strolled around and did his best to look as though he was in no hurry but had a destination in mind. This was a skill honed over many years, and not one that most people could pick up; it required a level of commitment and deception that had to be nurtured for years, practiced repeatedly until mastered. As a man of little means Skerrick was generally ignored when he was out walking, and this suited him perfectly. Blending in only aided his purposes.

He had successfully picked the pockets of three moderately affluent people in the street during the morning. A modest taking, but enough, for now. He started to feel the familiar prickling in his stomach, the result of skipping breakfast, as was his habit. Skerrick subtly altered his bearing to bring him close to a stall stocking various fruits, somewhat of a luxury within the Bowl. Such foods were hard to grow without being killed off by frost out in the spacious regions of the sanctuary. They were only grown in any number in the sweet spot between where it was too cold to be viable and the slightly warmer zone before the busy sprawl of Dralcea, where houses piled upon houses and there was no room for such extravagances as fruit trees, with all the space and water they demanded. The stall sported a few varieties of fruits grown in the cool climate and was well placed to tempt the more affluent residents of the sunniest, airiest tier of the city.

He drew alongside the stall, appeared to move aside to allow a rushing citizen to pass by more easily, and when the stall owner glanced at a potential customer Skerrick made his move. He swiped an apple from the top of the piled-high basket, deftly dropped it into the hidden pocket in the inside of his waistcoat and then sauntered down the road and away. It was pocketed in a flash; the stall owner did not know anything had gone and would not notice until someone else made a purchase, if he noticed at all.

Once a safe distance had been established, Skerrick turned off into a smaller side street where he plucked the apple from its hiding place and tucked into it eagerly, biting off a large chunk and relishing the juicy flesh. He took the opportunity to rest his legs and leant against a shop wall whilst he enjoyed the pilfered snack. What now? Not being tied to a job, his options this and every day were varied.

He took another bite with a satisfying crunch – it was perfectly ripe – and noticed a young Crinochin child wandering his way, shepherding a single flammula that plodded along on stubby, scaled legs. The Crinochin habit of using a short stick to expertly guide it spoke of the devotion they had for their fowl, and their reliance on them. It was possible that the extravagantly feathered bird, all rich oranges and reds, puffy as a seedclock, was all this young Crinochin had, both for company and sustenance. The child – Skerrick was unsure whether it was male or female, owing to its emaciated state – stopped a few metres away and stared at him with the large, round eyes typical of their species, the irises shining bronze. He could hardly continue under such scrutiny, noting the taut grey skin of their face and unusually thin hands, not yet wide and shovel-like as they would later become. Pity in his heart overflowed. 'Hungry, little one?' he asked.

The child gave no audible response but instead slowly nodded their head, seemingly shy.

'Looks like you need it more than me.' Skerrick gently threw the unfinished fruit to the child to catch before sucking the errant juice from his fingers.

Nimbly snatching the apple from the air and then calming the alarmed flammula, scared by the sudden movement, the Crinochin child tucked into the fruit hungrily. It ate the fruit core and all before shuffling off again, bird in tow. Roger Skerrick was no monster; the streets were home to such a wide variety of peoples, and in all of them he recognised facets of his own early life. It felt good to be able to assist this youngster in their survival, thinking back to his youth when he had struggled to survive himself. He watched the young one disappear from sight and hoped he had made some difference by sharing his stolen snack.

The day was wearing on and as he considered what he should do next, Skerrick touched both of his thighs at the same time in a subconscious gesture; the shape he felt there, the feel of his daggers strapped to his legs was comforting. He could slip his way into and out of buildings with a subtlety and quietness that people would never know he had been there, and he had more than enough skill in conversation to talk his way out of a wide range of situations. The sphere of his influence had limits, however, and he kept the daggers as a last resort in the event of his other skills failing to keep him safe – and whilst he was prepared to use them in the case of real trouble, he truly hoped never to have to. Every day they stayed strapped to his legs, unused, was a small victory for him personally and also a credit to his street survival skills.

He decided to re-join the main street and the people going about their business. Perhaps his hand might chance upon a pocket containing a jewel or a full wallet.

Skerrick's eyes automatically started scanning the street, as they had done before to stop him blundering heedlessly into the trouble that would be his undoing. He always had to stay aware of his surroundings, taking everything in, his ears picking up all they could. All of this was in aid of preserving his freedom, his way of life, against the biggest threat to both that he could possibly encounter – the Dralcea Guard, who were always looking to lock him up based on some petty crime or other. His nefarious practices being what they were, he had experienced many brushes with the authoritarian presence in the past and aimed – no, vowed – to minimise all future contact with them.

This aim was of course helped by the many-tiered landscape of the city, and he took advantage of this topography to help disguise his whereabouts by switching between levels regularly. He even knew the names of many of the higher-ranking guard members who walked the streets – as of course he was well known to their membership – and in a few cases he was even aware of some of their habits and foibles. *What better way to avoid your enemy*, he reasoned to himself inwardly, *than to know as much as you possibly could about them*? If, for instance, a particular sergeant carried a long-standing ankle injury that meant he favoured walking on the left of the street close to the buildings, lest his leg suddenly weaken and he needed support, then it would be best to stick to the right-hand side of the street when abroad in the area he walked his beat, correct? In this way he would keep out of the way of that patrol and make life easier for himself.

These were the minor details that Skerrick picked up on and calculated in his wily mind every day; minute slivers of information tucked away into his head that individually would look inconsequential, yet put together with countless other little observances added up to a huge library of specialist knowledge. In his experience, it was often the small matters he could affect that made large differences in outcome. It was with all this in mind that he went on his way – always seeing, always hearing, always taking everything in.

There was only one way to find out what lay ahead for his day. He would just have to get on with it and see which way his luck led him.

*

A few hours later, Skerrick was still out on the streets, but had noticed a change in the air. Something felt subtly different. He noted that the guards pacing the streets had increased in number, seemingly the result of the distant pealing of a large bell somewhere near the Promontory. The meaning of the bell itself he did not assign much importance to. Those officials loved their pomp and ceremony and relished any chance to make some noise in aid of some overblown matter or other; it just seemed to come with the territory. Skerrick still went about his routine, however – observing, avoiding, skulking around and trying pockets and door handles to see if he would find himself striking lucky today. Those were the things he knew he could rely on – his eyes, his hands and his wits; those factors in his favour that had kept him going all these years.

Skerrick was not a young man, being somewhere in his mid-forties, but he did not yet feel the effect of the years gone by even despite his difficult lifestyle. He felt just the same as he always had. Yes, his hair had thinned to balding on the very top of his head, his skin was a little less elastic than it once was, and he seemed to take a little longer to recover from minor cuts and scrapes he incurred these days, but really, what other difference was there? His mind was the same as it had been since his late teenage years – better now, if anything, since it contained so much more learned information than previously, and he was still careful as in younger years. Skerrick was nothing if not careful.

A large cloud passing overhead made the street darken considerably. The gloomy streets of Dralcea were rarely bright at the best of times, the buildings generally being made from whatever stone and timber was available at their time of construction. In such shadows those buildings became especially dark, although the effect in this instance was fleeting and the cloud moved sufficiently to allow the sunlight through once more. Skerrick's eye was drawn to the light shining off a collection of reflective surfaces – several guards in their well-polished armour. Worse still was their bearing, as they seemed to be heading directly toward him.

'I don't think so, not today lads,' Skerrick muttered to himself as he quickly changed direction and hurried off toward the nearby steps descending to the second tier, whilst of course appearing distinctly nonchalant. Sparing himself one subtle but informative glance backward as he went, he could see the guards had closed a good chunk of the distance already. *That isn't the best sign*, Skerrick thought.

Reaching the steps, he quickly began to descend them. Skerrick set foot at the bottom, now on the secondary tier. *What have I done this time?* he said internally. *I don't fancy letting you catch up to tell me. I'm not even sure you would spare the time to use words.*

His sandals slapped rhythmically on the bare ground as Skerrick broke out into a flat run.

Chapter Twenty-two – A Farewell

Once the injured had their wounds seen to satisfactorily, they agreed to leave The Crimson Duck behind and rendezvous with Cronto and the others. Fyrir had instructed his young employee, Aokir, to leave the preparations he had been undertaking in the kitchen for the evening's pies, and instead focus on serving those wanting a drink as his sole task. This came as a surprise to the young man, as he usually helped wherever needed on the few days of the week when he was required. Aokir had certainly never been left in sole charge of the pub before and did not enjoy the idea of it either. There was a reason he came in to help; there was a lot to attend to.

Aokir Takeuchi was a bright lad and lived close to the inn itself. Whilst he descended from a different Originator group to the Haþingvoðs and was accordingly represented in their government by a different Ambassador, that did not affect how he was treated or thought of in The Crimson Duck. He worked hard and was polite to the customers, and that was enough for Skula and Fyrir. Ryx was two years older than he, and often treated Aokir like a younger brother – occasionally teasing but usually just encouraging and passing on useful tips where she could. They had all gotten on well throughout the past few years of his employment in the pub.

Fyrir's instructions to Aokir were to deal with the few customers already present as best he could and then when the daily lull arrived, as it always did in the mid-afternoon, he was to shut and lock up the premises and take Piecrust with him. Fyrir promised he would send word to Aokir as soon as they were back; the implication being that he did not know quite when that would be, and that Aokir should not come back until that time. The most surprising part of it all was that Skula had pressed into his hands his pay for the next month, well in advance, and a little more besides that would cover Piecrust's invariable hunger and then some. 'We mustn't let you go without,' she had said as she handed the cash over in a way that would brook no refusal. Skula was nothing if not firm when it came to such things. 'And we've got to make up for the trouble of looking after the hungry one.'

'But, aren't you going to be back soon? What are you going to do? You don't need to pay me in advance, and I don't have a key either...'

Aokir was confused by this sudden change to his usual routine and myriad questions came to the front of his mind. Until called through to the bar, he had been in the back chopping up meat and vegetable snippets for the pies to be baked later. Seeing Skula come into the kitchen needing stitches had been a shock, alongside the later witnessing of her taking the kitchen's biggest cleaver and tying string through the hole in the handle before suspending it from her waist. The whole strange experience was making him uncomfortable, and that sense was only growing with each passing moment as more and more unusual events seemed to be unfolding. He had also just noticed Ryx, whom he liked but was also very slightly afraid of, holding a green-edged, threatening-looking weapon; this did nothing to calm his nerves.

'Well, that's all up in the air at the moment,' Skula had replied vaguely in response to his initial question. 'You just go on home once you've shut the place up, and we'll worry about when we return. Our regulars will cope, I assume. You just look after your mother,' she had said, smiling, whilst she patted him on the shoulder.

With that, they had each given Piecrust an affectionate tousling goodbye and left amongst the grins and waves of some of the more inebriated customers present; the early time of day had no bearing on the appropriateness of that for many of their clientele.

*

Rundup had directed them all in the direction of his troupe's camp and led the way accordingly. The extravagantly dressed man did his best to take them on a route that included the darker streets and subterranean levels to avoid being recognised and inviting further trouble. On arrival at the site of Rundup Ovygdalha's home, Rundup realised he had left the spear taken from the Promontory in a corner of The Crimson Duck. He would have to do without it. The need for more vigilance was apparent after the attack that Rundup had been central in foiling, an event which had prompted his invitation to the Promontory that day. His people now perennially kept someone on sentry duty at the entrance to the campground. As they approached, the strongman Eric Wurm, whose turn it was to keep watch, looked as Rundup approached hurriedly with his five accompanying travellers, four humans and one Ananeptide in tow. Eric arched an eyebrow.

Rundup simply said, 'They're with me.' He did not slow his pace and headed straight for his tent as the rest followed.

'You must get up to some weird stuff, Rundup,' Eric said as they passed, watching the procession.

'This is a bit of a revelation to me,' Julius said, gazing at the array of different lodgings on show. 'We're most used to seeing log cabins back in Thorntuft, simple but sturdy and warm when caulked with tree resins. I've never seen these...flappy houses before.'

'I wonder what it's like living in these. We live in the back rooms of the pub and all the housing we ever see is more or less the same, just variable on the scale of grandness and generally packed into the streets on all sides,' Skula said. 'Somebody is cooking something that smells good, too.' The many multicoloured rectangular tents appeared to inflate like huge lungs when buffeted by the wind, whilst there was also a smattering of wheeled carts, covered over with curved timbers and anchored to the ground to stop them moving off when not intended.

'Flammula egg omelette,' Rundup said absentmindedly. 'Tents have their advantages and disadvantages, but they suffice.'

Eventually Rundup reached his brightly coloured purple tent and undid the toggle holding the door closed. He left the others standing awkwardly outside, as none seemed to want to follow him inside uninvited – although in truth Rundup had no issues with them doing so. He had been shown hospitality that day already, after all. He was more than willing to reciprocate.

After a couple of minutes, he reappeared from inside with a simple two-strapped bag covering his back and a small wooden chest tied to the bag's underside. He bounced slightly, imitating a step, and seemed content that it would sit on his back reasonably well. 'All right, that should do. Now, onwards we go.'

'Yep, seems wise,' Julius replied.

'So long as you're ready, dear,' Skula said as they began walking again. 'It's actually quite surreal being here, seeing all this with you. We came to see your performance just a few days ago, Fyrir and I. It was very impressive.' She looked a little red-faced. 'I was embarrassed to tell you before in case you thought I was just saying so for effect.'

'No need to be embarrassed at all, my good lady. I thank you for the compliment, on behalf of all my colleagues. We do try to make the show as entertaining as possible, as far as our capabilities allow,' Rundup replied.

'Oh, it was very entertaining, make no mistake. The lady who ate fire as if it were nothing! And your friend with the huge great tower of balanced flammula eggs reaching right up into the top of the tent, and then when he whipped that one out of the middle and the whole pile stayed upright – incredible! We were extremely impressed.' Fyrir seemed very enthused about the spectacle.

'He has hardly shut up about it to me and Aokir these last few days,' Ryx said, sounding amused.

'Did you catch an egg when he threw those few into the crowd?' Rundup asked Fyrir and Skula.

'No, we weren't close enough,' Skula said.

'Perhaps just as well,' Rundup said. 'Occasionally they catch people unawares and they end up with egg on their face. His idea of having a little extra fun. Audience participation, he calls it. Not strictly endorsed by our leader.'

'I can imagine, especially if it makes them want their ticket money back. Does that ever happen?' Fyrir asked.

'Occasionally,' Rundup admitted. 'They usually end up being misdirected into spending even more money in one way or another, though. It takes a certain talent to do that.'

'Not entirely unlike our trade in that respect. Not that we ever encourage anyone to keep spending their somoni once they've had their fill,' replied Fyrir. 'We're good like that. Responsible.'

'Yeah, they don't need any encouragement to continue drinking,' Ryx chimed in.

'That's true,' agreed Skula. 'They're thirsty enough as it is.' She fell silent for a moment. 'Is the entertainment they provide here the sort Ananeptide are interested in, Nothro?'

'Never seen anything like this place before,' he replied. 'It's all new to me.'

'It's different out in the wilds of Thorntuft,' Julius said. 'Those guys love the more...ruthless forms of entertainment. You know, pulling the legs off goats and seeing how far they get before collapsing. Or submerging themselves in the icy river waters to see who lasts the longest before giving up and getting out – often with fatal results for the stubborn ones. Dark stuff like that.'

'Vicious rumours,' Nothro growled, pushing Julius with a massive paw. 'Nothing more. We're just as civilised as everyone else. Songs, art, crafting – we enjoy those sorts of things.'

'Art? I had no idea your people create art,' said Rundup, intrigued.

'We mostly keep it to ourselves,' Nothro said with his approximation of a shrug.

'Fair enough. I'd love to see Ananeptide art someday.'

'We'd better see how this turns out first,' Nothro replied.

Rundup nodded solemnly. What he was suggesting would be a ludicrous luxury right now and he knew it. Still, he really would like to learn and experience more of Ananeptide culture. He was sure it was as rich as Nothro had summarised, but their people gave so little away that it was hard to access such things as a human far distant to most of their culture. Perhaps one day the rifts between them and the human population would be healed enough for them to share their way of life. Nothro's relationship with Julius showed there could be trust and friendship between the species that went beyond simple business transactions and casual acquaintances – there was a real bond there. Rundup dearly hoped that was the way their world was heading, although he had seen little evidence of it. If anything, the opposite seemed to be occurring on the streets of Dralcea currently. He could, however, hope.

Rundup led the way to a clearing amongst the living spaces where a circle of stools and small crates formed a ring, providing seating for the performers and others who worked on the show to relax and socialise. A cordon of stones enclosed a blackened patch of earth where a fire was frequently made, to warm them and give an excuse to gather there. People have a habit of coming over and sitting down around to talk in peace when they see a fire at night-time, and this one was effective in entertaining the troupe and encouraging the discussion of new ideas. Rundup invited his guests to sit and, although early in the day and of a different ambience, the few stagehands that were relaxing there were friendly in greeting the strangers. 'Please make yourselves comfortable here for a moment. Before we depart, I need to speak to a friend and colleague of mine.'

'Of course,' Skula said. 'Take your time.'

'Probably best that he doesn't,' Ryx muttered under her breath. She received a tired-looking expression aimed her way in response from her mother.

Rundup bowed slightly and left, taking several turns before approaching a neat circular tent with a pointed tip from which a steady trickle of smoke emerged. The timber frame giving the structure solidity showed through the material, despite the quality of the latter. The doorway consisted of two overlapping flaps of tent wall, which Rundup gently pushed through as he made his way inside to see Lady Folodawa. She had long been more than a colleague to him, even as she fulfilled a motherly role to the whole circus – she was a frequent confidant, an advisor and a good friend. He couldn't simply leave without at the very least letting her know he was doing so.

As he entered the tent, a gentle swirl of scented smoke surrounded him, as usually occurred when he paid her a visit. The smell was herbal, heady and rich but not overpowering. Lady Folodawa was fond of her pipe and had a seemingly endless supply of different leaves which she would slowly puff on in her spare time; the source of which remained a mystery, as she never seemed to go anywhere to obtain such items. Rundup had once tried it when she had offered her pipe to him, but he had not taken to it – he thought the taste akin to food burnt to the bottom of a saucepan, but she seemed to enjoy it.

She was sitting in her usual place for relaxing, the rocking chair situated on the far side of the tent. In most people's tents and cabins that was where the bed would sit – but Lady

Folodawa's had no bed in it at all. Those privileged few invited inside assumed that she simply slept in her chair due to the lack of other options. Seeing Rundup enter, she continued rocking and smiled, her lined face creasing significantly. Whilst wreathed in smoke, her rocking motion gently stirred it into eddies that spiralled off into the room around her and into the tent roof.

'My lady,' he said, returning her smile. She had the great gift of relaxing all who enjoyed her presence, now evident in Rundup despite the traumatic day he had endured thus far.

'Come in, Rundup, sit,' she instructed, gesturing to the stool reserved for visitors. 'You're back already? I imagined you would be out celebrating your honour still.' She took a big puff on her pipe before the smoke billowed out of her nose and drifted upwards. 'How was it inside the Promontory? Such a grand building. I would love to be invited there myself, and wander through the halls. I'm no hero myself though, of course.'

You would want a better welcome than the one we received, thought Rundup as he perched on the stool, placing his pack on the floor. 'It wasn't quite what I expected,' he said diplomatically. 'The courtyards and gardens were beautiful though.' He fumbled for the correct words to say and failed to come up with anything he felt was particularly fitting. 'Something has come up that I need to attend to, and I will have to be away for a few days. Perhaps longer.'

Rundup was suddenly aware that he perhaps should not have come back here at all; the guard were sure to come to his home to find him. What if he was incriminating his people by returning here, innocent though he was? They would not be able to deny seeing him after his visit to the Promontory now, and that was due to his own actions in coming home for his possessions. He resolved to limit what he told Lady Folodawa so that at least she was not burdened with more information than necessary.

'Something has come up.' She repeated this as a statement, not a question. Her eyes still looked kind to him, but she stopped rocking in her chair.

Of course, she is far too perceptive to be fobbed off with such a vague statement, you fool. She knows this is not what you say it is. 'Yes,' he replied lamely. 'Unexpectedly. I have to go immediately.' He felt almost insulting talking the way he was, and hoped he didn't appear that way, whilst also wishing he had planned something more personal to say that would convey his gratitude to her for everything she had done.

'There has been trouble,' Lady Folodawa stated plainly.

'I'm sorry, my lady. I don't know exactly how long it will be for.' Rundup crossed over to her and gently placed a hand on her shoulder. 'I didn't want to just leave without telling you. Thank you for everything,' he said, emotion threatening to boil over and break his facade of calm. He struggled to keep it intact and could feel the scar on his cheek ache as he recalled her stitching the wound after the attack on their camp. Unbidden, the other times she had guided him and helped him with his personal struggles came to mind. 'You've been better to me than anyone ever has.'

She looked up at him in surprise. 'You will be back,' she said with the utmost certainty, and smiled. 'I know it. But you have no need to thank me. All that you have achieved is down to you, and there is more to come. Just promise me one thing.'

'Of course, anything.'

'Look after yourself, really look after yourself, and your companions too. They will need you.'

Rundup felt briefly confused. Lady Folodawa was always incredibly perceptive, bordering on the eerily insightful. But still, how did she know about the others? They had not come in, nor had he mentioned them. That was her way though, and he doubted he would ever fully understand it. 'I will do my utmost,' he said with complete sincerity. He gave her shoulder one more squeeze and turned to leave, a thought occurring to him that he could not ignore. 'It would be wise to forget that I was here today, for your safety,' he said quietly.

'I understand,' she replied. 'Goodbye for now, Rundup Ovygdalha.'

'Goodbye, my lady.' He kept his pace steady as he retrieved his bag before pushing his way back through the tent flaps. Once outside, he took a deep breath to calm his emotions and returned to the others waiting by the remnants of the fire.

'Are we done here?' Ryx asked.

'Don't be rude, Ryx. It's not easy leaving behind the ones you care about. How are you, Rundup?' Skula asked.

'Fine, I've said what I needed to.' Rundup thought of the countless other people he cared for in the group he was set to leave and how he wanted to say goodbye to them, but there was no time to do so – to get overly sentimental would only endanger them all. He was sure the other folk would understand. 'Let's get moving and meet up with the rest. I think it's best we see where this day takes us next.'

Rundup led them back out the way they had come and nodded as they approached Eric on their way out. 'Take care of yourself, Eric.' Rundup shook the man's hand firmly. 'This is a good place. I'll see you soon.'

Eric looked surprised at the turn of phrase. 'Everything all right, Rundup?'

'Everything will be fine.' Rundup ushered the others through the gateway ahead of him. He smiled at Eric warmly before departing. 'Look out for everyone!' he called over his shoulder.

Rundup and the strange group of friends left, slowly disappearing back into the main sprawl of the city and leaving any semblance of normal life behind.

Chapter Twenty-three – Cornered

Cronto was beckoned over by Zhin as he crouched under the window, keeping out of sight. Cronto left Jenker holding his newfound cutlass with a pleased look on his face, then crept over to join Zhin. Risking a glance outside, he counted a dozen guards led by an officer, all carrying the weapons they had been menaced by earlier. The situation looked dire as the authorities headed directly for Jenker's shop, their path unwavering.

'This is not good,' Cronto whispered. He realised the shop was filled with people simply standing around, and unless something changed they would shortly be discovered – and their escape would count for nothing once the guards entered the bakery and opened fire with their weapons. 'Jenker!' Cronto hissed urgently, as quietly as he could manage whilst still getting the man's attention. 'You need to get everyone out of here, into the back room where they can't be seen.'

'Hmm?' Jenker said, staring intently at the cutlass in his hands, turning it this way and that to let the light accentuate the details of the carved handle.

'The back, get everybody into the back, now! Quickly!' He still seemed to be struggling to break through Jenker's reverie, and so appealed to them all directly. 'Hide yourselves, immediately!' Cronto urged the seven people waiting around.

They began to comply, shuffling through the door into the back. Jenker had trouble moving as fast, distracted as he was, and so Wilfred guided the taller man through to where they would be hidden. Only Zhin, Cronto and Cedric Guyal standing behind the closed front door remained in the main room of the shop.

'So – what do you think?' Cedric said, flexing his arms as he leaned with his back to the door. 'Three of us and thirteen of them, all well-armed. Fancy our chances?'

Zhin looked Cedric straight in the face. 'Not at all. But what choice do we have?'

'If they get through the door, I've no doubt that they will start using those weapons indiscriminately. There is not much scope to hide either...but we can try. Get down, out of sight. There is a chance that they will simply go away.' Cronto could only hope that he was right.

He tried to stick closely to the wall and attempted to slow his breathing to reduce the noise, although he still seemed to be making enough sound to bring the guard crashing through the door at any second. Cronto realised that they had no concrete plan should the guards realise they were inside or just decide to force their way in anyway. The escapees by the door possessed little enough means to defend themselves, were outnumbered more than four to one and the element of surprise should they attack from their concealed places would only help them briefly. Cronto had Bulwark to hand, but Zhin only carried a short baton and Cedric was armed with nothing at all. Not an overtly religious man, Cronto was sorely tempted to clasp his hands together and offer his prayers to whatever deity happened to be the most popular in the current month. It was hard to keep track. A few moments later Cronto heard the guards arrive outside the door of the bakery.

'Mr Jenker! If you're in there, now would be the time to come outside. We urgently need to speak to you,' Cronto heard a guard yell from outside. 'It would be best for you to come out and talk to us now. We cannot guarantee your safety if we have to come inside. Come out, now.'

Cronto tried again to calm his terrified breathing and hoped against hope that the guards would simply give up. He then had a sickening realisation; as the last through the door when the entire group arrived, he had simply closed the door behind him and set about his task of uncovering the beautiful cutlass embedded in the wall. He had failed to get Jenker to lock the door behind them – it was simply shut, not secured in any way. It could not be locked now without being discovered; likewise any attempt to bar or barricade it now would have the same effect. Cronto's heart sank. Cedric was the main thing keeping the door seated in its frame as he leaned his weight against it. Big though he was, he was far from an immovable object.

'This is your last chance, Mr Jenker! Come out now, and bring anybody else with you, or we'll have no choice but to use force to make you come out!' the guard shouted.

The officer's yells reverberated through the door. Cronto stared down at the floor and his mind raced, unable to focus on trying to plan any defence or escape; instead he examined and took in the contours and signs of wear of the stones he slumped on as if he would be tested on their qualities shortly after. In that moment he was utterly confused about the sequence of events that had led to this point. Earlier he was in line to be given an award, and now he was hiding with nothing but a door between him and being shot by the very people he was supposed to be being honoured by. At this point he wished all of this would stop – so long as that excluded his violent death at the hands of the lawkeepers of their city. Nothing would guarantee that, however.

Having received no response, the officer in charge had to act. 'You there. Open the door.'

*

Cronto briefly wondered if he should shout to those sheltering in the back room to run. This could be the last chance for him to do so and perhaps they could exit through a back door and flee – they might yet live to see another day if he and his two companions in the front held the guards up enough. If the bakery had a rear door, that is; shouting might just betray their presence when there remained the slimmest of hopes that the guards may have just been about to give up and leave. It was an impossible choice, and not one that he felt the courage to make. Instead, he would leave fate to work as it deigned correct and see which path it led them down.

Cedric moved away from the door to Zhin's side whilst still crouching in a surprisingly lithe manner for a large man, and positioned himself there instead. Presumably, he did not want to try to delay the charge when the guards outside forced their way in, as now seemed inevitable. Cronto nodded to Cedric and Zhin, more in an amiable recognition and farewell than to convey any instruction. Zhin nodded back, looking miserable, whilst Cedric ground one clenched fist into the open palm of his other hand, softly cracking his knuckles.

The three huddled companions heard a muted sentence uttered outside and braced for the worst. A moment later, the door swung open violently and illuminated a long rectangle of the stone floor and all its unique patterning in the day's warm sunlight.

Cronto gripped Bulwark's handle tightly and took a deep breath. A pair of booted feet at the ends of navy-coloured trousers entered his view as the first guard crossed the threshold into the bakery's interior. Before he could get a look at his face, the guard was down at Cronto's side having landed heavily on the floor, his Ejector clattering loudly on the stones as it impacted under him. Cronto quickly recognised Cedric's arms wrapped around the struggling guard – he had sprung akin to a coiled snake striking his target, tackling him bodily and bringing him down with an efficiency that suggested he had done the very same before.

The next guard entered the bakery closely behind his colleague. He came through the door only to be tripped by Zhin's baton extended expertly at just the right moment, threading it between his legs and bringing him down to the floor face first. The man inadvertently triggered his Ejector as his subconscious kicked in, trying to stop the sudden fall but just enforcing muscle contractions; his fingers curled inwards sharply and activated the trigger, sending a cluster of Sweat of Hephaestus into the bakery at waist height. With the bulk of the group sheltering in the back room, the projectiles caused no harm.

The other guards attempted to rush in and put an end to this resistance with their Ejectors at the ready. In doing so, they allowed themselves to be concentrated into a close column, the bottleneck of the entrance forcing them to be tightly packed together.

*

Hearing the shot from the tripped guard's Ejector impact on the interior wall of his business, Jenker felt a protective emotion surge within him at this violation and he emerged from the doorway to the back room full of confidence and rage. This was his livelihood and home, and the door had just been kicked in! He pushed himself up off the floor where he had been squatting a moment previously, his newly-discovered cutlass tucked under his arm. In this way, the blade stuck backward with just the carved handle pointing forward and visible as it protruded from between his chest and arm. He faced those guards attempting to enter and getting in each other's way.

Jenker noted the big man, Cedric, who had been minding the door was seemingly crushing a guard in a vice-like bear hug on the floor to one side of the door. This action prevented either from getting up or indeed fighting in a traditional sense, although Cedric seemed to be enjoying success in bouncing the man's head off the floor, trying to knock him out. More frenzied was Zhin on the other side, beating a cowering guard dispossessed of his Ejector, desperately trying to shield himself from Zhin's baton blows, equally desperate and panicking in his will to survive. Cronto squatted near Cedric, axe held tightly, unengaged but looking ready to act. The whole scene, taken in over a few fractions of a second, gave Jenker heart and fuelled his protective urges. He briefly wondered if this was what battle was like, and if he felt now how his father had in one of the occasions he saw action.

'Bastards!' Came the cry from the officer as they tried to storm the bakery's front room, enraged by seeing two of their own floored. The next couple then made it through the doorframe.

Fear lanced into Jenker's mind then and, as if in reply to the officer, Jenker roared something incoherent back. He raised his right hand, catching the cutlass's handle as he released it from between his left arm and chest, and gripped it tightly. He practiced what he had learnt from his lesson with Cronto and willed the cutlass to perform its duty. The weapon duly obliged; a hissing blast of flame spat forth from the carved dragon's mouth and with his aim correct, it engulfed the doorway, the guards entering and also those beyond clamouring to make it through. Those at the front were lost from sight and flames were channelled through the doorway and into the waiting ranks of guards outside. Bottled up as they were, the attack was devastating and almost as one they dropped to the floor screaming. The fire burnt their exposed faces and hands first, and clung to the cloth parts of their uniform, lingering and burning as they panicked and writhed on the ground. It was a pitiful sight, but to see the attackers brought down in one sweep was pleasing to Jenker in his adrenaline-addled state and he spared them no pity.

Having witnessed the searing heat of the flames as they passed by and the subsequent screaming of the stricken guards, Zhin and Cedric stopped their attempts to subdue their respective opponents and stared in shock. Both unburned guards attempted to flee at this opportunity, before Jenker pointed the handguard of his cutlass at each until they were stilled out of fear of falling victim to its cruel fire. Neither uttered a word, too terrified to act or even move for fear of it being misconstrued as an attempt to get away.

'Stay where you are,' Jenker commanded, his voice wavering thanks to his body being in a fight-or-flight state of readiness, his blood surging and breathing rapid. Both lay on the floor, glaring at Jenker with defiance in the face of their own terror at ending up like their colleagues who continued to suffer mere feet away.

'You're just what they told us you were,' one muttered bitterly, only just loud enough for Jenker to hear as the blood pounded in his ears.

Cronto stood and approached Jenker carefully, hands out in a placatory gesture. 'You've certainly got the hang of using that – I can't say I thought you'd have to use it quite so soon though. You can put it down now.'

Jenker looked at the older man fiercely, the traces of his earlier meekness gone after that exhibition of power. 'I had to do something. They had the nerve to kick their way in here. I had to do what was necessary.'

'Yes, of course, and we wouldn't have survived without your intervention. Now, we should go. We have been here for too long already.'

Jenker stared at Cronto dumbly before nodding and realising he should put his weapon away, then did his best to tuck the blade between his belt and trousers until it sat on his hip. As he did so, Zhin and Cedric stood up to watch over their captives and did their best to ignore the cries of those outside. Cronto headed into the back to reassure the others hiding there and prepare them to move on.

The doorframe of the entrance to the bakery had caught fire following the blast and was smouldering gently. Jenker noticed and grabbed the water bucket to try to douse the glowing timbers.

'I don't think I'll be sleeping tonight,' Cedric commented. 'The smell is almost the worst part. Can you smell things in your dreams?'

Zhin looked at Cedric sidelong, as if he had just said the stupidest thing he had ever heard. 'We'll all be lucky to see the sun set tonight, let alone try to get any sleep the way this is heading. I'd appreciate every moment if I were you. We don't know how many more of them we have left.'

'I hope you're wrong, but I doubt you are.' Cedric sighed heavily. 'I've never wanted to be neck-deep in work more in my life than right now. Give me a lifetime of busy days getting my hands dirty mucking out the snorthogs, with only trivial worries to bother me, and I'll die a happy man. Anything would be better than this running and hiding, hoping simply to go unnoticed, and for what? I've done nothing wrong. That is the bit that really chafes the most. I've never done anything to anyone.'

Zhin shrugged before replying, 'Me neither. I live a quiet life and go about my business the same as most people, just keeping to myself and doing what I think is right. How anyone can take offence at that, I don't know. Best not to think about that right now though. What matters is keeping our wits about us and using them as best we can to save ourselves. I'm sure there will be plenty of time for wondering why later.'

Cronto reappeared with the rest of the group from around the corner. 'It's time to go, before any more of this lot arrive.'

'What about these two?' asked Cedric, nudging his captive with his boot. 'What do we do with them? They're witnesses,' he added darkly, adding to the fear of the man at his feet.

Cronto also noticed the smouldering doorframe at that point, and Jenker failing to put it out. 'Firstly, we help put that out. There's no need to destroy anything more than what has already been damaged. As for these two – we had better find something to tie them up with so that we can leave them here and get on. Jenker – find us something to do that with, please, and we'll sort this door out.'

Cedric looked at him incredulously. 'Leave them here, are you mad? We can't leave them here alone. They know who we are, what we look like and will be able to tell whoever comes along and finds them which way we have gone. We should restrain them and drag them behind us. Could come in handy as leverage later, too.' He was clearly of the mind that they should try to profit from the pair as much as possible.

'I'm not convinced about that,' Zhin chipped in. 'Seems a bit incriminating.'

'Supposing we took them with us,' Cronto posited. 'How do you propose that we keep them quiet? One yell at the wrong time and it's all over, they've caught us and whatever else that entails follows. I'm sure you can imagine well enough without me telling you. Also, there's the issue of motivation. If they were to drag their heels they could just as easily give away our presence to their comrades. It's not worth the risk – they would be a burden.'

'So we let them get away with it, that's what you're saying?' Cedric asked.

'Get away with what? Coming to find us, as they've been ordered to do? Terrible acts have been committed today, it is true. Rightly or wrongly, they happened. Now we have our part to play, and furthering that evil is not the right thing to be done. I won't let you kill captives under our supervision. We will not become murderers. What easier way is there for them to justify their actions against us than if we give them the very reason they need through our own actions?'

Cedric looked admonished, and more than a little ashamed at letting his emotions blind him to the sensible reasoning Cronto lay before him. He slumped, his large frame sagging visibly. 'You're right. It would do us no favours to repeat their violence. What happened to the rest of them was unfortunate, though – who knows how they'll interpret that.'

'Yes, it is most unfortunate, you're right. That is another of those things that have occurred today which we no longer have any control of, so try not to worry yourself unduly,' Cronto said.

*

As he readied the people to leave, Cronto wondered about his recent decisions. He had directed them all here based on a hunch, fuelled by his own interest and a desire to satisfy his curiosity. What resulted had proved him right, which was gratifying in its own way, but had also set them on this collision course with the guards. Had he been right to seek out this weapon? He knew beforehand the power it entailed and the damage that could result if he was correct, and had still proceeded. He had even passed it into the hands of a man he had met precisely once before without so much as a second thought, even if he was the rightful heir of the item; if not for Cronto, Jenker would have continued in blissful ignorance. Cronto's priority at this time was to protect these victimised people he seemed to have adopted, and help them survive. The last thing he wanted to see was more people being hurt to accomplish this aim, yet precisely that had happened. This thought weighed heavily on his mind. He tried to put it aside and focus on what needed to be done in the immediate future. At that moment, Jenker returned with a coil of ancient-looking rope in hand and silently proffered it to Cronto.

'All right, excellent. We'll restrain them and move on. We have been here too long as it is.'

With that, Cronto strode through the doorway and tentatively into the street to assess the situation outside, aside from the unlucky guards. All appeared calm, which seemed wrong after all they had just experienced. A few people were poking their heads around corners and out of doorways to see what all the noise had been about. He knew the situation would only worsen from here as interest intensified.

Cronto oversaw the restraining of the two men and mentally prepared his charges to leave and continue their journey. Then, after taking one last moment to appreciate the precious peace that had been all too rare that day, he led them all back out into the dangerous streets swarming with people intent on hunting them down.

Chapter Twenty-four – The Temple Gardens

Julius, Nothro and Rundup allowed themselves to be led by Skula, Fyrir and Ryx through the streets until they came into sight of the temple they sought. Ryx had insisted that they were the most able to act as guides around Dralcea given that they lived in the city, but Julius knew the job was made easy by the golden ball sat at the highest point on the temple, which could be seen from afar. They arrived at their destination safely, avoiding the patrols in the area.

Whilst Zhin Xofia had been correct about the temple being surrounded by trees and foliage, Julius assumed he had either forgotten, underestimated or disregarded the fence that ringed the perimeter. This fence was wooden with closely fitted slats to keep the noise and bustle of the city at bay, at least in some minor way. Julius could see the greenery within where it poked through the fence in places, or else crept over the top, and of course the trees inside the temple garden showed their branches fanning out as they stretched up toward the clear sky.

'Well this is a lovely spot, isn't it? I particularly like the trees; they remind me of home. One small thing though – how do we get in?' Julius asked.

'I suppose if we get in, we will be well hidden, that's for sure,' Fyrir said. 'Not sure how we accomplish that, though.'

Ryx didn't hesitate in pulling her macuahuitl out of the strap harness she had affixed to her back before they set off, and was about to swing Grænn Klær at the fence when her mother grabbed her shoulder to stop her.

'We're trying to stay hidden, Ryx, remember? We need to conceal where we are and where we've been. Smashing our way in leaves quite a telling trail,' Skula said gently.

'Here,' Nothro said, putting his back against the fence and cupping his hands in front of himself.

The Haþingvoð family and Rundup looked collectively confused at this until Julius stepped up to his friend.

'This is how we get in,' Julius said, and put his right foot into the furry platform made by Nothro's waiting hands. He was flung over the fence when Nothro quickly raised his hands up high in a well-practiced movement. Julius landed in the temple's garden with a soft thud, but without any sound of pain or discomfort; he was used to being treated roughly as he knew how to handle himself with regards to the Ananeptide. 'Easy!'

'I see. Is it safe doing that?' Rundup asked.

'Safe is a relative term right now,' Nothro replied in monotone.

'Fair enough. I'll go next then.' With that, Nothro repeated the action for Rundup, but warned him before he was flung over. Nothro then helped to get the others over the fence before anyone around paid too much attention to them.

Having safely made it over with no calamities and gathered on the other side of the fence with Julius – inside the garden – Skula spoke up. 'So, how does Nothro get over?'

'Just give him a second,' Julius replied. 'You'll see.' Pounding footsteps could be heard accelerating and before any of them bar Julius was ready, Nothro's large shape came vaulting over the tall fence and clearing their heads, making all bar Julius flinch, before he skidded to a stop some considerable distance inside the garden. In an instant he was back up on his feet as if nothing had happened and he had not just easily leapt over them all. Nothro gestured deeper into the garden. The humans aside from Julius looked awestruck at the unexpectedly athletic display from Nothro.

'This way,' he said in his best attempt at a whisper.

'You're right, we might as well go deeper to stay hidden,' Ryx said. 'Can anyone see the others around anywhere?'

'They wouldn't be doing the job of staying out of sight very well if we could,' Julius replied sarcastically.

Ryx shoved him hard by his injured shoulder and sent him stumbling into the nearest shrub. Julius had tried to stay on his feet but the potent spirit he had consumed earlier was still circulating in his bloodstream and he couldn't maintain his balance. 'You'd better check in there to see if you can find them, then,' she said before walking off.

'*Ryx, behave yourself*!' Skula hissed as she scurried after her. Julius heard Fyrir fail to disguise a laugh at his daughter standing up for herself.

Rundup offered his hand to Julius as he struggled to extricate himself from the clutching branches of the shrubbery he found himself occupying. Julius gratefully accepted, allowing himself to be hauled out with some minor catching of his clothes on the thorny foliage. He nodded his thanks to Rundup, his pride too injured to dare say anything in case he betrayed that feeling. He looked to his friend Nothro, who just shook his head.

'Is this a normal occurrence for him?' Rundup asked Nothro.

'When it comes to talking to women, yes,' Nothro replied. 'Rare as that is,' he added after a moment.

Rundup smiled at the response and patted Julius on the back whilst he scowled at his Ananeptide companion. 'We *do* live out in the woods in the middle of nowhere,' Julius grumbled.

'A nice problem compared to the ones we have at this moment in time,' Rundup pointed out. 'Let's keep an eye out for the rest and move onwards. It looks as though there aren't any Flowers of the Sun members around right now – and hopefully it stays that way, or we might have some awkward questions to answer.'

'Agreed, the quieter we keep it here, the better,' Julius said. 'Assuming *she* can refrain from shoving anyone over at critical moments.'

'Time will tell,' Rundup said. They followed Fyrir, Skula and Ryx up the grassy garden between bushes, trees and flowers. The large, pale stone temple stood ahead of them and gleamed slightly as it reflected the sunlight; an intended effect that matched their religion's philosophy surrounding light and its benefits. It was a loosely five-sided building with a peak of non-structural stone rising in the centre of each side to represent the petals of a flower. From the very middle of the building rose a thin flagpole-like tower with a golden ball at the top, intended to mimic a stamen.

Julius punched Nothro softly on the arm. 'Hiding out in a garden. What has happened to us?'

'The city changes people,' Nothro said, deadpan.

'Even after two days?' Julius asked.

Nothro simply shrugged in response, suggesting that it was clear that was the case. The Haþingvoð family had made their way further forward, zigzagging between the scattered bushes and trees to mask their movement from anyone who might be around up ahead. They covered most of the distance until they found themselves lurking behind one of the trees closest to the temple itself; all of the tallest plants stopped in a radius some fifty feet out from the stone walls, the nearest of which boasted a small door set in an ornate alcove carved to resemble two thick braids of vines meeting in a point at the apex.

As Fyrir, Skula and Ryx stopped to assess their next move, Julius looked to the door beyond them. It slowly opened and an old woman dressed in a long white dress began to shuffle out, her hands occupied with a basket of twine, scissors and small brushes in one and a small bucket of water in the other hand. It quickly became apparent that the worshipper was intent on tending to the plants and the direction she was heading in was only a few feet away from where the family now stood waiting. She would undoubtedly see them as she passed by, or might even bump into them. It was unavoidable. To continue forward was to break out into the open where they were not meant to be and expose themselves to the eyes of the Flowers of the Sun members who were sure to be watching from somewhere around the temple.

*

Julius desperately thought of an action to take but came up short. He noticed Rundup also looked ahead keenly and must have also spotted the danger as the old lady was steadily making progress toward those in the lead. They were surrounded by nothing but bushes and trees – nothing of much help in Julius's opinion. Just as the first tendrils of despair at being discovered began to encroach on his mind, Julius saw Rundup eyeing a small tree and the performer dashed over to it silently.

The performer plucked at the ends of the branches with both hands. Julius had no idea what Rundup was up to, noting that Nothro was also staring at him as though he had lost his mind. Rundup briefly looked back and held his finger up to his lips before turning back to the Haþingvoðs. Ryx was visibly agitated at having also spotted the woman, and she moved to snatch Grænn Klær from her back.

islandRundup acted quickly to stop her, launching the tiniest of the small, round fruits he had plucked from the tree in a shallow arc before it hit Ryx on the head, stalling her motion as she turned to see the source of the thrown object with a scowl on her face. Rundup held up his hand in the hope she would understand it as a signal to stop. Ryx gesticulated wildly yet silently in response, until her parents each put a hand on her shoulders to calm her. Ryx looked annoyed but did comply, and they huddled together to see what Rundup would do next.

Julius watched keenly as Rundup palmed the other, larger fruit he had gathered and carefully took aim. He expertly threw it into a tall tree far off to their collective left. The fruit entered the tree almost at the top before it crashed through the branches, bouncing off each one on the way down and making a cacophony. At length it reached the ground and had successfully attracted the attention of the worshipper shuffling her way toward the garden.

She altered her course with a smile when she realised there was a tasty morsel to be collected. Despite the distance, Julius saw her frown in confusion at the sight of the underripe fruit that had seemingly been produced by the evergreen tree she now stood beneath.

Fyrir grabbed his wife's and daughter's arms as he dashed toward the opposite side of the temple and away from the worshipper. The others quickly followed whilst their potential discoverer was distracted; Nothro launched into a run and grabbed Julius as he did so to accelerate their short journey, carrying the human under his arm as if he weighed nothing. It took a few heart-hammering seconds, but soon they were all in the shadow at the side of the temple.

'Good move back there, Rundup. You do have one hell of an aim on you,' Julius commented quietly.

Rundup shrugged. 'It's sort of my job. Now let's get up front and see if we can find Cronto and the others. Remember, keep quiet and if we stick close to the walls we should stay out of harm's way. I don't think these people have any particular love of the authorities of Dralcea, but it would be best not to test out my hypothesis.'

'Agreed,' Skula said with feeling. '"Quiet" sounds perfect after all this today.'

The six of them moved around the temple, avoiding attracting any undue attention. A handful of other worshippers also occupied the gardens but were some distance away and engrossed in the minutiae of some task or another – all except for one, that is; a man of middle age, lacking in head hair but with a sizable white beard. He was dressed in a long green shirt that extended down just far enough to cover his modesty and wore rough sandals, with just bare legs in between. He came strolling toward them and appeared just twenty feet away from them. He seemed deep in thought, his eyes cast downward and was jabbering softly as if discussing both sides of an argument by himself. *Must be pondering some religious matter*, Julius thought.

The man eventually broke from his reverie around six feet away from the approaching group. Julius headed the group and he tried his best to look nonchalant, but the worshipper looked up and started as if he was completely unaware of them until that moment after being so engrossed in his one-person debate.

The breath caught in Julius's throat and he spared the quickest of glances behind him. Fyrir put his arms in front of his wife and daughter in a protective manner as if he could physically protect them from the man's gaze, although Ryx looked ready to grab Grænn Klær if required. Nothro, who simply tried to look as non-threatening as possible, surprisingly enough succeeded in looking strangely serene, and Rundup looked understandably tense. The moment was only a few heartbeats in length, but it felt an eternity as they tried to hide the weapons they carried for self-defence. To Julius's amazement and relief, the man simply grinned broadly at them and waved as he passed by, a picture of joviality.

As the man tramped off the way they had just come, Julius could feel the collective release of tension – except from Nothro, who looked impassive as ever. They pressed on. There were no further incidents and they reached the side of the temple, where it faced the street with fencing holding back a ring of hedges, and paused there to take stock of the situation.

'Well, that's us here where we're supposed to be. Presumably there will be guard patrols out specifically looking for us now, so let's not leave this relative shelter without assessing the danger first. Can anyone see everybody else?' Julius asked.

'Obviously not,' Ryx retorted. 'If they were here, we would all be having a jig and a bloody good singsong by now, wouldn't we?'

Skula elbowed her daughter. 'Ryx, don't embarrass me! There's no need to antagonise Julius like that, you know it won't help anything. Honestly, I don't know where you get this tendency from, it's certainly not my way.'

'Come on now, you know she has a fire all of her own. You can't lay that blame at my door,' Fyrir said.

'Perhaps an inn was not the best environment to grow up in if you wanted me to be exceptionally courteous and meek? It was good for being assertive and confident, though, I'll give you that,' Ryx posited.

'You're not wrong there,' said Fyrir. 'Just so long as you remain in control and use those positive traits to our benefit now. Of course, I know you will.'

'Just don't go forcing divisions. We only have each other now and need to work together,' Skula said. 'Speaking of which, if we keep our eyes out for the others, they will soon show up I'm sure,' she said diplomatically.

'Let us hope so. It can only be a matter of time before a patrol comes by, after all,' Rundup replied. 'Everyone keep down and try not to look suspicious. Patience is our friend at this moment.'

A moment after speaking, their calm resting point ceased to be peaceful as a shrill voice pierced the air.

'Just *what* do you think you are doing in our *sacred* garden?'

Chapter Twenty-five – Blend In, Run for Your Life

Skerrick was making best haste to escape from the guards, but they were never too far behind him. He tried to keep walls separating them so their view of him would be limited, rounding corners or taking stairways whenever possible, though he could only run for so long. Youth was far behind him now; although physically fit and active for his age, he could only sustain intense activity for a limited time. Having been running flat-out for several minutes now, it was beginning to take a toll on him as his lungs struggled to keep up with his body's demand for oxygen. His leg muscles burned especially fiercely with the exertion, particularly from bounding up steps. Skerrick's sandals were not good for running in and slowed him down – thankfully, the guards' heavy boots and armour had a similar effect and evened out overall and prevented them from closing the distance, for now.

He dashed up another set of stairs before doubling over at the top, and his hands supported his upper body weight by holding onto his knees. A strong breeze stirred what remained of the hair on Skerrick's head – that which had not already been plastered to his scalp with perspiration. Realising he had emerged onto a much lighter street – one flanked by a hodgepodge of differently sized houses, each appearing akin to an individual and strangely independent stair in a multicultural staircase – Skerrick was now on the uppermost tier. He breathed quickly and as deeply as he could manage, trying to fill his lungs with the cool air of the surface to ease the burning sensation he felt deep within his chest.

Heavy rumbling and jingling sounds broke through the sounds filling his ears – largely his own laboured breathing and heart hammering – and intruded upon his compulsory rest stop. In an ideal world he would not be running at all, as that went against every fibre of his normal self; tricksters do not run, they scheme and manipulate to resolve their issues. His options in this respect appeared extremely limited however, as for reasons unbeknownst to him he had become the target of the guards' ire and they were on him relentlessly, not affording him the little bit of distance he needed to slip away.

Skerrick looked around wildly for something to aid his escape but, seeing nothing of use, again launched himself into a run despite the protests from his body. His sandals slapped on the cobbles as he ran. The jig was up if he failed to get away soon as he felt his energy waning. He wondered if hiding in plain sight amongst the other ordinary folk going about their business would work – the problem being that so far, they had all scattered when seeing the desperate man sprinting in their direction. That plan was doomed before it even started.

Various placatory shouts had come from the guards previously as they appealed to Skerrick to stop, promising merely a talk and he could be on his way, but he knew the score. If he stopped, he would end up in the dungeon where his days would surely be miserable and few, or he would simply be dealt with in the most extreme way right there and then. Unsurprisingly, neither option was desirable.

Skerrick turned right at a junction and emerged into a wider thoroughfare where fewer people roamed; not quite what he wanted. He ran on, despair beginning to extend its heavy tendrils around his heart and with each side street he passed without a plan forming, they tightened their icy grip. The pleasant smell of woodsmoke assailed his nostrils as he passed by a house that had already started its evening warmth ritual; an essential part of life, being on the topmost level of Dralcea where the temperature was lower than for those who lived further down the levels into the caldera. The sky was beginning to darken and the temperature was dropping. Small orbs of wavering light appeared in murky windows as people lit lamps and candles to illuminate the homes and small businesses packed tightly along the street that Skerrick traversed.

An unusual sight caught Skerrick's attention. Coming toward him from an adjacent street was a mixed group of around ten people and he automatically recognised what they were trying to do. Knowing the streets and the folk who walked them, Skerrick could tell their intentions just by observing their body language and the speed at which they carried themselves. These people were in a hurry and were desperate not to be noticed. 'This could work,' he rasped to himself.

Slowing to a stop, Skerrick dawdled just beyond the intersecting junction of streets and spared a glance back the way he had come as he caught his breath; the guards chasing him were rapidly gaining ground but appeared not to have spotted him yet.

He would have to be quick.

*

Cronto and his ragtag crew had been fortunate thus far since they had resumed their journey. Upon leaving Jenker's bakery they had attempted to use the most direct route possible to rendezvous with the other folk they had separated from earlier. That was assuming they avoided any guard patrols, of course. The plan was to go as covertly as possible, meaning they might have to change tack if there was any chance of being intercepted. This they had been forced to do twice – both successfully – and they continued their journey unmolested and unnoticed.

Mostly they had needed only minimal directing; they simply followed whoever best knew the area they were passing through at the time. One person had been more trouble than the others, however, and was irritating and raising Cronto's already monstrously high stress levels – the nervous young man named Wilfred. He insisted on lingering at street corners and intersections to scrupulously scan for danger and generally dragged his heels. In several instances they had to lead him by the elbow for fear of him derailing their whole effort. Cedric had grumbled at one point that they should leave him staring at a particularly picturesque carved stone archway if it meant the rest of them stood more of a chance. Cronto, however, had dismissed the remark and would not hear any more such suggestions. He would not willingly abandon any of them – even if they verged on being infuriating.

The golden sphere atop the temple they had chosen as their meeting point was getting ever nearer, the beacon providing a token of hope to all their minds. Cronto was pleased with their progress, along with the fact that Jenker seemed to be more alert than he had been after the discovery of his inherited weapon. For a time, it appeared that he was drunk on power with such an instrument in his possession – Cronto wondered if he had done the right thing in unearthing it. On balance, it should be of more benefit to them all than the potential harm it could do, the judge concluded. He would just have to ensure that Jenker was carefully shepherded along the right path for the safety of them all, and not allowed to be tempted down a dark road of seeking ever more power from which there would be no return nor safe conclusion.

He continued to lead the way as inconspicuously as possible as they approached a convergence of roads on the upper tier of Dralcea. Cronto deferred to one of the other members of the group more familiar with the capital city – in this instance, Zhin Xofia – for directions at the coming crossroads to take the best route going forward. After some brief discussion and subtle hand gestures as they moved, they picked their direction and checked for signs of guard patrols, only to see something that made Cronto's blood run cold. A squadron of heavily armed and armoured guards were huffing and puffing up the street as they laboured at a quick trot under the weight of their equipment. The saving grace was that they did not seem to be bearing down on them specifically, yet. Cronto made sure to cajole Wilfred into moving promptly as they shifted in the opposite direction.

*

Skerrick, who had been lurking in the shadows, sidled out into the street and walked alongside the gaggle of pedestrians distractedly before attaching himself to their group as if he had been with them the whole day. Most of their number failed to notice him, such was their rising level of stress with the guard patrol approaching.

One short young man did see Skerrick insinuating himself into their huddle though, looking up at the older man with a mystified look on his curious face. 'Who are you?' the man asked Skerrick in a surprisingly child-like way.

'I've been here all along,' Skerrick responded confidently, thinking off the top of his head. He hoped that directly dismissing the fact he was suddenly tagging along would be enough to convince them. His immediate safety lay in numbers and this was as perfect an opportunity as he was going to get; he had to grasp the chance with both bony hands. The man staring at Skerrick looked bewildered at his answer, but also as if he lacked the spirit to argue.

Skerrick was pleased; his bold statement seemed to have been accepted by the one person who had noticed his presence, and better still – the others seemed oblivious. The plan was working. He would stick with these people until he could break away again and slink back to his residence to hide out for however long necessary. Usually to evade detection, he would disappear down a narrow side street and melt away as morning fog when struck by the sun's warming rays. Being out of breath from his exertions, he doubted he could hide without his loud breathing giving him away. For the meantime, these people would form an excellent patch of shade for him to shelter in. He must now go unnoticed, and to aid this he stooped to hide himself more effectively from view.

'There, lads! In amongst that lot straight ahead!' shouted one of the pursuing pack just as Skerrick began to squat down. He noticed they had closed much of the distance, possibly noticed his distinctive pattern of hair and recognised it as belonging to their quarry who for a few moments they had lost. A satisfied roar ripped from the throats of the other guards, their blood up from the chase. Tired or not, they seemed to have a renewed sense of urgency now they had sighted their prey and they powered onward with vigour.

Skerrick noticed that these people he had joined had been trying to avoid looking at their pursuers, but many now involuntarily turned to look in the direction of the shouts. He felt the tension in the air around him soar as panic gripped these people. The man at their head, a dark-skinned man with a flat hat, seemed to be leading them and had also seen the danger.

'Run,' the leader said loudly enough to ensure that they all heard him. The time for Skerrick to use strategy had passed; his future was now completely out of his hands, and all that was left for him was to flee with all his remaining energy and perhaps offer up a prayer.

Chapter Twenty-six – Saving One, Damning Many

The roar of blood pounding in Skerrick's ears was almost matched by the pounding of boot soles rapidly striking cobblestones as the unfortunate group ran for their lives. Snatched breaths were never enough and none found the capacity to speak. *What could there be to say, anyway*? Skerrick thought. He knew that appeals to their pursuers were pointless. It was fair to assume that they were not in the mood for mercy.

Skerrick cursed inwardly, incandescent with rage that he had been a hair's breadth away from making good his escape before it had all gone wrong. He had also inadvertently drawn the ire of the guards onto those he had hidden amongst, who had seemed to have been doing an effective job of secreting themselves away from trouble – from what exactly though, he could only guess. A glance at those running around him gave no hint as to their origin; a complete mix of people from all the different cultural groups of Dralcea that he would see each day. There was no readily apparent link between them. He thought hard, racking his brain for some clue that could help steer the situation onto a more favourable route.

Then, Skerrick tripped.

He had been distracted. Skerrick had got too close to the person in front of him, tried to adjust his footing and his sandals had somehow caught on the pavement, pitching him forward. His brain tried to protect him from the impending collision with the ground and his eyes saw nothing as he fell into an untidy heap. Pain leapt through his forearms and knees as they broke his fall without any grace or dignity, losing patches of skin in an instant as his limbs collided with the unyielding stone underfoot. He was even trampled by those following who were unable to avoid him after he dropped at such speed, unintentionally adding insult to injury.

Skerrick was in shock for a moment. The sharp pains from his fall stalled his movements for a few vital seconds as the people he was surrounded by quickly left him behind. All except for one, a young man with a cutlass who left the others and returned to his side. Skerrick was grateful since it wouldn't take long for him to be overwhelmed and likely cut to pieces if he did not act quickly. The rest continued, either unaware of his fall or too caught up in their own adrenaline-fuelled dash to consider stopping.

He grabbed Skerrick by the arm and hauled him to his feet before they both glanced back to see the guards gaining on them. 'We need to get out of the open,' he said, and pulled Skerrick away to an alley that angled off at 45 degrees to the route they had been taking.

The alley was narrow, not helped by the clutter of refuse that lined the sides despite appearing to host some well-to-do businesses. The sky overhead was darkening, an occurrence exacerbated by the upper storeys of the buildings either side looming ominously above, crowding the space overhead. Skerrick had regained his senses and was keeping up with his rescuer, who had released his arm as he did what he could to avoid being tripped by the discarded debris of city life. A pungent aroma filled their senses, a bittersweet mix of the waste around them mingling with woodsmoke emitted by the chimneys of the surrounding houses and businesses; the wind failed to dissipate the smell in the close confines of the alley. Their running disturbed a stray mlem-mlem hunting for unwitting rats amongst the rubbish and it sprinted away before they could reach it, startled by unfamiliar humans hurtling toward it.

'What's your plan?' Skerrick hissed. He was used to traversing these thoroughfares, although not usually at this kind of speed and much less with a squadron in full-on pursuit.

'I'm really just acting on instinct here, rather than having a plan as such,' he replied. 'This way angles roughly toward where we were headed, I know that much. Hopefully, we can catch back up to the rest.'

'Heading toward what?' Skerrick asked.

'Where? The temple we agreed on earlier, remember?'

'Of course, of course, the temple,' Skerrick said as if feeling daft for having forgotten. He ought to be safe – this was hardly the time to stop and be questioned. Behind them, he could hear at least two of the guards chasing them enter the mouth of the alley, crashing through the rubbish in their haste and letting their armour deflect most of it away from them.

'Just keep up if you can. Are you hurt from that fall? It looked nasty. Not to mention the boots landing on you too.'

'I've had worse, it's nothing that will keep me from running. I could use a breather though – what about ducking out of the way up here and letting them pass?'

'No chance,' he replied. 'This goes straight along, no recesses or anything worth hiding in – they would stumble across us as easy as a snorthog snuffling out mushrooms on a tree stump. Besides, we must catch up – we're endlessly better off sticking as a group, and Cronto hasn't led us wrong yet.' He paused to think for a moment. 'Are you armed?'

'Just for my own personal protection, you know,' Skerrick replied, suspicious for the first time. 'Nothing significant, just my daggers.' He touched his thighs where they nestled, reassuring himself with their comforting presence, and again noticed the extravagant cutlass hanging from the man's belt.

'Probably not enough to fight with then, not if you want to win anyway. That's perhaps obvious enough anyway given their armour and ruddy great spears and whatever those other things of theirs are.' He sighed, a tough thing to do when breathing heavily during running.

'In my experience,' Skerrick puffed between breaths, 'it's always better to avoid the fight. It either ends up with you hurt or in the brown stuff because you've hurt them.' He considered a little more. 'Sometimes both.'

'Believe me, I don't want to be fighting them. I just want this to end without me being perforated for my troubles. I'm a baker for the gods' sake! This is absurd!' He was getting noticeably angry with the injustice, but was looking around for something to help them. The density of waste increased ahead of them before peaking in a great slope up at either side of the alley, separated by just a metre or two. Broken fruit crates, dung and other detritus of a busy city was gathered there. 'Come on, up here,' he said, waving Skerrick ahead of him. Skerrick looked back again to see four guards labouring along in their direction yet making reasonable progress.

Skerrick squeezed through the piles surrounding them and stopped on the other side. 'You aren't planning on taking them on in some heroic last stand, are you? I mean, look at me, I'm no brawler, but look at you – no offence, lad, but you're clearly not either.'

'Nope, just something to give us some breathing room,' he replied, and began pulling the heap to his left down and into the centre of the narrow alley, before doing the same with the remaining pile until the passage was loosely knee-high with rubbish. He left a gap so that the heap didn't directly lean up against the buildings. Drawing his cutlass, he placed the broad blade under his arm, the dragon's head pommel aimed at the barricade and on one wrecked wooden crate in particular. 'I just need to focus on my rage and frustration,' he mumbled, and after a momentary pause out spilled a jet of flame from the gaping mouth of his weapon's handle. He adjusted his aim back and forth, clumsily spraying the fire across as much of the waste as possible until it all roared with flames reaching up into the ever-increasing gloom. Sap boiled in some of the pieces of younger wood within the flames, hissing and spitting as it escaped into the atmosphere where it competed with the popping sounds of discarded fruit exploding due to the intense heat.

Skerrick stood with mouth agape. 'What in the world have you got there? What is this trickery?' he said with wonder. He didn't want to admit it, but he was terrified by the display – it was unlike anything he had ever seen before, something beyond what he thought was possible. He had seen his share of unusual talents in street performances aimed at parting passers-by with a coin for a few moments of entertainment, but this was something else entirely. Not bad for an apparent baker.

'Come on, we can still catch the rest – this should hold those guards or at least slow them down. No time to watch the pretty colours.'

'All right, no need to be a dick,' Skerrick muttered quietly. They continued down the remainder of the alley and Skerrick decided to try to learn a little more. It could only help his cause. 'How did you do that back there? It's one hell of a party trick. I could do with being able to do that myself.'

'Trick? It just...does it. I don't know how, I've only just discovered it myself. You saw it back at my bakery, surely? Or the after-effects at least.'

'Yes, of course, I just wondered how you do it. You can just do it when you like?'

'It seems so. I'm far from knowing its full capabilities though, as I said, it's new to me. What is your name anyway? I'm Harold Jenker. I don't remember you telling me yours.'

'I've kept myself to myself so far,' Skerrick said with a shrug. This was true of his general life, so it was not a lie per se. 'There hasn't seemed to be time.' This was also technically true. He assumed there was little to lose in using his real name now, in as deep as he was. 'My name is Roger Skerrick. Thank you for helping me back there – I don't think any of your friends were going to. I appreciate you taking the risk.'

'Friends would be the wrong word; I don't really know any of them. We've got to help each other out though, haven't we? The Dralcea Guard seem to have it in for us, the gods only know why. If we don't stick together, we're that much easier for them to pick off I'd say. Honestly, I've seen far too much of that already today and I want to make it at least until the end of the day without witnessing another instance.'

'Hear hear! Those blue-cloaked bastards have been after me for years for no good reason, and they never ask anything nicely. I've seen them take friends and acquaintances down and I for one have no intention of being another to fall to their brand of justice.'

'You've had encounters like this with them before? What is it you do? From what they've said, I didn't think any of our lot had ever really had any trouble with them.'

Skerrick knew he may have said the wrong thing here and tried to step back slightly. 'Well, you know, I'm an entrepreneur, and they don't appreciate the way I do things and the way I live.' Realising that sounded like vague nonsense, he opted for diverting the conversation instead. 'I don't think they've braved that fire back there, thankfully. Looks as if we're near the main street here too – do you know the way from here to this...temple?' Skerrick had to rack his brain to remember where Jenker had said they were heading. They were close to the end of the alley.

'Roughly, yes. If we go this way...' Jenker said.

Both men slowed down as they approached the junction with the main street. Poking his head out afforded Skerrick a good view and as he did so, his brief erstwhile companions raced past. His heart leapt at the sight; the main street must curve at such an angle to have slowed their companions down enough for Jenker and Skerrick's own progress to be equal to it as they cut across at an angle. Behind them followed the guards, still pursuing their targets but losing ground as they tired under the weight of their protective armour.

'My father once said something to me about his time in battle which I think might be relevant here. *"Attack the flank, shatter their formation"*. I rarely understood what he told me but I think in this instance I do,' Jenker said. To Skerrick's ear it sounded as if Jenker had an opportunity presenting itself to him, and he seemed emboldened by his success in blocking off the guards who gave pursuit.

Jenker waited for the right time and as the guards were just about to pass by the mouth of the alley he stepped out, unseen by them all in their haste. Cutlass drawn, he blasted the dragon's mouth-flame at them as he thought of those the group had needlessly lost over the course of the day and the fear they felt as inspiration to feed the fire. Their ornate blue cloaks, sashes and helmet crests were set alight in a hellish maelstrom that enveloped them all as he pivoted the flame around. Their world became a swirling red vortex, their only hope of surviving was to drop and try to roll and extinguish the flames; there was no time to try to remove their burning clothing. The acrid smell of flaming cloth and hair assaulted the nostrils of the two men lurking at the alley's mouth.

At a stroke, Jenker's actions had freed the others from their chase. Having stepped out into the open and so brazenly set a terrible fate upon these men must be testament to the man's character, Skerrick concluded – he had a caring enough soul to help when he had fallen, but now showed that he must carry some darker element inside to be able to attack in such a way.

'My word…' Skerrick was appalled at the sight of the guards before him – as wary of them as he was – suffering in such a manner as the flames ate at their unprotected skin amidst their helpless howls. Whilst grateful to the young man for saving his life, he wondered just what he was getting into with his association, and what these people were wanted for exactly. This one seemed dangerous enough despite his ordinary outward appearance. *No wonder they're trying to bring him in,* Skerrick thought to himself as bright orange and yellow light rippled across his pinched features in the diminishing daylight. *Criminals! Killers! They were fleeing for a reason. Who have I got tangled up with here?*

Jenker returned his cutlass to his belt and the pair moved off, anxious now to leave the scene of such savagery behind. It was an unpleasant business and only their desperation to escape had necessitated it. They quickly caught up to the other nine and Skerrick tried to ignore the horrific noises as they receded.

*

Wilfred had been the first to notice the sounds of anguish behind them and drew Cronto's attention to it, who halted the whole group as several had already turned to see what was going on. A set of figures frantically whirling greeted their vision in the unnatural glow of deliberately set fire, as if some supernatural performance were underway in the street for their amusement.

Cronto's heart suddenly felt heavy. He knew at once what had happened and felt responsible. Having uncovered and literally put that unnatural weapon in Jenker's hands, he had given him the tools to ruin his own conscience and turn a good man cruel. The knowledge that Jenker's actions had probably saved them all from a violent and possibly fatal confrontation did little to ease the burden. They were really committed to their course now; the actions taken at the bakery had been forced upon them when they were backed into a corner, but this instance was performed with the luxury of choice, and that was damning evidence against them all. All Cronto could do was try to ignore that fact for the moment. There was no time to consider his professional career as a judge and how this would ruin all that he had worked for. All that mattered was survival.

Cronto could make out a pair of men running toward him, one of whom appeared to be Jenker, the other he was not sure that he recognised. It was hard to tell with all the trauma that they had been experiencing; things were flashing by so quickly that it was difficult to retain every detail.

Jenker slowed down as he drew up to them, his companion closely behind.

'We dealt with that lot,' Jenker said, throwing his thumb back over his shoulder casually.

'Certainly looks that way.' Cronto was not impressed with the way Jenker disregarded the men's lives behind them so carelessly. Whilst aware that he was most probably trying to act tough now that he had the means to help them out, Cronto did not think Jenker really had the strength of will to stand up and do the right thing when it mattered, or if he was dispossessed of his cutlass. Time would tell on that matter. For now, all he could do was keep an eye on him and get them moving again. 'Let's continue,' he said blandly, which was all that he could muster in the face of the horror they had all witnessed, then ushered them all away from the abhorrent scene.

Chapter Twenty-seven – Reunions

At the shout they all just heard, Julius turned to see a small woman with long black hair had emerged from the temple and was marching over toward them standing around by the limits of the grounds, her floral gown swishing behind her as she went. The door she had exited through was still swinging shut as Julius watched; she must have spotted them immediately and noticed they looked out of place. From her purposeful stride he decided that she was probably quite used to dealing with those she deemed troublemakers, and he imagined the criteria for this was likely flimsy. *No doubt she will have more to say about our presence*, he thought. *Although, to be fair, we are visibly armed. She looks as if she relishes telling people off, probably thinking it earns some kind of advancement in the eyes of the deity these lot revere.*

'Are you here to *worship*?' she demanded sarcastically. 'The temple is *that* way!'

The woman did not seem at all intimidated by the assembled men, women and one imposing Ananeptide, which would have surprised Julius if not for his previous assessment of her. She drew herself up to her full – albeit limited – height and jabbed a thin finger at Fyrir, the nearest person to her. 'What is your business here, hmm?'

'We heard all about your unbelievable flowers here from our friend and we had to see them for ourselves,' Skula stepped up and said as earnestly as she could, clearly trying to improvise in this difficult situation. 'They certainly don't disappoint!'

'Our devotees do as good a job as they can with the time they are able to spend here,' the worshipper said. 'As you probably know, the art of growing our floral companions is central to our faith and consequently it is imperative that we do all we can to help them grow. What is your interest in them? Do you wish to join us here in our noble work?'

'Some use that would be,' muttered Julius to himself, though not quietly enough.

'As I thought. I'm sure our hardworking followers would like to hear your opinions.' She took a breath and shouted over her shoulder. 'HORACE! PIOTR!'

Two large men looked up from their tending of the flowerbeds and hedges and quickly made their way over to where the angry woman waited, arms crossed. One of the men, in a dirty pair of overalls, brought his garden fork with him whilst the other wore simple farming clothes and hefted a sizable hedge knife under his arm as he lumbered onwards. On arrival, Horace and Piotr stood at the ready, their tools held as improvised weapons. The threat was clear.

'Trespassers again, Edwina? They don't look like the usual teenagers that skulk around here trying not to be noticed,' the man with the hedge knife said.

'Yes, but they look like more trouble than teenagers. They're even carrying weapons openly!' the woman, evidently named Edwina, exclaimed; she must have spotted Grænn Klær on Ryx's back. 'Perhaps we should enlist some more help to evict this lot.' Edwina suddenly moved toward the front gates with surprising swiftness and purpose before peering out into the street. 'There must be a patrol coming past before too long. Guards! GUARDS! Trespassers over here!'

'Oh, damn,' Rundup said.

As Edwina shouted and waved, Julius craned his head and noted that she did succeed in catching the attention of a pair of guards who were some distance up the street, strolling along at a casual pace. Upon hearing the call aimed at them, they broke into a run to arrive at the disturbance quicker.

As Julius stood by, Ryx began to pull out Grænn Klær, presumably as a display of force to the two gardeners. 'Don't provoke them,' Julius hissed to her. 'They aren't our enemies. Save your ire for the bastards in blue – a couple of them are on their way now.'

'Fine, but we still need to get out of this jam. Better think of something quick,' Ryx replied.

'I'm trying!' Julius whispered back. 'We can't stay here,' he said to Nothro on his other side as he saw what was coming, subtly touching his friend's arm. 'Any ideas?'

Nothro quickly looked around toward where Edwina was still waving her arms as she leant over the gate, urging the approaching guards to hurry. 'Follow my lead,' he said quietly and in a low register to Julius. 'And move her, gently.'

Before Julius could reply, Nothro surged forward in one flowing movement as he skipped around the others with a grace that belied his massive size. Not giving the men chance to react effectively, he had reached Piotr and Horace and dealt with their improvised weapons in short order. Piotr's hedge knife was quickly sent spinning away with a precisely aimed punch to the long shaft of the tool, whilst Nothro grabbed the fork just behind the iron prongs and yanked it forward, wrenching it from Horace's grip before hurling it into the branches of one of the nearby trees where it became entangled and lodged fast.

The two men, neither of whom seemed to Julius to be the sharpest thorns on the rosebush, stood in shock at the events that had rapidly led to them being disarmed. Julius knew that although Nothro had his utility knife and gauntlets hidden in his fur-pouch, he doubted very much whether he would use them. Yes, these men had been a threat, but Nothro had taken away their means of harming anyone – and they were well within their rights to defend themselves against armed trespassers, which they could not deny that they were. 'Play nicely, Nothro,' Julius called out.

Nothro grunted and dropped to one knee, then whirled his right arm around in a low, wide sweep that took out the legs of the two men. They dropped onto their backs with a thud that caused them to gasp as the air was driven from their lungs with the force of impact.

'My older sibling's trick for ending fights,' Nothro said to Julius.

'Very effective it is too,' Julius replied, impressed. He then acted on Nothro's lead and bundled Edwina away from the gate – their only real escape route – and into a fairly soft-looking bush as gently as could reasonably be managed, given the circumstances. 'Quickly! They won't stay down for long,' Julius half-shouted as he waved the others toward the gate. Fyrir quickly opened it as Skula ushered Ryx and Rundup through urgently. Julius and Nothro followed without hesitation. In a blur borne of the drama they faced, they were through the exit and into the street seconds later.

'Stop right there and drop your weapons!' one of the two approaching guards shouted. They began to close the remaining hundred yards separating the two groups at a run.

'These lot are usually handing me somoni for yet another drink. I don't enjoy being the focus of their professional attention,' Fyrir said.

'Since you're familiar with their ilk, do you have any insight into them that could help us out here?' Rundup asked Fyrir.

Fyrir puffed his cheeks out. 'Only that they are fond of a strong drink of galumph, no, several strong galumphs after a shift, and sometimes a pie to help soak it up. Neither of which I have right now,' he said with a shrug.

'All right. We can't go back in there,' Rundup nodded to the temple gardens, 'so I suggest that if violence is to be avoided, we run very quickly that way,' he said, pointing in the opposite direction to the approaching guards.

There was no time for Julius or his companions to suggest any alternative options, so they broke into a run with their two pursuers close behind. Julius was grateful to see them only armed with the standard patrol spear favoured by the Dralcea Guard, and not the horrible, ranged weapons he had yet to learn the name of.

'Stop! Stop, you bastards! Running will only bring more charges against you!' one of the guards yelled after them.

'I'm not sure how much more running I can do,' Skula said as they were under way again. 'I thought it was a good idea bringing this bag of supplies from the pub, but it's weighing me down with all this dashing around.'

'We can't give up now, Mum,' Ryx said, as they ran. 'We've come too far. I'll help you along – or fight them if necessary.'

'No more fighting,' Skula insisted. Julius knew from her tone that she was ever the protective mother. He ran closer to her and scooped the bag from around her neck, taking its weight to help her focus on continuing forward.

A few hundred feet were traversed, and two corners turned as the group continued running without saying any further words to each other. What was there to say? A quiet despair was settling upon Julius, and he thought it must also be affecting the others. They had seemed to be on the cusp of making a breakthrough and so remarkably close to safety and escape. To have that ripped away was to have their very hope trampled upon.

At length they spotted another group heading toward them from the opposite direction, also in a hurry. Julius was the first to recognise the man heading up this group from afar; he wore a disc-shaped hat and loose robes, and it could only be one man. Molefi Cronto.

'Look, there! It's Cronto and the others! They were on their way to join us, we just beat them to the meeting point.' Julius slowed down as the others approached, who also looked as if they recognised their fellow survivors.

'What now though? We still have these two after us,' Rundup replied. Both groups had stopped and several people exchanged smiles, nods and comforting pats on the shoulder now that they were reunited.

Julius looked around to assess the situation and noticed that Jenker had spotted the pair of guards rapidly approaching. 'I have a little incentive for them to find another way to spend their afternoon,' Jenker said with a grim expression on his face.

Cronto looked pained, as if he could stand no more of this from the younger man. Cronto put himself between their pursuers and Jenker. 'You were always meant to inherit that weapon and it is only right that you now have it in your possession. It is a great tool, a piece of beautiful craftmanship in its own right and it contains more than a little mystery. Yet it also has the ability to make good men tempted into doing evil, even if they don't realise the way it is leading them at the time – and I fear that temptation might become all too enticing to you soon. Please, *please* consider my words carefully, Harold.'

Jenker stepped around Cronto without a word in reply. He drew his cutlass and stood ready as the guards closed in. The two approaching men slowed, eyeing the suddenly much larger crowd than the one they had begun chasing and looking increasingly nervous with every passing second. Jenker pointed the gleaming white dragon's head in their direction but tilted it downwards. Julius watched as Jenker performed this strange stance with an ornate-looking weapon he was not in possession of previously. *He looks angry and determined – nothing at all like the meek man he was earlier*, Julius thought. *No doubt it's fuelled by thoughts about all that these men's colleagues have done over the course of the day. I feel the same, but surely he's not going to stand up to them on his own?*

Jenker looked more and more frustrated and a little confused as he continued to point the pommel of his cutlass at the stone pathway ahead of the guards.

'Is he expecting something to happen by standing there with a fancy sword held the wrong way round?' Julius wondered aloud.

With the guards a mere fifteen feet away from now, Julius realised their best chance here stood in making the most of their superior numbers and he stepped forward intimidatingly, coming shoulder to shoulder with Jenker. The large figures of Nothro and another bulky man also stepped forward, evidently understanding Julius's intention. Others swiftly followed until the pair of guards had all seventeen people bearing down on them menacingly.

Being so close to this determined mob seemed to dissuade the guards to continue their pursuit. They looked at each other with wide eyes, then backed off slowly before turning tail and running for the nearest side street to escape.

'They came to their senses. It wasn't worth them risking their lives because some old bat started shrieking at them from a temple garden. Good for them,' Julius said.

'Good thinking taking the fight to them,' the large man who stepped up with Nothro said to Julius, offering his hand to shake. 'I'm Cedric Guyal.'

'Julius Dominguez, thanks for backing me up.'

'My pleasure. We're all in this together as far as I can see,' Cedric replied.

Julius felt Jenker jump beside him as Cronto gently placed a hand on Jenker's shoulder. He carefully put his cutlass away again and turned around. A wide smile split Cronto's face as he looked at Jenker. 'You made the correct decision there, my boy.'

Jenker smiled faintly in response. 'Actually I tried to make it act as it did before, but it wouldn't this time. I was going to direct it at the stones by their feet to scare them off. Clearly there is much more to this cutlass that needs to be worked out yet.'

'You wanted it to obey you, but it refused? Interesting. The important fact is that nobody was hurt this time,' Cronto said.

'I only want to protect us all, you understand. Those two looked like frightened little boys compared to some of those others that were after us. They seemed as ordinary as...well...me.' Jenker appeared a little sheepish at the admission.

'What are you talking about?' Julius asked, confused.

'We'll explain later. Those were probably new recruits on a simple patrol, unlike those others who looked to be seasoned professionals. You were right to exercise restraint there, intentionally or not. Now, where is Zhin?' Cronto looked around for the man who appeared knowledgeable of the area. 'Zhin!' he called out.

'I'm here,' Zhin replied, working his way through the crowd. 'The Temple of the Sun is up ahead, the way these lot came from in fact. We're close.'

'I see. Why are you coming this way? You were heading in the wrong direction. We were supposed to be meeting at the temple,' Cronto asked those who had branched off to go to the pub, plus their new addition, Fyrir.

'Yes, well, we weren't exactly welcomed at the temple,' Julius said. 'We waited there but were...uh...escorted out, I suppose you could say. Our Nothro here made it a little less forceful for us than it might have been, though.' Julius pointed vaguely in the direction they had come from. 'A woman took exception to us waiting in the temple gardens and called those two guards for help against us menaces. She had a few of her fellow worshippers there to kick us out too.'

'This is true, they did not appreciate our presence. I'm Fyrir Haþingvoð, Skula's husband and Ryx's father,' he introduced himself to those he was meeting for the first time. 'Did the guards turn on you all?' he said with astonishment.

'Sadly so, but for what reason we cannot fathom. We're all here now though – those of us that made it at least – so we will do what we can to stay safe together,' Cronto said, looking heartened that they had managed to reunite. 'For that matter, dark is falling. We must quit the city as soon as possible.'

'I certainly like the sound of leaving. This city has been nothing but trouble since we got here. Screw this place I say. Let's go.' Cedric spat the last few words.

'As much as I hate to say it, I think he's right. I can't think of anywhere we could hide where they wouldn't eventually find us, especially as a large group.' Fyrir shrugged.

'At least outside of the city and away from the Dralcea Guard we might stand a chance, even if it is harsh outside the walls,' Ryx put in her word at last.

'My sibling lives east of the city – they might provide us with temporary shelter,' Nothro said.

'I don't think there's any doubt about it being the best thing to do, if your family member wouldn't mind us visiting their house, Nothro? It gives us some direction at least. Let's get ourselves to the walls.' Cronto patted Zhin on the shoulder, who nodded and led the way toward the Eastern Gate that looked to be their only chance of escape from being hunted.

Chapter Twenty-eight – Choosing Loyalties

Janos tried not to sigh as he jogged around yet another corner before visually searching the side street, the Ejector he was told to bring remaining strapped to his back aside Hilde, unused. 'Nothing, again,' he grumbled. 'Are we really going to find this lot when we have virtually nothing to go on?' Doubts were certainly creeping into his mind.

He at least had the comfort of knowing that his fellow sergeants, along with their sections, were also busy searching. It was highly unlikely that Souo would get anywhere with his search – he would almost certainly keep stopping his contingent to catch his breath, something that his men would not grumble about. The other sergeants – Sluss, Tanbry, Disheart and Pelovir – were a different matter, although he would not begrudge his long-standing friend Tanbry the honour of dealing with these elusive foes. Janos would still obviously pick himself to be the one to tackle the interlopers, were it his choice to make.

Janos gave a large huff as he pondered on this, knowing the facts were that he had no say in how it would go. All he could do was look for the time being. 'At least the men assigned to my command today are performing well, unlike some of those we've taken on recently,' Janos muttered. 'Some of them couldn't find their arse if they were sat on it.' They were covering the ground effectively and with vigour, and for the moment he could ask nothing more of them. Recruit Paul Gantle had been showing himself to be particularly enthusiastic in his endeavours and showed good initiative. *That lad is going to go far*, Janos decided, *sooner rather than later.*

After yet another predictably empty alley, containing nothing more than a few wandering mlem-mlems picking through the litter and a loitering Crinochin adult who scrabbled away into a hiding place under his scrutiny, Janos found his earlier enthusiasm all but evaporate. 'This could turn into a long day,' he sighed. 'Not what I had planned for my day off.'

The clear, cool air at surface level had blown away much of the stuffiness inside Janos's head caused by his drinking the previous night and he now felt much fresher, although chilly. It had been difficult to think ahead with much clarity as the hangover made his temples throb and tightened his stomach, and although those symptoms had now mostly subsided it still felt as though he had a mouthful of sand. What he wouldn't give for a nice cool drink right at that moment to flush the dry feeling away.

Janos moved on to the next street over, another narrow one, when one of his newer recruits came running up to him, his face flushed with exertion.

'Sergeant, sergeant!' the recruit said excitedly.

'What is it,' Janos searched for the young man's name for a second before it surfaced in his mind, 'Verrin? Report, recruit.'

'Sir, I came as quickly as I could. We might have spotted the suspects nearby. Recruit Gantle sent me to find you whilst he keeps track of them – I can lead you back to where he is,' Verrin said.

Gantle sent you? He's delegating now, Janos thought. *Good for him, showing some leadership.* 'Where? What makes you think they're the ones we're after?'

Verrin looked nervous as he was questioned further. 'They're a big group, sir...and some are armed. They were making their way down Slate Street at a fair pace. Looked very suspicious. Got to be them.'

'Got to be, eh? Stake your wages on it?' Janos asked. Verrin looked even more perturbed, as if he had overstepped the mark by being so forward, but did not reply. Janos didn't think the recruit realised he was joking. 'You're probably right though. Slate Street...they must be making for the Eastern Gate, thinking they can slip away from our reach. Well, we aren't going to let them. Lead the way.'

Recruit Verrin nodded and set off back the way he had come at a jog. As they went, Janos gave a coded whistle to let his other men nearby know to come after the source of the sound and follow him; a high note, two lower notes and then the same high note again. Those guards – Hamza, Waucus, Goshin and Alapich, a mix of guards and recruits – dutifully gave up their own searches and tagged on behind their commander and colleague.

They eventually reached the spot where Gantle had been and Verrin then quickly followed the logical course and found his fellow recruit a few streets away, crouching in the shadows as he subtly kept watch on the progress of the bizarre-looking group. As they approached, Janos ordered the guards under his command to stay back around the corner, keeping them out of sight. The increased likelihood of a group of guards being spotted was not a risk that Janos would take – he would call them forward when he decided to make his move, not have his hand forced.

Gantle glanced behind him as he heard the heavy tread of his companion's boots and stood up to address his sergeant who approached on his own. 'Sergeant Boltfoot, I believe this is who we're looking for. They fit the description you relayed to us, sir.'

'Indeed, recruit. Well done for spotting and tracking them. It looks almost certain that they're heading for the Eastern Gate and presumably from there, back out to whatever dump of an exile settlement they came from.'

'Do you think they are exiles, sir?'

'Must be. Who else would have an axe to grind with the city? It's the only conclusion that makes sense, especially if they're trying to leave Dralcea again now.'

'They're coming down the road now, sir. They should cross at the junction if they maintain their current course.'

Janos gently pushed Gantle back and out of the way so that he could flatten himself against the wall at the corner of the street and peer out. He caught sight of the group on their way down the road, true to Gantle's projections, and the breath caught in his throat. He saw a variety of figures and their diversity baffled him; a man in an elaborate high-collared jacket, a man in traditional Olrofi clothing, a huge Ananeptide padding along amongst others – it was impossible to see all of those making up the crowd. He also saw a head of long blonde hair belonging to a woman, a shorter blonde haircut of a man roughly his own age, and a braid of strikingly red hair belonging to a young woman.

The latter three belonged to his friends, the Haþingvoðs.

Janos was stunned. He could only stare, not believing his eyes that these could be the people he saw almost every night in their tavern, those whom he had known for so many years. This family who had always been so welcoming to himself and all the other guards who had come through their well-worn wooden door over the years, regular customers and those who stopped by infrequently, or even just once; not all who visited found The Crimson Duck as charming as Janos did. Fyrir and Skula had become like an extension of Janos's own family years before, and when Ryx had arrived he had shared in their joy. The situation was simply unfathomable. *How could they have possibly been involved in the attack at the Promontory*? Tanbry's earlier words of doubt returned to the forefront of Janos's mind before Gantle interrupted his line of thinking.

'That's them all right, sir, I've kept track of them. They look a real mixed bunch, for sure. Much better turned out than I expected too, but who knows how these outlaws usually dress.'

'Yes, looks like it...' was all Janos could manage to say as his mind raced through the ramifications of what he had seen and what he should do next. His orders were clear; stop those responsible at all costs, preferably with violence to make an example of them. There were too many in this group to simply arrest and bring in with the handful of men at his disposal – that simply could not be achieved safely since they outnumbered his squad more than two to one. His men had been amped up with the prospect of a fight and he doubted they would be willing to just forget that and walk away. Janos had always respected the strict hierarchy of the Dralcea Guard and had never before questioned an order, but for the very first time, he simply couldn't countenance following his orders and initiating an attack on his friends, who he was convinced were innocent. He was caught in a quandary and his mind reeled with the permutations of the choice facing him.

'Sir? What is our move? We could send a runner to summon one of the other sergeants and his men before we attack, or perhaps strike out ourselves and try to surround them?' Gantle said urgently. 'We will have to move around again quickly to stay parallel with their course and keep them in sight. We can't lose them, sir.'

'Lad, there has been a mistake. This isn't right.' Janos suddenly felt that this matter took on a different level of authority than the Dralcea Guard should be dispensing and turned to look at his subordinate full in the face. 'These people aren't our enemy,' he said, not as a sergeant now but as a citizen.

'*Of course they are our enemy*!' Gantle exploded quietly, extremely animated but keeping his voice down to remain hidden. 'Those people *murdered* our colleagues in cold blood! They cut them down with no hesitation at all just to satisfy their selfish agenda, whatever that may be. It is *our duty* to stop them,' he punctuated with a jab of his finger. 'If we don't act, we're as bad as they are, and I won't let that happen, sir.'

'You forget yourself, recruit.' Janos fought to ease the fury building inside him; he knew that if he lost control and let his rage take over, his command would be compromised. 'You do not decide our course of action. Stay here, Recruit Gantle. That's an order.'

'An order – to not act, when we've been specifically briefed to do the opposite? You must be mad. You know what needs to happen, and quickly, before they get away. There is no time for this delay, sir.'

'Mad?' Janos chuckled without humour. 'Not mad, boy. Experienced. I've been following orders for most of my life and I know when they stink – this is one of those occasions. Somebody has got it wrong, Vilipas most probably, the slimy turd. Those people there are no killers, I can guarantee that. And if we go after them, *we* will be the ones committing the crime. So, you are not to go after them. I will deal with the consequences.'

'Like hell I will,' Gantle said, and stepped forward to enter the street after the fleeing group. Janos was too quick for the younger man and slammed an open hand on his breastplate, swirling Gantle around with one strong-armed move to trap him against the wall with a dull thud. Gantle dropped the Ejector he had been holding ready which clattered to the dusty floor of the alley, and looked up at the much burlier, older man in surprise, the friendly demeanour when he had previously encountered him in The Crimson Duck completely forgotten. After a moment he regained his composure. 'You aren't fit to command, sir,' Gantle said with renewed confidence into Janos's uncomfortably close face. 'I'm taking over from here.'

Janos shoved Gantle against the wall anew using the flat of his hand in his anger. 'Don't be stupid, lad. You have such potential, that much you have shown already, but if you try to subvert the order of authority here you will be finished. I know you're thinking you can somehow pull this off and become a hero, gain a rapid promotion probably, become the darling of the Dralcea Guard, but it doesn't work like that. You will rise through the ranks, that is already obvious, but you can't do this on your own. Don't ruin your chances for the future, Paul. It's not worth it.' Janos removed his hand and stepped back. 'Believe me, take your time and use your head as I did – you will get there eventually. Frankly, you've got much more between the ears than I have so it should take you a fraction of the time. The Dralcea Guard needs men like you, with initiative and the bollocks to put it into action – but now is not the time to go running off dramatically to play the hero in the way you've heard the skalds tell of.'

'You're not the legendary sergeant that they make you out to be, Boltfoot. You've gone soft. I will do what is right – on my own, if necessary.' With that, Gantle lunged down to retrieve his Ejector from the ground.

Janos had been in enough brawls and merciless street fights to know what Gantle intended. He instinctively reached down with his right hand for the knife strapped to his left thigh and quickly drew it in one smooth motion. In the same time Gantle had picked up the fallen Ejector and was bringing it round to point at Janos, point-blank. The sergeant managed to get his left hand under the swing of the weapon and pushed upwards, forcing the Sweat of Hephaestus-laden chamber at the tip safely over his head, and the pair struggled briefly. Gantle's face was all grimace as he realised he had been foiled, and tried to smash his Ejector down onto Janos's head.

Janos reacted instinctively to defend himself and whipped his knife up, then lanced it down below Gantle's left shoulder, slicing into the flesh at an angle where it remained without Janos's intervention. Gantle's eyes opened wide in shock as he gibbered a series of half-formed words, none of which Janos could make out.

Janos pulled his knife out, aghast at what he had done. It had been a natural reaction to preserve himself in the face of danger, but he felt sick for having done it, nonetheless. His shoulders slumped as he released his grip on the younger man. 'It didn't need to be this way,' he said to himself as much as Gantle, the sadness in his voice a rare event as he wiped the stained knife on his leg before returning it to its sheath. Janos stepped back as Gantle spluttered wetly and made a distressing choking sound before falling back against the wall and sliding down it until he half-sat, half-lay slumped against the wall and bled profusely. Gantle's eyes never left Janos the entire time.

Janos knew he had little time now. He had acted on his own instincts, but they ran counter to the will of the higher ranks of the Dralcea Guard and he would not get away with this indiscretion now that he had harmed one of the men under his command. He would not be able to explain away the events that had just occurred – the men stationed just around the corner would be sure to work out what had happened and would likely make that known for fear of being the next victim of such an act whilst under Janos's command. They would not accept the necessity of his actions.

He had trusted that Skula, Fyrir and Ryx could not have been involved in the earlier attack at the Promontory – now he had no choice but to use that same trust and go after them to discover the truth. It was also his only recourse to save himself from being stripped of his job in the best-case scenario, or else sentenced to die which was also a possibility if he was caught. As a man who had always wielded his authority with a casual ease since it came so naturally to him, it was difficult indeed to be forced into this position where he had little to no control and had been compelled to act in such a devastating way.

'I've failed my men, and, what's worse, cut short the life of one of the most promising newcomers to the Dralcea Guard in many years,' Janos whispered, aghast at what he had done.

The realisation of it all came crashing down onto him in an avalanche of grief and shame. Janos made Gantle apply pressure to the horrible wound with the recruit's own sash to help stem the bleeding, then called his men waiting around the corner so that they would come to tend to their fallen comrade. He gritted his teeth and ran, head down, after the group who had disappeared down the gloomy road.

Chapter Twenty-nine – The Eastern Gate

Julius watched as Zhin Xofia got as close as he could to the street adjacent to the Eastern Gate without becoming too noticeable from afar. Zhin then motioned for the others, who followed a few feet behind in a cluster, to stay where they were. The cover provided by the buildings he was sticking closely to the side of petered out as they neared the gate, before a large, paved area stretched the remaining distance between them and escape. It would be extremely difficult for them to cross this open area without arousing suspicion, especially if they attempted to cross in their entirety, as they had been travelling so far. Zhin surveyed the surroundings a little more before turning back a few paces.

Julius took the opportunity to lean on a wall and rest a little while he could. Nothro crouched down next to him, trying to make himself less conspicuous. Molefi Cronto was close by also, still trying to direct the effort to escape wherever he could. Zhin addressed Julius and those nearest the front who seemed to be contributing and making decisions whilst the others, more happily led or simply too scared to speak up, stayed back and attempted to hide for the moment.

'The Eastern Gate is across the square there, it's perhaps fifty feet of open ground. It's not as simple as that though. Although we're all technically free to come and go through the entrance as we please, there is the small matter of the guards manning the gate itself. They're a more specialised subdivision of the guard rank, known sensibly enough as gate guards. There are four of them on the ground on our nearest side and there could be more on the far side. I also saw one atop each of the redoubts – those storey-high walls flanking the passageway. Each one must enjoy an unparalleled viewpoint of the square and the passage through to the outside world. Looks as if there are guards currently patrolling way up on the top walls, too – I spotted dark shapes moving against the light backdrop of the sky behind them.'

Julius had been keeping watch from his resting place and spotted some of those guards Zhin mentioned who were in view. 'There are quite a few of them over there. We must assume that they've been told to look out for us, too. They'll be on high alert for sure.'

'Presumably, yes. They are some of the more unusual guards in the city too, in terms of kit and training if nothing else,' Zhin said. 'They use bows to discourage any invaders from getting close enough to have to fight face-to-face – it's only them and a limited number of officially sanctioned hunters who go out into the countryside who are allowed to use bows. Somebody has to help feed the population, after all. These gate guards are specially picked and trained to use bows effectively. This experience puts them a half-step closer to achieving the rank of sergeant, too.'

'How do you know all that?' Cronto asked.

'I've seen them practicing on the outskirts with targets to simulate what they would have to do in the event of a real attack on the gates,' Zhin shrugged. 'That's what it looked like at least.'

'Well it's lovely to know that they can kill us before we get close, even if they don't have those weapons we saw earlier,' Julius said. 'So, what do we do about it?'

'The light is fading. Could we wait for night to fall and make a break for it, so they can't aim at us so easily?' Cronto ventured.

'There's still the actual gate to get through if it isn't already open. The light won't make any difference to that if it is closed,' Nothro said.

'Pretty sure they'll close it up for the night once it gets dark. No more traders to come in, so they will shut up shop,' Ryx chipped in.

'I don't think waiting is a good idea either – what happens if another patrol comes by and finds us in the meantime? We'd be stuck between them and the garrison in the gatehouse, and I wouldn't put any money on us succeeding in that situation,' Fyrir said as he came forward to add his own input. 'I fought at a couple of the gates as a citizen during the Great Border Raid Retaliation and I can tell you that they aren't easy to get through if they don't want you to pass. That attack on the gates by exiles only happened at all because they had come up with a sophisticated plan that involved scores of them working in unison and was executed very carefully. I daresay we don't have the same resources at all, nor the vicious intentions.'

'You fought at the gates? Maybe you have some information we could use. Anything that could give us an advantage,' Cronto suggested.

'Not as a guard, and obviously we were looking out, not inwards. They had everything very well drilled though, that was obvious – it's all designed to make it extremely difficult for the enemy to gain any ground,' Fyrir said. 'We would have to ensure the gate was open already or we wouldn't stand a chance. Beyond that? Distraction could work I suppose, but we would still have to run and hope for the best.'

'Those up on the walls must have an excellent view, and shot, down into the passage we'd have to take. I don't fancy our chances,' Julius said. 'And it's a fair run through that walkway by the look of it. It would have to be one hell of a distraction. Any suggestions, anyone?' he asked the group in general.

Jenker stepped up at this point. 'I could use this,' he said, patting the sword hanging at his waist. 'I could take on the ones on the walls, and—'

'And what exactly? You're not a warrior, or even a guard. What was it you do again?'

'I'm...I run a bakery.'

'A baker! So you don't know how to use that cutlass, and if you try using it against them they will very rapidly target you with their bows. You won't stand a chance on your own, so stop trying to play the hero. Enough people have died unnecessarily today,' Julius said, not knowing the ability Jenker now possessed with his inherited cutlass. He assumed that the man had intended to run headlong into the gate guards swinging his weapon wildly, which would only end in the baker's violent death.

Jenker fell silent and looked at the ground. 'I'm just trying to help,' he said meekly, the earlier traces of confidence gone. 'Somebody has to do something. I'm not intending to put myself in harm's way for nothing.'

'Of course, I didn't mean to hurt your pride. It's just there must be a better way, which we need to establish pretty quickly.'

Cronto intervened. 'Now, now. All suggestions are welcome.' He turned to Jenker and put a hand on his arm. 'We need to try something a little more peaceful in this instance, you understand.' Jenker nodded, though seemed to shrink further back into himself.

'Any other ideas then?' Julius asked, looking around at the others.

Nobody came forward this time, but many of those huddled in the shadows looked at each other as if willing them to come up with a plan. Julius saw Wilfred let his jumping spider, Zebedee, out of the box hanging around his neck and cupped him in his unsteady hands as he started jabbering. 'There's no way to get out, the guards will catch us. We're doomed...'

His words started to spread to some of those around him who already looked nervous and Wilfred seemed to spark panic in a few of them. An uneasy shifting began in the crowd and Julius feared they might break and run for it, which would lead to them being exposed and almost certainly sealing their fate.

Cronto acted first. 'Wilfred, put your...friend there back. You need to focus on what is ahead, and he needs you to look after him to the best of your ability. Do you understand?'

Wilfred looked up, his eyes full of tension; he looked only just in control of his senses. He nodded suddenly. 'Yes. I'll try.' As Zebedee restlessly jittered in short, mechanical circles like the second hand of a clock, Wilfred gently tipped him back into his resting place in his box before closing the lid reverentially and letting it slip back inside his shirt.

'Good man,' Cronto said.

'I have something that might help,' Rundup said quietly. 'I think distraction might be the best course of action. It's not guaranteed though – anything could happen.'

'That pretty well sums today up, mate,' Julius said grimly. 'What is it?'

Rundup put his chest of belongings down and undid the latches, then took out a palm-sized object with each hand. 'Not it. They.'

He showed the group the dried pepper-like fruits, both with a stubby point at the bottom and a short stump of stalk protruding from the top. Each had been swaddled in a protective wrap of dried grasses to safeguard against breakage; the drying process made them brittle and they needed the protection. In this case one of the fruits was a bright yellow colour whilst the other was vivid purple with a mottled whitish band near the top where the stem lay.

'I use these dustpeppers in my act – they're carefully dried, prepared and filled with a mix of coloured powders. When broken they release a cloud of smoke that I use on-stage to mask my exit. They could be utilised here, provided we are organised enough to make best use of the cover.'

'How do they work? I'm afraid I am unfamiliar with what it is that you do, my friend,' Cronto replied.

'They contain delicate chambers within their skin – separate segments which alternate between being empty and being filled with the dyed powder. I break the skin, usually by dropping them forcefully on the floor, then the membranes separating the chambers break and the powder rushes out and fills the air. If I could throw them accurately enough into their midst...' he shrugged. 'It might just obscure them enough to let us by.'

'They could provide us with a facade...do you have a few of those dustpeppers with you?' Cronto asked.

'All the ones I have recently dried and prepared, which amounts to a reasonable number, yes.'

'Then you might just be able to save us,' Cronto said, clapping Rundup on the shoulder slightly awkwardly due to their height difference.

All agreed that it was necessary to move as quickly as possible if they were to stand any chance of success. There was little doubt that once they started to move, everyone would be in a rush to get it over with and – if all went to plan – leave harm's way. The variables they could not control were precisely how long their cover would last and exactly where Rundup's thrown projectiles would hit. They mostly had faith in his abilities from what he had told them of his skills, but only Skula and Fyrir had seen them fully in action; they at least knew exactly what he was capable of.

*

Their vague plan settled – it was drawn up in a hurry, as they had no time to waste – Rundup folded down his oversized collar and patted dust gathered from the street onto his bright clothes to attract less attention. He was pivotal to their success and so he would venture out into the open space before the gate first. The rest would spread out a little to lessen their own conspicuousness as they left the relative safety of the street's mouth, with the more confident near the fringes to shepherd them all along.

Rundup took a big breath and strode from cover, walking quickly despite his best efforts to appear casual. He had taken two more of his dustpeppers and stashed them inside his jacket to complement the first two he held, one in each hand. It was agreed that he would not look back to see the others making their move as it would look too suspicious if they were being observed. For his part, Rundup tried to keep his gaze level as he approached the gate. He had already picked the points he would target; to look at them again now, before he reached the appropriate distance at which he could throw his fruits, would only increase the chance of failure should he be spotted and challenged.

He was however able to see the lettering carved into the stone of the gate above him. It read:

AN ISLAND OF SANCTUARY IN THE RAVAGING, HOSTILE SEA.

Rundup tried to dismiss the phrase. *That doesn't seem to be true anymore,* he thought sadly.

On reaching his mark, Rundup did not hesitate. He had already roughly gauged the distance from his earlier observation and so threw the dustpepper in his left hand with his best effort, aiming at the left of the upper walkway that ran above the gate itself, meaning to obscure the view of those gate guards with the best vantage point.

It was a miss.

The object travelled more efficiently through the air than he had anticipated, and his eagerness had lent a little extra force to his throw. It sailed harmlessly over the top walls, out of the city and out of sight. Rundup was sure he must have unintentionally caught the attention of the gate guard situated on the walkway. No doubt they would be used to occasionally having rotten vegetables or something even less pleasant and worse smelling thrown at them by street urchins or idlers, and would likely now be looking for the responsible party.

Rundup acknowledged his miss but did not pause to lament the failure. Instead, he quickly adjusted and, switching the dustpepper from his right hand to his dominant left, threw the second projectile at the upper right of the walkway.

He learned from the first shot and compensated well. The brittle fruit struck the stone flagstones of the high walkway where it splintered apart, and bright yellow powder gushed forth in a cloud that rapidly expanded outwards. The gate guards nearby were quickly lost from Rundup's view thanks to being surrounded by a dense fog that would likely confuse and terrify them in equal measure. One of those obscured began to yell instructions and curses to the other men to find the culprit.

Before his second shot had landed, Rundup had plucked the remaining two dustpeppers from inside his jacket and threw them both at the same time, his weaker right arm capable of making the simpler, shorter throw straight in front of him. His peripheral vision noticed the billowing cloud at the top of the gate and his heart lifted at the sight, then saw his lower throws strike their marks by the redoubts that flanked the passage. More yellow powder filled the right side at ground level, whilst a green fog enveloped the left as a chlorophyll-tinted flour emerged from that broken dustpepper.

Rundup heard the bellowing from above and finally risked a backward glance. His fellow refugees had seen the plan beginning to be enacted and all sixteen were on their way toward him at a sprint. His position, standing where he was in the centre of the plaza and ahead of the passageway, marked the point they would go straight forward from so that they wouldn't become disoriented and end up going in the wrong direction. None knew how long the cover would last, or if it would even be enough to see them through. Some of the more inquisitive citizens present in the area stopped to stare in wonder at the coloured clouds obscuring the gate as they went about their business – the more cautious simply fled away from it, fearing trouble and being wrongly caught up in the strong-arm response that would inevitably follow from the Dralcea Guard. Fortunately, no bystanders got in the way of the group running for their lives.

The first arrows started whistling out unannounced from the unseen interior of the powdery stormclouds and striking the cobbles around the survivors as they ran onwards.

Chapter Thirty – Chaos in the Cloud

The shots were wild and panicky and must have been fired blindly into the cloud of obscuring fog. Julius assumed that the gate guards would have little idea what was befalling them, and that they were in full fight mode in response – flight was not an option, since they were pinned in place by being unable to see more than a foot or so in front of them. Those factors did not make the arrows flying toward himself and the fleeing group any less deadly, however.

Most of the arrows clattered harmlessly to the cobbles of the square, bouncing along a little way before eventually running out of momentum. Some arrows, fired at a sharper downward angle than most, were unable to withstand the force and the thin wooden shafts shattered when the iron heads struck the solid stone pavement.

Fear urged those fleeing onward, although mercifully none were struck by the missiles as they neared the mouth of the passageway that would lead them to relative safety. The firing stopped, perhaps discouraged by not hearing any screams of pain, Julius thought. He came close to Rundup's forward position and the tall man moved forward carefully enough to still be seen so they could follow his lead.

Nothro was just ahead of Julius and had donned his steel gauntlets in preparation for whatever might imminently happen, and he now headed up the mass of humans. Julius readied himself for the part he was to play, wondering briefly what he had been thinking volunteering himself. *Too late now, the wheels are in motion*. Once Nothro was near enough to the redoubt on his left, he motioned to Cedric Guyal, who followed close behind. The human allowed the Ananeptide to grab his waist and swing Cedric up onto the redoubt heavily, but succeeding in effectively putting the man onto higher ground.

Julius was relieved to see that Cedric rode the clumsy assistance well, not least because he would imminently be treated in the same way, and then Cedric straightened up, brandishing the spear he had taken from one of the fallen guards back at Jenker's bakery. He stalked carefully along the walkway, ready to take on any gate guard that waited there for him. Julius joined Nothro, moved over to the end of the right-hand redoubt and let himself be unceremoniously thrown onto the raised protrusion from the gatehouse. Julius did the same as Cedric opposite him, cautiously moving forward with his retrieved work-knife in hand. It was not much of a weapon, but it would have to do.

*

The gate guard's view rapidly diminished as the coloured clouds below him blossomed outwards in all directions. There was also one spreading quickly along the walkway to his left, shrouding it from view.

He had never been so confused.

The training he had been given over the previous two years had not prepared him for this. He had learnt to use his bow quickly enough, and even gained some proficiency with it after a few months of practicing when he had chance. He knew to keep watch over the approaches to the city and being a gate guard, this had been simple enough – you just look in one direction, patrolling up and down the top of the walls. Exiles would be easy to spot; they would be the ones without carts of goods to sell, dressed scruffily and wielding vicious weapons with which to hack innocent citizens to pieces. At least, that is what he had been told.

Clearly, this was a different scenario altogether; the object hurled up at him, and narrowly missing his head, had originated inside the city. This was not so unusual in itself, but usually it would be something rotten hitting the walls. He had never seen anything thrown so far and high, nor that had an effect such as this. Something was amiss. What was it he had been told by that runner earlier? Oh, that was it. Some miscreants had attacked the Promontory. He should be outraged about that, he supposed, but he did not see much of the place as he was always on duty at one of the gates. They failed to give much detail to him either, so the information was of limited use. Still, he had a job to do here, and he would perform it to the best of his abilities.

He could not see much, and his colleague over the way from him would be able to see absolutely sod all, but maybe his men down at ground level could. At least, he hoped so.

'Guards! Fire on the attackers in the square!' he yelled down to them. After thinking for a moment, he added, 'Just do your best!' He then lent his own arrows to the ragged barrage which had already begun, aiming purposefully further out than his men would – or so he hoped, anyway.

After loosing half a dozen arrows into the void in quick succession, he stopped. There was no way of knowing if he was being in any way effective. He could not see a damn thing and heard nothing either, denying him any feedback.

The man sighed in frustration and stared down at the billowing yellow and green haze below him for a few moments, hoping to get a glimpse of something that would enable him to make an informed decision on his next course of action. The noise of arrows striking cobbles far below slackened before it stopped entirely. His men had obviously come to the same conclusion as he had and ceased firing as they were unable to see enough to warrant continuing.

If these attackers got away – if indeed that is what they were, and he was not going to afford them the benefit of the doubt – then it would be his neck on the line. His blood boiled with the impotence he felt at being unable to control his own future. He fitted another arrow to his bowstring, the nock making a satisfying *click* noise as he did so, then angrily fired downwards as his frustration got the better of him before he could calm himself. This last arrow was shot closer to the gate than all his previous attempts.

He stepped back, trying to calm himself down. As it stood, he could do no more.

*

Following the way Rundup had gone, Fyrir was just able to see his outline through the spreading, consuming smokescreen. Nothro was also useful for keeping track of the direction they should head, owing to his size, and the Ananeptide was keeping pace with Rundup. He seemed to be powering forward at pace to be as quick as possible without leaving behind his friend Julius, and the bulky Cedric was also inside Nothro's orbit.

Fyrir held the guard's spear that Ryx had liberated in his clammy hands as he ran on. He was keeping ahead of his wife Skula, unarmed as she was, bar the large meat cleaver she had brought with her from the pub's kitchen which remained tucked away out of sight. He intended to keep her out of harm's way so she would never have to use her culinary tool.

He had intended to do the same for his daughter, Ryx, but enacting that was a different matter. She had her inheritance now, the macuahuitl which had finally passed to her in this time of need, and she now had Grænn Klær drawn and ready. Ryx had refused to hide behind her father for protection and instead strode beside him confidently. Whilst naturally fearful of anything happening to her, Fyrir also knew that anyone getting in her way was in for one hell of a fight. Fyrir had every confidence in her coming out on top in such a scenario.

Arrows began to whistle and clatter toward them all and Fyrir felt a different kind of fear altogether – that of the indiscriminate violence that could strike anyone down at any moment, and which you were powerless to avoid. He had thankfully not felt such an emotion for many years, but it all came rushing back in an instant. There was nothing to do but run. He did his best to continue in the right direction as accurately as he could, given extra speed by his fear.

Fyrir saw Nothro help Cedric and then Julius up onto the high redoubts, one on either side, and they at least appeared to be successful in ignoring the rain of arrows. Glancing back, he saw a couple of the other more confident people, Cronto and Zhin included, corralling the rest and making sure they made best speed forward. A slim man with thinning hair seemed to be glancing around particularly nervously from near the edges of the group and looked as if he might bolt in a different direction at any moment. He held firm though and continued onwards with the rest.

One short young man near the rear seemed too nervous for his own good and through the fog Fyrir only just managed to see him trip and fall, sprawling on the stones in a shocked heap. The others were too busy guiding the group to stop and help him, and he disappeared so quickly that they might not have noticed him drop at all. In a flash, Fyrir was over at his side and helping him back to his feet. He didn't like to let his wife and daughter get too far ahead without him but he wasn't able to simply ignore the young man in distress – although he hadn't personally been through the initial trauma that the others had, he had seen enough since to bond them in kinship. He did not know the man's name, but they were a group now. None would be left behind or deemed less worthy of help.

The hail of arrows noticeably slackened and then stopped completely.

Fyrir got him to his feet, gave a smile and with a firm hand on the lad's back steered him urgently on after the rest. He found himself at the rear of the pack now – the others having already passed by – and not wanting to be left behind, Fyrir followed them as quickly as he could. The idea of being permanently separated from his beloved wife and daughter was too much to contemplate and the mere thought of it felt as though it clawed at his guts.

Fyrir was momentarily aware of a faint whistling sound before he was struck to the ground as if punched down by the unseen fist of an angry god. For a few seconds he lay stunned before the piercing agony hit him and he gasped deep, cold breaths with the suddenness of it. The arrow had driven down into his shoulder deeply and was firmly lodged there. With difficulty he got back up using only his uninjured arm and tried to retrieve his dropped spear, which he accomplished, but only with much reduced movement in his right arm. He endured more horrible stabs of pain with every muscle contraction.

Fyrir staggered after the others, slightly dizzy with the pain, and noticed the young man he had helped standing a few feet away, staring at him in horror and seemingly unsure what to do to help. Catching up was Fyrir's priority now – getting back to his family. He had to protect them. Although, he conceded mentally, he was going to be restricted in how much protecting he could do now.

Before he got too far, however, another figure appeared alongside his fellow escapee and grabbed the young man by the wrist. A member of the Dralcea Guard manning the gate, or one on regular patrol passing by and deciding to interfere, Fyrir couldn't tell in the haze. It was the glimpses of shining armour that gave him away, otherwise he might have mistaken the much taller man for one of their group.

Fyrir lurched forward faster to intervene as the guard yelled and grappled with his catch. 'Just what do you think yer playing at, eh? Playing tricks on us lot who're here to look after you all,' Fyrir heard the guard shouting whilst receiving nothing but panicked jabbering in response.

The youth was held fast by his wrist and could not twist away. The guard continued to question him and began to lower his spear towards the lad's unprotected body. 'Let him go!' Fyrir shouted before he could close the distance. 'He hasn't done anything!'

Fyrir's shouting caught the guard's attention, and the sight of the arrow shaft sticking almost vertically up from his shoulder now kept the man's eyes locked on him. Fyrir drew closer, trying to interject himself, able to see more clearly all the time. He looked to the young man and saw his free hand scrabble desperately at his shirt, then draw a small box on a chain out from within its folds.

With the guard distracted, the youth fumbled the box open and brandished it at his captor. A tiny form sprang from the box's interior and directly into the guard's exposed and unprepared face. Fyrir suddenly realised what it was – the jumping spider the lad had been nervously playing with before they had come up with their impromptu plan.

The guard shrieked and let go of both the youth and his spear as he succumbed to blind panic himself. The spider had landed square on an eyeball and proceeded to jump around the guard's face, avoiding the frantic slaps attempting to crush the small beast. The man spun crazily, arms flailing and legs kicking as primal fear overtook him, and he stumbled to the ground as a gibbering wreck.

Seeing the guard overcome in this way seemed to calm his young charge, and Fyrir watched as the spider leapt onto the cobbles. 'Come back, Zebedee,' the young man said, and scooped the spider back into its protective box before tucking it back into his shirt. The guard seemed thoroughly incapacitated to Fyrir, even with the removal of the spider from his vicinity; he continued to writhe, seemingly still convinced that he was being crawled upon. Fyrir was simply happy to have the youth freed without his overt intervention, impeded as he was. The pair exchanged a look before running after Fyrir's family and the others, keen to regroup.

*

Cronto jogged on with the twelve others loosely around him, lending them some of the calmness he exuded but barely felt at that moment. Their plan was in action now and there could be no going back. They had left a man on each wall flanking the passageway the rest of them now ran through – those two, Cedric and Julius, would be hot on their heels as soon as it was safe to rejoin the rest – whilst Nothro and Rundup went forward first to probe the way ahead.

A thought struck Cronto as they progressed. In their discussions a few minutes earlier – which felt like an eternity ago courtesy of the stress they endured – it had been assumed that Rundup's concealing powder would largely cover the Dralcea-side of the gate but leave the passage through it relatively clear. That did not seem to be the case; they could still see as little of the way ahead as when they first ventured forward and entered the swirling cloud. The major drawback was that they could not see who – or what – was ahead and about to run into them, or vice versa. This was beyond Cronto's control anyway, so not worth dwelling on, he reasoned.

A body heading the opposite way pushed by Cronto heavily, catching his right arm, confirming the validity of his thoughts moments earlier; he had not seen anyone approach due to the low visibility that they created. In that moment, his heart skipped a beat as he realised that it must be a guard defending the gate that had just brushed him. Cronto spun on his heel and waited for the man's inevitable return whilst taking up a wide-legged crouch for stability given that he would get little, if any, notice of their arrival.

As expected, the guard came charging back, having also belatedly realised what had happened. Cronto however had prepared himself well and used the guard's momentum to grab and push him away from the group, sending him reeling into the wall of the passageway. The moment of shock it afforded Cronto whilst his opponent crashed to a sudden stop was all he needed to strike the decisive blow; he used the head of Bulwark end-on to strike a blunt blow to the guard's helmet, knocking him unconscious.

Cronto breathed a heavy sigh of relief, then moved after his group of more vulnerable people that Zhin and Jenker were helping to keep moving. The disguising factor of Rundup's dustpeppers meant that Nothro and Rundup had passed right by the guard unseen but also unseeing. This encounter had swung in their favour. Cronto could only hope that it was also the last one.

It was not to be. Another guard came stumbling through the fug much more carefully than his colleague had done moments earlier, taking each step carefully as if the floor could fall away at any point in front of him. He walked centrally through the middle of the passage and as such went headlong into the midst of the group moving at a faster pace.

*

The guard's face was a mask of surprise as he collided with Roger Skerrick. On Skerrick's part, he had spent most of his life avoiding the authorities as best he could, and of course on this day especially, for all its strangeness. He was frankly terrified to have one of them slamming into him. It seemed to be just his luck for things to go wrong at the last second. He disentangled himself from his foe and shoved at the gate guard desperately.

A little distance having been achieved, the guard drew his short sword. Skerrick's neighbour, a man a little younger than himself who hadn't said anything during their sprint side by side, ran back to assist and was promptly cut down by a vicious back-handed slash that dazed the man with a cry before a well-aimed stab to the left of his chest stopped his resistance. He sputtered briefly and then was still.

Skerrick was aghast. He fumbled to free his daggers from their place bound to his thighs and tried to bring them to bear. His fingers betrayed him and, in his desperation, would not accurately obey his commands; every pluck at their bindings missed its mark and he got nowhere. Panic gripped him increasingly tightly with every failure. The guard closed in to stab with his sword, as he had just exercised on Skerrick's erstwhile running companion; exactly the work it had been wrought for.

The Haþingvoðs caught up to Skerrick at that moment, the women of the family supporting Fyrir in his wounded state. He had quickly learned many of the names of those around him and was grateful for their presence, thinking it might take the focus off himself. Ryx was quickest to react; she hefted a terrifying-looking weapon edged with glassy blades and left her father to be supported by Skula on her own. 'Time to try out Grænn Klær,' Ryx half-shouted.

Skerrick stared as Ryx closed the gap in scant few heartbeats, looking enraged. The distraction almost cost Skerrick everything. The guard thrust his sword at him, but Skerrick succeeded in twisting aside at the last second to let the sword pass agonisingly close by his waist, nicking his shirt. Ryx reached him and, swinging the fearsome weapon, slashed it down upon the sword-wielding guard as he drew back his arm to strike at Skerrick again. It struck heavily and the uneven obsidian blades cut mercilessly into the guard's lightly protected elbow.

The unfortunate guard sustained a horrible, wedge-shaped wound and lost all control of the arm, which flopped uselessly to his side and released the sword from his grip. As he saw the mess which had been made of the limb he began screaming. He then dropped heavily to his knees and stared at the wound, clamping his good left hand over it as if being unable to see the problem might solve the issue.

Skerrick stared in horror for a moment before profusely thanking Ryx for her intervention. He then snatched up the dropped sword as they hurried on and left the injured guard wailing on the ground. His daggers were all that he was used to using and he had no idea how to use the sword effectively, but the larger weapon would come in useful, he was sure.

It was at that moment that Skerrick heard the piercing yells sounding from the way they had just come, rippling through the yellow haze surrounding them, the source unseen and unseeable.

Chapter Thirty-one – Personal Battles

All had been going well for Cedric Guyal so far – his part in the plan was going smoothly. He had run forward and been hoisted onto the wall, then held his scavenged spear ready.

The idea was simple; he was to occupy the guards present on this part of the gate and in doing so allow the rest of the group to exit without harassment. Julius would perform the same function on the redoubt opposite. The coloured haze swirling around was an aid and hindrance all rolled into one. The walkway was only four feet wide and it was taking all of Cedric's concentration to walk straight ahead and not veer off to the side, where he risked falling off. He walked on warily, knees bent slightly in an almost-crouch and holding the spear so that the tip was at midriff height.

For a dozen feet he ventured forward, not able to see much. Occasional sounds could be heard from where the others were presumably leaving via the passageway, including the echo from hurrying footsteps, although it all seemed strangely muffled as it reached his ears. Cedric wondered briefly whether Julius was finding it as odd as he was. Barely able to see ahead, he could not tell how the other man was getting on.

The one thing Cedric was grateful for was the cessation of the hail of arrows raining down from above. He was happy to admit that those had frightened the life out of him, and getting up to his current position had been a relief for the slight protection it offered. The terrifying way the arrows just seemed to appear out of nowhere and clattered among them indiscriminately, and with their origin concealed, appalled him. Cedric was more than happy to meet an enemy face-to-face and fight them, courtesy of his tempestuous nature, but potentially being cut down at random whilst knowing nothing about it did not feel right to him. Thankfully, they had at least avoided the wicked arrow points in the dash to the gate. He dearly hoped that he and Julius would not face any more when they broke from their positions and ran after the others to form the rear-guard. He was not sure that he could take the tension of such an attack were it to happen again.

Cedric was just beginning to struggle to focus his eyes forward as the cloud swirled all around him when a figure resolved from it, hidden until that moment. This gate guard was probably not expecting to encounter somebody encroaching on his redoubt; he was busy fanning his left arm in front of himself, as if doing so would improve the visibility around him. He held his bow in his right hand, strung and ready.

The guard's eyes widened and his mouth sagged open a little at the sight of Cedric facing him from just a few feet away. Both men stood in shocked silence for a moment before reacting. Cedric rushed forward as the guard drew an arrow from the quiver slung over his shoulder, managing to do so quickly despite the restrictive armour he wore.

Cedric held the advantage, given his superior reach with his spear, and as such he struck the first blow. The guard was fast; he already had an arrow fitted to his bowstring by the time Cedric lunged. As the bow came up, Cedric's spear-thrust knocked it aside before he could draw the string back and the bow clattered to the walkway at their feet.

As Cedric's momentum from the thrust carried him forward, his weight leading the way, he came in close to the guard; too close. The hand newly freed from trying to pull back the bowstring quickly balled into a fist and swung at Cedric's unprotected face, catching him heavily in the cheek and eye socket. *He really is fast*, Cedric thought as the blow resonated in his head. *The reasons for him being assigned a gate guard are clear – he reacts quickly. He must be a valuable asset in defending Dralcea.*

White spots leapt across Cedric's vision following the blow and reduced what he could see even further for a few seconds. He blindly stumbled a couple of steps past his adversary but crucially kept hold of his spear. Cedric turned as quickly as he could so that his vulnerable back was not facing the guard who had already exhibited swift reflexes; it would be madness to give him an opportunity like that. He was faced with the onrushing guard who snarled as he approached.

The pair clashed before Cedric could adjust his grip on the spear to use it, so he released it since he needed his arms free for balance. He had no desire to pierce the man with it anyway – to do so would be to give legitimacy to their hounding and abuse, and he would not provide them with any excuses in that regard. Cedric only just managed to hold his ground as they came together, the two men being of a similarly large frame with plenty of strength at their disposal.

It was a stalemate for a few terrifying moments as they heaved at each other, pushing and grunting, each aiming to gain the upper hand and control of the situation. Cedric had a slight height advantage and a fraction more muscle; the guard counteracted this by virtue of being heavier due to his armour.

Cedric decided that the time was ripe to try something different. A pushing contest would exhaust them both and he wanted to retain enough energy to escape after this encounter, assuming he prevailed. Cedric faked a grimace and glanced to where his left arm was pushing on his adversary's right shoulder, then waited for a reaction in the man's face. The guard obliged with a triumphant look in his eye and the corners of his mouth very slightly upturned. He had taken the bait and the man started a renewed effort on Cedric's supposedly weakened left side.

As his opponent reacted in this way, Cedric quickly dropped his left hand away, stepped to the right and then used both hands to shove his opponent from the side. It worked beautifully; the shove came right after the guard stumbled forward from his own pressure and Cedric's quick sideways movement. He went down hard onto the paved top of the redoubt thanks to his armour and lay on his front, stunned for a moment.

Now what do I do with this man? Cedric grabbed his spear again as he desperately tried to think – there was no possible way they could take him with them, he didn't want to seriously hurt him and he had no real method of restraining the man. *Do I just run and hope for the best*?

Cedric had a sickening realisation at that moment. Neither Julius or he had any way of knowing when the others had got clear, which marked the point that they could leave their positions. It was the one part of their plan which had been overlooked in the rush to get it formulated. *Should* he just make a break for it now?

Indecision rooted Cedric to the spot. What he failed to notice was the guard's fallen bow on the ground and the fact that his foot was planted in the middle, right in the space between wood and cord.

The guard managed to suddenly manoeuvre himself forward with his forearms and grab the span of his dropped bow with the string facing himself. The man used all his strength to heave the bow toward himself, taking Cedric's leg with it before he knew what was happening.

He had no chance to extricate his leg before it was pulled out from under him and Cedric fell backward, landed heavily and hit the back of his head on the stone. The shock made him release his grip on his spear which proceeded to roll off the edge of the redoubt and into the passageway below. Cedric lay there stunned, his head feeling hot and wet in the area that had struck the ground. He could only watch as the man moved in front of him.

Cedric's nemesis used his hands to push himself up and then got back to his feet. The action took some considerable effort having been flat on the floor in his armour to begin with. He exhaled heavily at the exertion of it and fiddled with the bowstring where it looped over the nock at either end as if checking it for damage.

'The thing that you lot don't realise – whoever you even are – is that you don't stand a chance.' He pulled the bowstring back with no arrow fitted, before gently releasing the tension again to avoid dry-shooting and potentially damaging the bow. 'You bunch of bastards are just a rabble, trying to do whatever base thing it is that drives you. You don't appreciate what you'll come up against.'

Cedric's head swam as he lay there prone. The blow to his head must have been serious; he struggled to think clearly and wanted to protest, but couldn't work the connection between his brain and mouth to speak the words. He could hear fully though, and wondered if he understood what the man was saying correctly – did he think they were exiles? If so, why would they be trying to leave Dralcea rather than enter it? Unless of course it wasn't obvious which way they had come from. That seemed entirely possible, given the smokescreen Rundup had created.

'See, they hired Gate Guard Manolete Roque here because I'm good at this. I'm quick. Most of all, I'm not thick, unlike some of those that get taken on. Add to that the training we have, and, well, I'm a bloody good choice to have manning this gate to protect it from louts such as *you*.' He looked over to Cedric's side where the spear had vanished from sight, likely having heard the *clang* as it hit the floor as Cedric had, and pulled a mock conciliatory face as if he could see it was safely out of reach.

'Oh! Wait. The other thing is also an important factor.' Gate Guard Roque pulled out his short sword from the scabbard at his side in a purposefully slow action to heighten the menacing effect. 'I'm a bastard, too. A cruel one.'

Roque thrust the sword point into Cedric's unprotected stomach with undisguised relish etched on his face.

Cedric stood no chance of getting out of the way in time. Instead, all he could do was let out a gasp of surprise at the explosive pain. His mind came into sharp focus for the first time since he had fallen and hit his head; it was as if the horrific pain snapped his senses back to how they should be by blotting out everything else in his fogged mind. He howled as the full realisation of what had happened struck him.

'I bet you didn't think I'd do that, eh? The Dralcea Guard are here to enforce the law after all. The problem is, sometimes what needs to happen, needs to happen quickly and decisively. You're a danger to the population and so that seals your fate!' Roque stabbed Cedric again, in the chest this time, more lightly but no less cruelly.

Cedric could not bear to just lie there and be toyed with in this way. *This man is going to take pleasure in causing me as much pain as he possibly can – until he either tires of the sick game and finishes me off, or I die of my injuries in the process.* The wound to his stomach was severe, he knew. The blade had gone deep and every heartbeat felt as if he was losing a little more of what kept him alive. His chest, although less seriously wounded, bled freely all the same.

He had lost. It was unlikely Cedric could recover from his stomach wound, even if someone could come along to carry him away. The others had gone on ahead and nobody was coming back. A cold feeling swept through his entire body with the certainty of the realisation.

I'm not going to be treated like a piece of meat, Cedric decided. He mentally recalled the brief conversation he had had with Julius before they embarked on this hastily drawn-up plan, aside from the others and out of earshot so that only they were privy to the details. Cedric looked up at the guard – Roque, as he had just learned he was called – and stared straight into his grey eyes and saw nothing but violence and spite there. With a huge effort of will to ignore the pain that pervaded his head, chest and stomach, Cedric heaved all the muscles that would still comply with his wishes and rolled himself off the redoubt and down to the street below.

It was no small distance, and as Cedric had no way to cushion his fall, he was unable to avoid hitting the stones hard. His arm suffered the most as it caught the full weight of his torso, but his shoulder seemed wrong somehow too. *No matter now*. Lying on his stomach, he glanced around for the spear he had lost. Perhaps he could still even things up a little. Cedric heard a voice from above him.

'You won't get far rolling away, mate.' With that, he heard a clatter as Manolete Roque jumped down after him heavily.

Cedric moved his head as much as he was able to see where Roque was, and in doing so noticed a significant red splatter dripping down the side of the redoubt along with a fair amount around his sides. *Is that all my blood? There is so much. I probably don't have long…*

Heavy footsteps approached.

Cedric reached for the spear shaft. His fingers were tantalisingly close to it. One fingertip, then two, brushed the smooth wood.

The footsteps stopped suddenly. 'Behave, you haven't the strength for that,' Roque said, sounding almost sad. Cedric heard one more step, then another, heavier, a second later. Roque stood over him now with one foot placed either side of his waist.

Cedric's fingers managed to flick the spear handle so that it rolled two inches closer to him. He closed his hand around the shaft.

'Seriously. Too late,' Roque said.

He slammed his sword down two-handed into the base of Cedric's back. Cedric screamed a horrible, animalistic noise of sheer agony as his muscles writhed in a primal attempt to escape the pain; all his muscles spasmed, except those in his legs, which seemed distant and unresponsive now. The spear rapped out a tattoo on the stone street as his arms flailed.

Roque laughed as he stood over the squirming form of Cedric. He had now lost all control to this man he had pointedly avoided harming. Cedric felt himself becoming steadily colder and his pain started to subside slightly. He thought upon the conversation he had had just minutes ago when everything was vastly different. It felt as though it had occurred years ago. *Now is the time to break what we had agreed.* Cedric drew as deep a breath as he could manage, as deep as his injuries would allow him without being completely overcome with the agony.

'JULIUS!' Cedric yelled as loudly as he could. 'RUN!'

*

Julius had experienced an easy time on this mad venture so far. He had not seen anyone on top of the redoubt he was exploring – securing? – although there had been at least one guard on there before the smokescreen had taken effect. The walkway was not wide, but he wondered if he had passed a guard unknowingly. He could not really see anything around himself, after all.

He briefly considered if not being able to see had scared the guards on duty back into their offices built into the gate and wall itself. Julius had no idea where those might be, but the blonde-haired man he had met in The Crimson Duck, Fyrir, had assured them that they would be there somewhere. If this were true, there could be any number of guards inside that could spill out at any point. The thought was far from comforting. All he could do was continue and hope their plan worked out.

That nervous calm was broken when the guard emerged from the green-yellow haze. He looked young and small to Julius, and as though his armour was a size too big, such was the way it seemed to dangle off him or else wobble in place. Julius had his knife up in an instant and held it at arm's length in front of him, aiming to be threatening. Whether this would work against a man in armour who carried a sword and bow, he was not confident of at all.

The tactic appeared to work. The slight gate guard looked terrified at the man emerging from the murk and brandishing a knife in front of him. He paused and presumably mentally weighed up what faced him in that time before he backed off and retreated the way he had come.

Julius let out the huge breath he had not realised he was holding and laughed at the sudden release of tension. It took a conscious effort to lower the knife which he had been rigidly displaying in front of him.

That relief was short-lived however, as it took only a few seconds for another, much burlier guard to push past his retreating colleague, cursing him for his inaction. The man appeared particularly infuriated by his fellow guard's cowardice and approached Julius quickly with a snarl. He had his sword out already and lunged forward, intending to end the engagement quickly.

The advantage was with Julius, however, who was wiry and muscular from his outdoor work and used to dodging out of the way when cut branches fell, a skill he used now to sidestep the sword point thrust at him. Both sword and the guard wielding it sailed past Julius harmlessly, the momentum throwing him forward uncontrollably.

Julius took the opportunity to utilise one of the tricks he had learnt growing up. He quickly turned to get behind the guard then kicked his foot firmly into the rear of the man's knee and sent him sprawling, dropping his sword in the process. He lay on his front spluttering with rage and unable to attack. Julius acted fastest and rolled the fallen guard off the edge of the redoubt; being prone on the floor the man was unable to resist, and resulted in him hitting the street on the other side from the passage with a crash. The guard lay there cursing ever more fervently after being so unceremoniously dumped out of his own stronghold and being incapacitated in the process.

He grinned with the success of his actions. 'Good effort there, mate. Now where did your friend go?' Julius had dealt with the aggressive attacker swiftly, but there was at least one more through the obscuring powder and potentially more – how many more could there be? If they turned out in force it was unlikely he would be so lucky again. Julius swiped the dropped sword so that he at least had more to hand than just his knife, then gave it a test jab. 'Heavier than my knife, but more useful I suppose. I'll have to get used to it.' He stopped, wary of going on without knowing what lay ahead of him. The next move was far less certain.

That quandary was solved for him when Julius heard the sudden yells from nearby. He quickly realised they were horrible screams of pain. Julius could not be sure of the source, but it seemed to be close. Was it just people caught up in the general confusion brought on by the smokescreen? It was impossible to tell from his blind vantage point where he was unable to see any distance.

A clatter sounded from roughly the same direction, and Julius decided it was time to investigate. The alternative was not one he particularly wanted to explore, and in any case, he thought he had probably left enough time for the rest to escape now. He started to try to climb down from the redoubt but struggled to get any purchase on the sides, unsurprisingly; it was not intended to be climbed. After a quick weighing up, Julius dropped down and landed heavily on his feet. As he took a moment and regained his bearings, he heard something unexpected.

'JULIUS! RUN!'

It was Cedric's voice, and it was strained and raw. The sound made Julius's heart sink. It was clear that Cedric's situation must be dire for him to yell out and warn him, specifically breaking what they had agreed earlier.

Julius moved cautiously forward to try to clarify what was happening. He quickly came upon the terrible scene and was horrified. Cedric lay prone on the ground, a sword protruding from his lower back whilst a guard stood over him. Julius's blood ran cold at the sight.

The guard, who must have put the sword there, spotted Julius at that moment and grasped the handle to pull it free. His intention was surely to put a similarly grisly stop to Julius. The guard struggled, however; the sword would not move despite his pulls and jerking motions trying to bring it to bear. His own savage glee in skewering Cedric had now hamstrung the guard as he failed to retrieve his sword, having wedged it in the bones of Cedric's lower back.

Julius tried to get closer to check on Cedric whilst the guard was occupied with re-arming himself. Cedric had been moved around slightly with the jerking of the attempts to free the sword and Julius had been unable to tell if his newfound comrade still lived. Julius finally noticed the man's eyes rove around to fix on him and he gasped at the agony of being wrenched around, though he looked weaker with every passing second. Julius edged closer, ever closer, wanting to help.

He got close enough for the guard to think that Julius was about to rush him and let the sword's handle go as he lurched forward to intercept the approaching woodsman. Julius panicked at this sudden movement and swung his newly acquired sword wildly to ward away the danger.

The guard stopped in shock, then put a hand up to his face and his fingers quickly turned red as hot blood flowed over them. Julius glanced at the sword now held at his side again; the tip was stained where it had flashed across the man's face and laid his cheek open from lip almost to his ear, severing the flesh all the way through to the inside of his mouth. The result was disfiguring – when the guard took his hand away, Julius could see the man's back teeth clearly thanks to the awful wound.

Julius backed away as the guard stood frozen in shock at his injury, although it was doubtful this would last long. He looked at Cedric again but could see no movement now. His eyes were still, staring at a point somewhere over Julius's shoulder, and his hands no longer grasped at the flagstones of the street.

Cedric Guyal was dead. There was no fight left in him now, nor any way to help, but he had used his last words to try to ensure the same fate would not befall Julius. He would not forget that. He would not let it be in vain.

Julius took the narrow window of opportunity afforded him before it closed entirely, bought as it had been so dearly with Cedric's life, and attempted to preserve his own existence. He turned and ran into the amber-shrouded passageway after his oldest friend, Nothro, and everybody else he had met that day whilst he was still able. He could not know what fate awaited him there, but hoped against hope that they could all attain salvation.

Afterword

My sincerest thanks to you, the reader, for taking the time to read this book. It is the result of countless hours of writing, rewriting, editing, doubts, more rewriting, further doubts, discussion and finally, publishing. I dearly hope you enjoyed what has been my pleasure to create.

Thanks must also go to my family for reading the first draft, giving feedback and offering support when I needed it. Your help has been invaluable.

*

Julius, Nothro, and their newfound companions will return in the sequel – they are far from safe yet. To find out what the future holds for them all, look out for Book Two of The Bowl Series – coming soon!

For Reference

Heart of Dralcea Award ceremony attendees (notable)

Julius Dominguez, a woodsman

Nothro Grafanc, an Ananeptide woodsman

Molefi Cronto, a judge

Wilfred Wolfscope, a clerk

Ryx Haþingvoð, a barmaid

Skula Haþingvoð, a pub owner

Cedric Guyal, a farmer

Rundup Ovygdalha, a performer

Zhin Xofia, a tailor

Harold Jenker, a baker

Dralcea Guards (major)

Grand Branch Drachvas Rizon, head of the Dralcea Guard

Branch Godfrey Vilipas

Branch Matthew Arnold

Sergeant Gengran Dalbahan, a Crinochin

Sergeant Janos Boltfoot

Sergeant Zygfryd Tanbry

Sergeant Egil Sluss

Sergeant Younes Souo

Recruit Paul Gantle

Gate Guard Manolete Roque

<u>Dralcea Guards (minor)</u>

Sergeant Pelovir

Sergeant Disheart

Guard Potas

Guard Hornak

Gate Guard Kelly

Recruit Goshin

Recruit Alapich

Guard Waucus

Guard Hamza

Recruit Verrin

Recruit Pascal Oso

Helfred Onnson (newly enlisted Recruit)

<u>Other citizens of Dralcea</u>

Fyrir Haþingvoð, a pub owner

Roger Skerrick, a petty thief

Alfred Omphalos, an inventor

Aokir Takeuchi, a barman

Lady Folodawa, a performer and leader of the troupe

Eric Wurm, a strongman performer

Wilbur Warburton, a barfly

Edwina Posan, a keyholder at the Temple of the Sun

Horace Evelyn, a worshipper at the Temple of the Sun

Piotr Mazel, a worshipper at the Temple of the Sun

Races

Humans

Ananeptide, large bear-like furry mammals with a head similar to a sloth but with pointed ears

Crinochin, squat humanoids with grey skin, copper-coloured eyes and wide hands used for digging; native inhabitants of the chasm around which Dralcea is built, who originally began excavating the subterranean streets

Specific animals of Dralcea

Piecrust, a mlem-mlem adopted by The Crimson Duck

Zebedee, Wilfred's pet zebra spider

Other creatures of Dralcea

Snorthogs, woolly porcine

Flammula, plump, chicken-like birds of vivid orange colour which lay cooked eggs due to being adapted to live in the hotter areas of the chasm around which Dralcea is built

Mlem-mlems, stray dogs that rove Dralcea; smaller versions of their much larger, wild cousins

Frostmites, mythical creatures said to stalk the frozen world outside of The Bowl, which are large, multi-legged creatures with a blue carapace and a pair of savage claws

Significant cities/areas

Dralcea, capital of the civilised cities, based around a caldera with layers of subterranean streets like an anthill with a chasm in the centre

Olrof, the second largest civilised city, a place of shifting sands in a cold, windy climate

Thorntuft, a largely forested, snowy area near the Western limits of The Bowl with a loose collection of small settlements

Significant buildings

The Promontory, seat of government in Dralcea, also home to the Dralcea Guard headquarters

The Crimson Duck, a pub run by the Haþingvoð family, popular drinking place for Dralcea Guards

Jenker and Son, Bakery, a bakery with a secret hidden in its walls

Named weapons

Hilde, Sergeant Janos Boltfoot's monstrous hammer

Bulwark, Molefi Cronto's axe

Grænn Klær, Ryx Haþingvoð's macuahuitl

Other terms

Somoni, the main currency used in The Bowl

Galumph, an alcoholic drink made by fermenting whatever is available and thus often being extremely pungent and unpleasant in taste

Ejector, a blunderbuss-like weapon utilising tension rather than any chemicals, invented by Alfred Omphalos at the behest of the Dralcea Guard

Sweat of Hephaestus, the small, droplet-shaped pieces of iron used as the official ammunition of Ejectors

Dustpepper, a bell pepper-like fruit containing segments like an orange which is dried out and filled with coloured flour or other powder by Rundup Ovygdalha for use in his act; when broken or thrown, the dustpepper releases the contents in an obscuring cloud, akin to a smoke bomb

Exiles, former inhabitants of Dralcea expelled from the city or those who have fled to escape justice, who generally head Eastward and settle elsewhere in their own communities

Ambassadors, the government of Dralcea and the civilised cities who represent the people of their own original cultural groups before they came together as one upon reaching The Bowl

Printed in Great Britain
by Amazon

24598911R00152